WITCH, PLEASE

BOOK 1 OF THE NOT YOUR BASIC WITCH SERIES

A.J. MACEY

JARICA JAMES

BLURB:

Aris Calisto, newest student at Aether Academy of Crystal Magic and Witchcraft not only stands out with her quirky outfits and bubblegum pink hair but also draws attention by being what's considered the lowest of the low in the Akasha society- a Mixta.

When mysterious things start happening, including unexpected bindings, things going missing, and being claimed by a not-so-traditional familiar, Aris realizes she's in over her cotton candy-colored head. Enter in the five guys who have been magically roped into Aris's rodeo:

-Caspian, the playful potions brewer,
-Drayce, the summoner who never seems to get overwhelmed,
-Kye, a broody rune drawer who Aris can't help but pester,
-Xan, the spell caster with no sense of humor to speak of,
-and Torryn, the history professor who seems to demand every waking hour working on mastering her power.

With a cauldron full of men behind her, can Aris use her i'magic'nation to figure out what's happening to her capricious coven? Or will she find out that life's a real witch?

Book 1 of the Not Your Basic Witch Series
Legends of Asteria Trilogy 1

WARNING:

The Not Your Basic Witch is a WhyChoose/Reverse Harem trilogy featuring MMFMMM meaning there is M/M content, and the female main character doesn't have to choose between her love interests. This trilogy is the first in a series collection consisting of six trilogies titled Legends of Asteria. Each trilogy should be read in order.

This book contains references involving violence, and other themes that some readers may find triggering.

CONTENTS

Chapter 1	1
Chapter 2	13
Chapter 3	29
Chapter 4	45
Chapter 5	53
Chapter 6	65
Chapter 7	78
Chapter 8	89
Chapter 9	103
Chapter 10	119
Chapter 11	134
Chapter 12	149
Chapter 13	161
Chapter 14	173
Chapter 15	195
Chapter 16	208
Chapter 17	219
Chapter 18	233
Chapter 19	246
Chapter 20	256
Chapter 21	276
Chapter 22	291
Epilogue	306
Resting Witch Face	309
Acknowledgments	311
Also by A.J. Macey	313
Also by Jarica James	315
Stay Connected	317

Copyright © 2019 by A.J. Macey and Jarica James
All rights reserved.

No part of this book may be reproduced in any form or by any electronic or mechanical means, including information storage and retrieval systems, without written permission from the author, except for the use of brief quotations in a book review.

Cover: Moonstruck Cover Design and Photography
Editing: Personal Touch Editing
Formatting: Inked Imagination Author Services

Dedicated to:

A.J.-
My daughter, Evelyn Rose.
I believe in you.

Jarica-
My sons Owyn and Kellan, who make my heart full every day.
I love you

CHAPTER 1

September 2nd
Monday Morning
Aris

As the magic driven carriage rattled down the cobblestone road, the wind whipped through the open window, shifting my hair around my shoulders in a wave of cotton candy pink. My eyes scanned the passing trees and buildings as the carriage pulled me through the long, winding roads, hoping to catch a glimpse of what would be my new home. The summer weather was slowly giving way to cool crisp air, and the leaves were ever so slightly turning into beautiful golds, reds, and browns. The trees and cooling weather were pleasant changes from the dry desert heat of my home territory, Ignis. The reminder of home had my expression tilting down into a frown. Home had hardly been welcoming, anything but. Witches weren't very accepting of those without affinities, or Mixtas as they named us, and my family was some of the most judgmental.

Shaking off the downward spiral of thoughts, I turned back to watching the world pass by. The anticipation of reaching my destination grew from a small niggle to complete antsiness as my legs bounced anxiously. After traveling for over a week to get to Aether, I just wanted to see where I would be spending the next four years of my life. A week stuck in a carriage with no one else to talk to was making me go crazy. At least I had snacks and a few books to keep me company.

Humming softly, I shifted for what seemed like the hundredth time to stretch my cramped muscles. The rhythmic sound of the spoked wheels turning over the stones set the perfect rhythm for the tune I had made up on the spot, singing quietly to myself to help pass the time. It was slow going, but after another little while, I finally saw the stone structures of my ultimate destination. I couldn't peel my eyes away from the prestigious buildings. The dark stone of the school was a perfect contrast to the crystal clock tower I'd read so much about. Iridescent crystals in light blues, purples, opal, and pink swirled around the cylindrical structure in the center of the school grounds. A new feeling started to brew in my chest as I took it in, a mixture of freedom and hope. A wave of lightness lifted my spirits, pepping me up as I drew closer. After years of being made to feel like a failure, I felt as though I would finally get a chance to be myself. To finally use the power I did have with less judgment and accusation. *At least none of these people can practically disown me for what I can or can't do.*

As the cart finally reached the main gateway of the school—after what felt like another hour when in reality it was only a few minutes—I felt the magic fueling my mode of transportation dissipate abruptly, forcing me to jerk forward at the unexpected stop. *Ow*, I thought, rubbing the spot on my head that had smacked into the front of the carriage. *They really need some safety precautions on these things.* An older witch came forward as I opened the door to exit. As I stepped out, I made sure to give my sore muscles time to adjust to movement. Giving me a tight smile before pulling my bag from the back-luggage racks, he didn't speak a word as he put it in front of me, opting to focus on his tasks rather than small talk. *That's fine, not like I've been alone for the last week or anything.* Squashing the irritated thoughts, I focused on the witch next to me as he quickly whispered an incantation under his breath. The carriage started its journey back home as soon as he finished his spell.

"This way," he mumbled quietly, turning on his heel, heading for the gate without a backward glance. Gathering my bag, I lugged it onto my shoulder as I struggled to keep up, my muscles rebelling at such sudden use. The massive wrought-iron gates swung open as soon as we neared, and a wave of magic swept over me as I officially entered the ground of Aether Academy of Crystal Magic and Witchcraft.

Holy shit, I'm finally here.

I made sure to keep the excited dance I wanted to do contained, but only just, as we continued to stand right inside the gate while it swung shut behind us. After a few quiet and frankly tense moments where I shuffled back-and-forth, another man came striding down the stone walkway toward us. He wore a navy-blue blazer with a silver tie and burnt orange sweater vest. The colors seemed to be an odd combination until I recognized the school crest was embroidered on the pocket, identifying him as Headmaster of Aether Academy. *Huh, he doesn't look as scary as I imagined.*

His gray hair and beard trimmed to perfection, everything about him prim and proper, except his wide, toothy grin. The excited expression made him look kind and carefree—if not a bit eccentric—but if my past had taught me anything, I shouldn't take anything at face value.

"Welcome! You must be Aris Calisto! I'm Headmaster Tallis. Your mother called to ensure your belongings arrived safely. I assured her they were up in your dorm room, waiting for you. I trust the ride was pleasant?" he asked in a rush, barely giving me a chance to respond before taking off up the path. I ground my teeth at the mention of my mother. *Of course, she didn't bother to ask about me.* It had been hard enough to be shipped off, but that reminder was just a slap in the face. *Though I tried to look at this as a positive... maybe this is a blessing in disguise.*

"Unfortunately, since your trip took so long, you'll have to jump right into your schooling. But you're definitely early enough today to see the campus before your first class, which is in a half-hour. Let's get you to your room first. Wouldn't want you to have to carry that bag around with you all day, now would we?"

My head spun to the point of dizziness from his quick ramblings and the overwhelming newness of everything. I attempted to use my powers to ease the weight of the duffle on my shoulder, but I couldn't focus long enough to do so, meaning it was up to me to lug it to my room. *No, Headmaster Tallis, I wouldn't like help or anything. Thanks for not asking.*

"That would be lovely," I managed to squeak out as I power walked to catch up to him, my arms screaming in protest at the weight of my bag. Despite saying there was enough time to tour the place, he stayed silent, focused on getting wherever the hell he was hurrying to.

If I hadn't been huffing and puffing, I might have had the chance to look around as we reached one of the buildings. Instead, I was trying not to die from lack of oxygen or collapsing from the exercise my body wasn't used to. Headmaster Tallis slowed when we entered one of the other buildings outside of what seemed to be the main cluster on the campus grounds. They all looked similar, but each had a unique picture on the wall. I could see crossed wands over one and the school crest on another.

The hall we stopped in front of was made of stone and brick, two similar images painted on the door. It was easy to recognize the symbols representing the gods and goddesses. The first was an image of a circle with crescent moons on the sides while the second consisted of another circle, only this time the crescent moon was lying on top. When we entered, I noticed the arches rose high above to allow little folded papers to whizz from one location to the next to reach their designated readers.

Nice to know I'll be able to message people whenever I want.
Although I have to make some friends first.
I also need to figure out how to enchant the little airplanes.

"This is the student dormitory which houses both males and females. Everyone here is above eighteen, which makes you all adults, and we expect you to act as such. However, each section has its own Resident Advisor, and any squabbles or issues should be taken to them first before approaching a teacher or faculty member. Although most freshmen are on the top floor, you're in the north tower room since it was the last we had available due to your late arrival. It's a bit offset from the other students and quite a walk up the staircase, but it should suffice. It was previously storage, but we had it converted for use. That means you get a bigger room," he added the last part with a hint of teasing in his tone, but something about it set me on edge. He seemed nice on the surface, but the more I listened to him talk, the more I realized he also seemed annoyed at this whole interaction.

Great, did he have it out for Mixtas too?

The walk up the staircase was worse than I anticipated, leaving my cheeks flushed and my legs quaking by the time we reached the top. *At least I'll be in shape by the end of term,* I thought as I hurried after him. He finally stopped when we reached the end of the hall, a wide, wooden door the only one left. It seemed older than the rest of the building, clearly not part of the update when they did a remodel. He pulled out an old-fashioned key and unlocked the door, handing it to me and ushering me inside. *Well... somebody certainly is in a hurry.*

When I stepped into the room, my jaw dropped. The tall, peaked ceiling of the tower was overhead, making the room seem huge. The room was circular instead of square, which made it unique—perfect for me. Squealing internally, I dropped my bag on the bed and spun in a circle, taking it all in. The furniture was still piled in the middle of the room, along with the boxes my mother had sent, which meant I'd get free rein to set it up however I wanted after dinner. *This is exactly the kind of fresh start I need.*

"Alright, ready to get on with the tour of the rest of the campus?" the headmaster asked, clearing his throat and looking annoyed. Not wanting to go to class unprepared, I grabbed my messenger bag with my school supplies from my duffel and followed him out of my room. I paused to lock the door behind us, tucking the key into my bag as we shuffled down the spiral stairs.

"Kyelerian," the headmaster called as soon as we reached the main floor. A tall boy with a wash of five o'clock shadow covering his jaw stopped at the sound of his name. Sighing to himself, I watched him grind his teeth before walking over to where we stood. He gave me a quick once over, his eyebrow quirking up at my pink hair before turning his eyes to the headmaster. I tried to listen to what Tallis had to say but couldn't help but stare.

His eyes drew me in first, a gorgeous rich brown with flecks of gold in the hickory depths. The furrow in his brow didn't make him look inviting, in fact, he looked downright hostile at being called out. *Thanks, headmaster, this will surely help me make new friends.*

My eyes moved lower, taking in his lean build and apparent muscles under his black shirt. Tattoos peeked out from under the sleeves he had pushed up slightly. I caught a small symbol but couldn't tell what it was before he crossed his arms over his chest. When he glanced back over at me, I quickly moved my eyes back to his, though my flaming cheeks definitely gave me away. *Clearly, my social skills leave something to be desired.*

"Perfect!" Tallis' cheerful exclamation pulled me out of another round of intense—probably a little creeperish—staring. "I'll leave you two to your tour." The headmaster scurried off, looking relieved at having a way out of showing me around. Taking a steadying breath, I glanced over at the broody boy in front of me as he looked less than pleased with the fact he'd been stuck with babysitting me.

At least he's nice to look at.

Kyelerian

The new girl's eyes trailed over me while I tried to pay attention to the task Tallis wanted me to do. Of all the damn students to pick from, he chose *me* as the face to represent

Aether... *why*? I was hardly the poster boy for friendly and welcoming. I glared at the headmaster's back as he hurried off, leaving me alone with the most cheerful-looking witch I'd ever seen.

"Let's go," I mumbled, leading her out of the dormitory building. "Five buildings. That's the Elemental and Spell Casting building to the left. Behind there are the staff housing buildings and the greenhouse. The forest separates the two. The library is next to the Elemental building, then administration and dining, and finally, Potions and Summoning. Your schedule should be marked with which building to go to. We all have lunch at the same time, so there's no confusion." When I finished my quick explanation, I turned to see her gaping at everything she saw, still lagging several feet behind me.

"Does the tower chime?" she asked quickly, clearly missing everything I had just told her.

"Yes, at the beginning and end of each period," I said, starting to walk around the courtyard to the Administration building. I didn't see a schedule in her hand, which meant she would have to start there. *If she can focus long enough to make it there.*

"What's your affinity?" she inquired, her cheerfulness dampened for a moment with the question. *Huh, if she's so down about affinities, she must be a Mixta.* At that realization, her cheerfulness seemed even odder. Mixtas were accepted here but rarely anywhere else. *Maybe it's just a mask, trying to seem friendly to fit in. Who knows? Witches can be weird.*

"Runes," I answered, steering us around to the Administration building, hoping she wouldn't come up with any other questions.

The girl next to me, whose name I realized I didn't know, bounced on her toes and stared wide-eyed at every little thing we passed. Her bubblegum pink hair was as bright as her personality, it seemed. My gaze narrowed as she somehow seemed to perk up even more as we rounded to the front of the crystal clock tower and got the full view of the silver clock hands. *How is someone this cheerful over every single thing? She has to have smoked some of the hexing herb*, I thought as we turned down one of the paths.

"Are you always this happy?" I couldn't stop myself from asking, my irritated tone making it clear it was a complaint rather than a playful tease.

"Is that a problem?" she sassed, flashing me an obnoxiously bright smile. Along with the grin, I could see a hint of feistiness in her eyes. Interesting. Her cheerful nature made me want to push her, pester her until the girl she was beneath that sweet cotton candied smile broke through, and I could see what she was truly made of—sugar, spice, or something definitely not as nice.

"Yes. I need more coffee to deal with that cheerfulness," I mumbled back, realizing what I had said once it was already too late. She stopped abruptly, rounding on me with fire in her eyes—*definitely a hint of spice in those steel depths.*

"Excuse me? What is so wrong with being happy? Did someone brew on the wrong side of the cauldron this morning? That's why you're so cranky, isn't it?" She gave me a sympathetic face, but her eyes lit with amusement at her teasing.

Did she just seriously use a witch pun on me? The corner of my mouth quirked up at the pun before I could stop it, but I dropped it just as quickly as she started to look proud of herself. I rolled my eyes and continued toward the main office in the admin building, content to ignore the hyper bundle of joy next to me.

The building was on the opposite side of campus from

the dorms, which meant with the way she was walking, we would get there by third class. She studied each door as we passed as if she was committing their images to memory. *It's not like they're hard to decipher; the library literally has tomes on the door.*

"Do you like the professors here?" she asked with another excited smile.

"Some, I guess," I muttered, holding back an eye roll at her constant questions.

"Is there a lot of bullying on campus?" she asked, her smile faltering for a moment. Clearly, it had been a problem before... I could see why with her odd behavior and strange peppiness. *Being a Mixta definitely wouldn't help*, I noted absently.

"Not really." I gave her a shrug. She had the wrong guy if she wanted to ask about other people. I tended to keep to myself, and that was the way I liked it.

"Do you have a familiar?" This time her question bothered me even more—*nothing like having one of your failures called out.*

"No," I answered after a long pause. She gave me a curious look but didn't stop her bouncy, upbeat peppering questions as we walked.

"It'd be nice to have a companion, especially in that tower," she mused, completely ignoring the tone in my voice.

"Tower?" I asked, confused what she could be talking about. All the floors were the same, and none of the rooms were in the towers. She turned around to face me, the grin spreading impossibly wider as her voice turned teasing.

"The north tower was converted into a room for me," she said, "and it's probably bigger than the other dorms."

"Good for you. I'll take my room on the third floor and

not have to walk up all those stairs," I deadpanned, hoping to catch a falter in her smile. She just shrugged and chuckled before continuing down the walkway, leaving me behind.

"I don't mind all those stairs; my ass will look amazing in a couple weeks." She threw me a smug smile and a tiny wink over her shoulder. My eyes dipped down to the curve of her already too alluring ass as she continued to stride away. *I can't argue with that logic.*

Yanking my eyes away from that temptation, I stuffed my hands in my jean pockets and glanced around. The courtyard was basically empty, most of the other students either at breakfast or getting ready for the day. *Lucky bastards,* I thought as my stomach growled. The grass was still green, but knowing Aether's weather, it would be turning brown with the impending winter in the next month or so. As much as I tried to keep my focus away from the new girl, I couldn't stop my gaze from drifting over to her. Something about her just called for all attention on her. *It could be, despite her damn incessant cheerfulness, she's hot as hell, although I can't imagine having to deal with her intense happiness all the time.*

Discreetly taking her in, I finally glanced at something other than her pink hair. She wore a black tutu that brushed above her knees while a plain white shirt barely brushed mid-stomach, a sliver of fair skin peeking out from between the hem of her top and the elastic band of her skirt. Dragging my eyes away from her creamy skin, I found myself staring at her shoes.

Why does everything have to be pink?

Low-top Converse chucks in a bubblegum pastel pink adorned her feet, her steps nearly silent as she practically bounced down the path. She paused when she reached our destination, turning to me with eyes full of anxiety before her usual perkiness took back over. Huffing, I walked around her and opened the door. She looked relieved for a moment as she followed me down the hall. I turned back around and made a right, opening the office door for her. Mrs. Briggs greeted us in her usual way, enthusiastic way, an almost sing-songy musical quality behind each word.

"Good morning! Did you bring me the new student?" she asked, turning her smile to the new girl. "Aris Calisto, I presume?"

"Yes, ma'am," Aris responded, stepping forward and aiming that cheerfulness at someone new. While she was distracted, I gave her one last glance before quickly ducking out of the office. Disappearing into the crowd, I headed for my first class, the sound of the clock's chimes echoing through the courtyard and urging me to class... and away from Aris. Whose name I still didn't care to know.

Hope she can figure out where she's going.

CHAPTER 2

September 2nd
Monday Morning
Aris

Collecting the materials in my arms to tuck into my bag, I turned and realized my grumpy tour guide, Kyelerian, was missing. I guess I shouldn't have been surprised since he wasn't the most enthusiastic of tour guides. *Can't wait to see him again; I'm going to throw a whole cauldron full of sassy smiles and happy greetings his way and see if I can push him far enough to throw more than two obligatory words my way.* Holding back a sigh, I made my way out into the hall before pushing the thick wooden door of the Administration building open, immediately overwhelmed by a cluster of other witches in the courtyard, bustling from one location to the next. Bracing myself, I squared my shoulders and started toward my first class. The schedule said I was in Mixta Basics for two hours with Miss Ballerio, in the

Elemental and Spell Casting building *he* had pointed out earlier. I looked for the picture of the crossed wands and elements to make sure I was at the right place.

When I stepped into the building, I realized just how big the campus really was. The outside of the buildings all looked the same to me, but the insides were worlds apart. On the other side of the entryway stood two large arches, an image of the five elements depicted above one and the crossed wands over the other. The students around me separated and filed into their respective corridors, working their way around me seamlessly. Thankfully, this building had silver plaques that helped direct me to the correct room, and I quickly veered the winding corridors toward the spell casting wing.

Unable to help myself, I stopped outside the door, my hand resting just above the doorknob. It felt like such a monumental moment, and now that I was facing it, I wasn't sure how I wanted to feel. On one hand, being a Mixta in a new place made me pretty nervous, but on the other hand, I was ready to begin, excited to be surrounded by those who knew what it was like to be on the bottom of the societal totem pole. *Finally, a place where I might fit in for once.*

With that in mind, I turned the knob and stepped over the threshold, moving out of the doorway when another student came up behind me and darted toward the closest open desk, almost knocking me over in the process. With my swirling emotions continuing to build, I wanted to scream and bounce around, but by some magical intervention, I stood still and quiet as I waited for class to start, unsure of where to sit. I didn't want to risk sitting in the wrong seat and causing drama. *Witches be petty.*

The professor swept into the room, her flowing dress and robe fluttering behind her, her frizzy, gray hair poking out of her ponytail, making her look slightly unhinged. Vibrant green eyes zeroed in on me as soon as she perched behind her desk. With a quick sigh, I walked up to her desk and put on my best cheerful smile.

"Welcome, dear. You must be Aris!" she exclaimed excitedly, her hands sweeping out in an extravagant flourish as if she were speaking to a theater audience instead of just me.

"I am," I said with a tentative smile, her wild gesturing and excited speech making me feel awkward.

"Class, let's welcome our newest student, Aris Calisto! She comes all the way from Ignis!" she flourished, pausing while she waited for the students to react. When silence answered back, she waved me on to say something.

"Hi," I squeaked, throwing my hand up in a quick wave. My cheeks heated quickly as the other students stared. Feeling incredibly uncomfortable, I turned to face the teacher with a wide smile in an attempt to urge her to start talking.

"You haven't missed much so far this year since we just started focusing on practical work this semester. Today, we'll see what you're capable of and go from there," she barreled on, not even acknowledging the weird greeting. "Go ahead and take a seat over there while we wait for the rest of the class."

As soon as the words left her mouth, I hurried toward the desk she had indicated, tucking myself behind it, finally relaxing now that I wasn't the center of attention. The other students slowly trickled in, filling the desks surrounding me. Curious glances were thrown my way, but I focused on the professor. When everyone was seated, she finally got up from behind her desk, sweeping to the front of the classroom.

"Since we have a new student, I figured I would briefly

touch on the basics of why you're in this class. As most of you know since you've been here since January when the school year began," Miss Ballerio started, "Akasha society has five major power classifications—Potions, Divination and Scrying, Elementals, Spell Casters, and Summoners. Witches who don't fall within those five specific umbrella terms are classified as Mixtas."

My eyes fell to the scuffed wooden top of my desk as she explained the very basics of how we functioned. Her soft, sympathetic tone grated on my nerves as she continued to talk to us—a class full of Mixtas—as if we were stupid.

"Since Mixtas don't have a designated or easily identified affinity under one of the main classifications, we need to figure out exactly what you can do... if anything." She turned toward me with an encouraging smile, but her vibrant green eyes couldn't hide the hint of pity in them. "Aris, why don't you come up here, and we can try a few things to see if we can figure out what's going on with your power. While we're doing that, everyone, please pull out your designated work plans for this semester and begin on those."

Unable to refuse, I slid out from behind the desk and walked to the front of the room. The others were supposed to be practicing their own tasks, but every set of eyes was on me. *Gulp!* Professor Ballerio pushed a rolling cart from behind her desk, an empty flower vase and several wilted flowers scattered on its surface. She gestured for me to begin, and I assumed she wanted to see what I would do on my own. *Here goes nothing—probably literally.*

Using all my concentration, I focused on one of the flowers. My nerves were so high strung, knowing all eyes were on me, it did little more than twitch at first. After a calming breath, I tried again, this time bringing the flower into the air and lowering it into the vase. A collective gasp echoed sharply through the room, startling me so much, the flower jerked, knocking the vase over where it tumbled to the ground and shattered.

"She moved that with her mind," one of the students hissed, not even bothering to keep it low enough so I couldn't hear.

"She didn't even say an incantation!" another whispered, openly pointing at me.

"Very impressive, Miss Calisto," Professor Ballerio said with a slow clapping of her hands. Her slightly narrowed gaze and the accompanying hint of suspicion was one I was used to receiving. Mixtas shouldn't be capable of doing that kind of magic, yet here I was.

I was a mystery even within an academy accepting of Mixtas. *Ugh.*

"Can you move the cart without any spells or invoking hand sequences?" she asked, walking to my side and peering down at me with a calculating gaze.

Rolling my shoulders slightly to loosen the tightening muscles, I ignored the stares burning my back and the feel of her breath on my face. After a few seconds calming myself, the cart started to roll at a steady speed until it rammed into the far wall. *Not my most eloquent work, but the best I could manage under these conditions.*

"Well done, Miss Calisto. Why don't you take your seat and look over the rule book you should have received from the office for the rest of the class? I'm going to discuss these results with your other professors this evening to determine a proper work plan for the semester," she said, the shrewd look not leaving her eyes, scurrying behind her desk and jotting wildly in her notebook.

Ugh, I'm a puzzle to figure out. Fun.

Turning, I made my way back to my empty seat. The critical stares and oppressive silence seemed to radiate throughout the room as the other students watched me. The open judgment wasn't lost on me, so I focused on doing what the professor said. *You'd think Mixtas wouldn't be this rude.* I dug out the leather-bound rule book and flipped to page one, resting my elbow on the desk to cradle my cheek in my hand and cover my face from the prying eyes surrounding me.

Hopefully, this doesn't continue throughout the day.

Although it's better than being kicked out of my own house for being different.

Positive thoughts.

September 2nd
Monday Midday
Caspian

The smell of the sleeping potion I had been making still lingered on my jacket as I made my way to my next class. It was almost noon, and here I was, already needing more coffee or a long nap—though that could be thanks to the aforementioned potion. My rusty brown hair flopped into my face as I weaved through the other students. Huffing, I raked my fingers through it to clear my vision.

A flash of pink hair caught my eyes, and my interest piqued, a strange pull calling my gaze to her. My energy picked up even more when I noticed the peppy, petite girl who was rocking the pastel wave of curls turning into the same classroom where I was headed. *Today just got interesting.* That weird pull grew stronger with every step in her direction.

I took my usual seat in the back of the room as she stood

awkwardly in the front, waiting for the professor to come in. I could see the new kid jitters all the way back here as she shuffled foot-to-foot, looking completely out of place. Professor Ruslan walked in, his bald head shining in the warm glow of the floating lanterns above us, perpetual scowl in place, not even faltering as he greeted the new student. When his raspy voice echoed in the classroom, she squeaked out an answer in return, backing up several steps as she spoke.

"You can take a seat next to Mr. Kersey in the back," he said, not bothering to look up at her as he took out his binder of notes. My attention perked up when he mentioned my name, a grin making its way across my face at the perfect opportunity to figure out this vibe I was feeling. She turned around with a confused look since he hadn't bother to mention where I was, and she was clearly too scared to ask. I gave a quick wave to catch her attention, gesturing to the seat beside me. The look of relief on her face was almost comical, but I knew how intense Mr. Ruslan could be, so I kept my chuckle contained, not wanting to make her feel more embarrassed. My eyes roamed over her form as she made her way to my table. The only word I could use to describe her was cute... no, *she's fucking* adorable. Between her bubblegum pink hair, short stature, and pretty smile, she seemed exactly the kind of person I wanted to get to know. *Thank the gods he sent her to my table.*

"Thanks," she said as soon as she reached me, setting her bag on the table before slipping into the seat next to me, a gleam of curiosity in her gaze. The scent of candied strawberries wafted over to me as she flipped her hair behind her shoulders, turning to me with a dazzling smile.

"Anytime. Rough first day?" I questioned, giving her a

half-grin. Her cheeks took on an adorable pink tinge as she eyed my smile.

"Not terrible, just a bit overwhelming. I just got here this morning," she explained, her voice chipper despite the obvious anxiety rattling her. Her spirited nature seemed to seep into me, my previously tired state slipping away as I sat up a bit straighter, a wave of unexplained energy brushing over me, shaking the last of the sleepiness away.

"Like, *arrived* this morning?" I quirked a brow. *Why would anyone want to start school the same day as traveling? That's just setting yourself up to fail.*

"Yup, I got off the carriage, and the headmaster sent me straight on a tour. The tour guy left me in the admin office," she explained, her voice holding a hint of annoyance. I felt my fingers twitch at that news. *Who just leaves someone to fend for themselves in a school of five hundred witches?* "After that, I got my schedule and started my first class. Now, here we are."

"What was your first class?"

"Mixta basics," she mumbled, her eyes dropping to the desk, her shoulders tensing.

"Cool, cool," I say with a bob of my head. *Why would I care if she's a Mixta? It's not like they asked not to have an affinity.* She relaxed at my answer, her bright smile back in place.

"Yeah, it went well. Professor Bellario was a bit intense, but she had me show her what I'm capable of..." Her words were cut off by Professor Ruslan calling class to start.

"Get your books out and read the next chapter," he barked. "There will be a quiz Wednesday on the basics of what you've read, so I suggest taking notes. No talking." The teacher glared at us, his eyes flickering between Miss Calisto and me, in a not-so-subtle hint to stop chattering. "If I catch anyone talking or trying to send aerial messages, I will write you a detention slip, and have you report to the Assistant Headmaster for disciplinary action."

Pulling out the textbook from my pack, I dropped it with a thud on the wooden top before flipping to the proper page. When she didn't move to follow the directive, I slid the book over between us. Flashing me another gorgeous smile, she turned her attention to doing our work, but no matter how hard I tried to focus, sharing a book with my new tablemate distracted me from getting any reading done. Her sweet, sugary scent tickled my nose with every tiny movement of her head. As I pretended to take notes during the rest of the period, I kept mulling over what she'd said. The way she said 'capable of' made her seem like it was something big. *I never could resist a good mystery.*

September 2nd
Monday Afternoon
Aris

The clock tower rang its little melody, signifying the end of class. Standing, I grabbed my bag and pulled out my schedule before my tablemate nudged my elbow.

"I'll show you where to go for lunch," he offered, his head tilting toward the door. "Only if you sit with me though," he tacked on the end with a small, teasing curl of his lips. Narrowing my eyes on him playfully, I pretended to consider his offer. His deep blue eyes stared back shamelessly, his long fingers shifting his backpack strap on his shoulder as he waited.

"I suppose I can do that," I teased back, shrugging a single shoulder, feeling my cheeks heat up at his blatant flirting. One side of his mouth twisted up in a cocky half-grin like he'd already known I'd agree. Inside, I was squealing at the rush of excitement that filled me. This was only my second class, and I had already found a potential friend. It certainly didn't hurt that he was cute as hell with his chiseled cheekbones and messy russet hair pushed off to one side of his face.

"Come on, short stuff. I want to get some of the good dessert, and if we take forever, there won't be anything left except fruitcake." He shuddered at the thought before slinging an arm over my shoulders.

The moment his arm moved around me, a tingling burst of magic flowed through me. *That was weird.*

"So, what's your name? Probably don't want me calling you short stuff for the rest of your time here."

"Aris," I gushed in a completely undignified manner. "And you are?"

"What? You haven't heard of me?" he gasped, feigning hurt.

"Wait?! You're Alfred, the famous alchemist?" I teased with wide eyes and a loud, exaggerated gasp.

"What? No. Do I look like an Alfred to you?" he laughed, unable to keep the facade going. "Who the hell is Alfred the famous alchemist, anyway?"

"Well, you're the one who freaking asked for it, so you could just tell me," I sing-songed. "And don't be hating on Alfred. He's a great alchemist, little plushy witch's hat and everything," I babbled, thinking of one of my handmade stuffed toys I'd made sure to pack.

"You're weird." He squeezed me to his side in a hug. "I love it. I'm Caspian, the coolest kid you'll ever meet."

"Yeah, yeah, whatever you say," I scoffed with an eye roll but couldn't hide the smile I knew I was sporting. I hummed, passing through the door into the dining hall, my eyes finally focusing on the space around us. Long rectangular tables lined the room with enough chairs to fit the hundreds of students bustling around the busy space. No one was wearing any type of uniform, though I would occasionally see one or two wearing collegiate wear I knew you could get from the town down the road. I remembered seeing a shop or two that had clothing with the Aether Academy crest or the school's colors of navy-blue, burnt orange, and silver.

Looking closer, I could pick out cliques among the witches, easily identifying who was considered one of the five affinities and those who weren't. It wasn't based on their clothes or their status, seeing as how the affinities weren't exactly tattooed to their foreheads, nor was there a giant scarlet M stitched into our clothes for us Mixtas. Yet I could easily identify the groups of Mixtas, smaller clusters scattered throughout the room, while those considered one of the major categories were packed together in noisy groups who seemed to prefer sticking with their own affinities.

Elementals and Spell Casters were the easiest to identify, their confidence and obvious powers radiating attention from around the room. Small bursts of fire and ice magic swirled through the air as two elementals playfully battled above their lunch table. Two others sat a few chairs away, growing herbs in small flowerpots before wilting them and starting again with a new one. Their blatant displays of power left me in awe and a bit jealous—though I'd rather not admit it.

Summoners, Potions, and Rune Drawers were harder to separate from one another since their powers required magical items, ingredients, and supplies. Some had potion bottles and bags of runes or stacks of cards in front of them, but that was the only sign I noticed to identify what kind of witch they were.

An obvious gap was visible at the edge of the student section, separating them from the faculty. A shimmering magic barrier engulfed the staff section, making it look as if they were underwater. As I inspected the dome, I felt a wash of prickling on my skin. Try as I might, I couldn't ignore the pinpointed feeling of someone staring. Scanning the tables beyond the barrier, my eyes fell on a pair of curious seafoam-green eyes watching me intently.

"What's with the bubble?" I asked, pointing to the staff tables without being too obvious.

"It's soundproof, so they don't have to listen to all of this noise. Or so they can gossip about us in peace," he joked, glancing away from the barrier. I tried to pull my attention away as well, but the prickling feeling wouldn't stop. Under the new sensation that wouldn't ease was that continual pull I couldn't place. *What in the world is going on with me?* Shaking my head, I forced myself to focus on something other than my frazzled nerves and jumbled thoughts.

"So, how's the food around this joint? On a scale of 'fucking fantastic' to 'Belladonna,' where we at?" I asked, shifting my attention away from the room as more gazes had started to drift in my direction.

"Eh, I'd give it a solid flying around on a broomstick, but not when it's nice out. You know those kinds of rides where it's bumpy, and you get a splinter in your ass? Yeah, it's like that," he explained, slipping easily into my witchy puns and joking mannerism. The fact he seemed to get my humor made me like him, even more. "The dessert, though? I'd say it's definitely up there with a good soul cake."

"Well, dessert is better than regular food, anyway," I shot back cheerfully. His laid-back and flirty mood made mine seem more natural, making my awkwardness less apparent. Some of the nerves that had been eating away at me today finally seeped out. *Maybe this school won't be so bad after all.*

The cafeteria had several long buffet tables arranged on one side, each displaying an insane variety of foods. An overflowing stack of lunch trays and plates stood on the edge of the lines, students grabbing one as they passed by. There weren't cashiers since meals were free to the students and staff. The workers simply focused on refilling the emptying dishes and trying to keep up with the crowd. Everything smelled so good, my stomach grumbled as we stepped up to the nearest line.

Caspian grabbed two trays, handing me one and putting the other on the counter. I watched in awe as he piled it high with a ridiculous amount of food. Despite his comparison, the food didn't look too bad, which was reassuring since I'd be eating here several times a day. Following behind him, I picked out two big slices of pizza; I couldn't choose between the toppings, fries, and a salad. When we stopped behind the dessert bar, my eyes went wide as I took in all the selections.

"Told you," Caspian sang out at me, picking out two huge cupcakes and putting them on his already packed tray.

"How am I supposed to pick?" I asked, unable to tear my eyes away. He chuckled and grabbed a few different things, plopping them on my tray. He cocked his head toward the tables and gave me a smile.

"Let's go, Aris."

"I like food, but even I can't eat all this," I mumbled, following as he weaved his way through the cafeteria.

"Don't worry, I can help with that," he joked, throwing a wink over his shoulder.

I was a bit surprised when he stopped at an empty end

of one of the tables. With such a friendly personality, I expected him to have a table packed with friends. We each took a spot on either side, separating us from the other students. I was thankful for that bit of isolation in all the chaos of the new changes I was fielding today. We didn't talk as we scarfed down our food. While we worked our way through the array on our trays, people kept passing by and greeting him.

"Okay, I can't take it, what are you capable of?" he asked with a big sigh, suddenly looking serious.

It took me a few seconds to figure out what he was talking about. A grin spread across my face as I considered the best way to handle it. Focusing on the cupcake making its way to his mouth, I used my magic to pluck it from his fingers and brought it to my open mouth. I took a bite and groaned as the rich chocolate exploded over my tastebuds. His mouth hung open in shock as I flashed him a smug smile, still chewing the bite I had taken from his stolen dessert.

"Holy shit," he muttered, still sitting there, shell shocked. "You freaking stole my cupcake."

"You asked for it," I hummed with a single shrug. Taking another bite, I lifted a challenging brow. He huffed and reached out to take his cupcake back. I decided to take pity on him, releasing my hold on his chocolate deliciousness.

"Next time, just tell me you want a bite, Cupcake, and I'll share." He winked, and the flirty smile he threw me caused my cheeks to flare again. The fact this guy had me blushing this much was crazy. I mean, I had never cared much about the guys around me before. *That could be because of my stuck-up family and the people they deemed worthy to associate with.*

"Cupcake, huh?" I challenged playfully, taking a bite of my own dessert.

"Yup, got a problem with it?" He leaned forward, his elbows resting on the table as he took another bite of his cupcake for emphasis.

"Nope, just wondering." I didn't have a better response but felt confident as I held out a bite of my dessert, offering Caspian some. After a brief moment of surprise, he ate the bite of cheesecake right off my fork, his sapphire eyes holding mine. Unable to stop the flare of desire that shot through me, I squeezed my legs together, thankful the table covered the motion. When he finally tore his gaze from mine, he leaned back with a smirk, clearly able to tell the influence he had on me. *Why does he have this effect on me? He's making me feel like a boiling cauldron over the fire.*

The bells ringing successfully ended the moment, both of us looking surprised at how fast lunch had gone. I gathered my bag and dumped my tray before Caspian tossed his arm over my shoulder, and another wave of electrified chills ran through my body. Him snatching my schedule from my hand distracted me long enough not to question the funny feeling.

"Perfect." He started walking, practically dragging me behind his six-foot-two frame.

"What?" I huffed, my skirt flaring around my legs as I struggled to keep up with his long legs.

"We have history together, so it might just be a bit less boring now. The teacher is kind of a douche though," he said, glancing over his shoulder and laughing at my attempts to keep pace. "Sorry, Cupcake." His steps slowed slightly, giving me a chance to catch up, only having to power walk instead of jogging to keep up.

"Oh, Caspian, I didn't know your little sister was starting school with us!" a girl's voice shouted out, making me cringe. *Oh good, here we go.* Caspian pulled me forward, so I was tucked into his side, his arm possessively holding me to him.

"Witch, please. Last I checked, I wouldn't fuck my brother," I responded with a flip of my bubblegum pink hair. Caspian's cheeks flared pink this time, his mouth falling open at my words. I wasn't usually the crude type, but the witch deserved it.

And it wasn't a lie. Caspian is cute as hell.

"Well, Cupcake, feel free to come brew this potion anytime." He started to say more, but a biting baritone voice cut him off.

"Mr. Kersey, you're late. Take a seat."

Oh, shit.

CHAPTER 3

September 2nd
Monday Afternoon
Aris

I recognized the man with the piercing seafoam-green eyes who had watched me in the dining hall. Now, those eyes glared at us as he waited for Caspian to follow his order. Now that he was closer, and no barriers stood between us, I took in his handsome face and fiery red hair. His eyes moved over me for a moment with a hint of the same intensity as earlier before simply pointing me to a seat right in front, next to Caspian's. As I hesitantly made my way past him, a wave of magic pulsed between us, making my steps falter. I pitched forward, the professor's hands reaching out to steady me, and the magic intensified at the simple touch. Yanking his hands back, he looked even more off-put than before. *Wonder if he felt that too?* I scurried to my seat as quickly as possible, getting a small surge of comfort when I felt Caspian's foot nudge mine.

"We left off yesterday talking about the five main classifications of Magic—Elemental, Summoning, Spell Casters, Potions, and Divination." The teacher's eyes locked onto mine as he explained, Caspian making a grumble of annoyance next to me at the obvious attention. My brows drew low as I glanced at him in confusion.

"Miss Calisto," the professor bit out. "Is there something more important that Mr. Kersey has to say than I do?" My face flared, my gaze snapping to his. I shook my head, trying to keep from slouching down in my chair. *Geez, I barely looked over at him.*

"No," I mumbled.

"Good, then keep your eyes on me." His green-blue gaze sharpened as he stared, almost as though he was waiting for me to acknowledge his dominance. I dipped my head, doing as he said.

"Douche," Caspian coughed under his breath.

"Detention," the professor snapped at Caspian. "Now, I suggest you stay quiet for the rest of my class unless you're on fire or dying."

"Yes, Professor Callahan," Caspian nearly mocked his name, throwing me a wink and a tiny smile, despite our teacher glaring between the two of us, his jaw clenching in irritation.

"Miss Thana, why don't you tell us what the five affinities are and why they are so significant in Akasha society," he asked, his voice softening slightly as his focus changed to someone other than Caspian and me.

"Elementals, Spell Casters, Summoners, Scryers and Divination, and Potions. The significance of the number five stems from the Treaty of Five and the Five worlds our ancestors moved to after The Great War," a girl answered from Caspian's other side, giving me a small smile when she looked my way. That was all the surly professor needed to start back into his lecture. Deciding not to tempt fate, I took out my notebook and started taking notes. Unfortunately, my attention span was short, so as soon as he started droning on about Akasha history, he lost me. Instead, I studied him as he spoke, his eyes flickering to mine every few minutes and holding them. Each time he did, I'd sink a little lower in my seat, not wanting the added attention. I was already the weird Mixta in school, and it was only day one.

"I want each of you to write a paper on which of the five affinities you have, including history and famous witches in your magic classification. Start now, work on it for the rest of the period," he demanded, settling in behind his desk.

Not sure what to do, I stared down at my paper, a mix of anxiety and dread washing over me for a moment. *The reason I came to this school was to avoid moments like this.*

"Miss Calisto." This time when Professor Callahan spoke, it wasn't harsh or demanding but soft and questioning. "Could you come here for a moment?" He stood, waving a single hand toward his desk.

Sighing, I slipped out of my seat, purposely ignoring the stares I felt against my back. What caught me off guard was the fact he'd stepped out from behind his wood desk and started toward a door off to the side. I followed him, my eyes taking in the muscles shifting under his white dress shirt before they drifted lower.

Well, then, that's quite the ass.

"In here." His voice had me nearly jumping out of my skin, but thankfully, he wasn't looking at me, seeing as how I had been checking out his ass just seconds ago. He held open the thick wood door for me and closed it as soon as I walked into what looked like his office. "Is there a reason you weren't working on the assignment?" His voice still held that underlying command, but it was softer here.

Maybe it's just Caspian he doesn't like?

"I wasn't sure how to proceed. I don't have an affinity, sir," I explained, my voice low as I waited for his reaction. I studied his face to distract myself, noting he could only be a few years past graduating himself, making him the youngest teacher in this place, I was sure. He was definitely handsome even with the serious expression on his face.

"So, you're a Mixta?"

I nodded, unable to look at him, knowing I would more than likely find one of two emotions—disgust or even worse, pity.

"What can you do?" he asked, no judgment coloring his question.

"Uh," I hesitated, trying to explain, "I can..."

"No, don't tell me, Aris. Show me."

Relenting, I took a deep breath and looked around his office. The small space was cozy, bookshelves lining one wall and a plush couch under the window. A large oak desk rested to the side, papers and binders stacked meticulously on its surface. The bookshelves were lined with color-coded tomes, organized to perfection, the walls bare other than a large picture of Aether's landscape that hung above the small fireplace. A magical blue fire was burning brightly, giving the room a calming glow.

Finally, I decided on showing off, something about his challenging gaze making me want to prove myself—the urge to show I wasn't worthless flowed through me. Turning my attention to him, I kept my eyes locked on his. I couldn't stop the tiny curl of my lip when I saw his eyes widen as he witnessed what I was doing.

"What the..." he breathed, striding over to his desk where his pen was scrawling across a page. "How are you doing this?" he asked in wonder.

Though his office is so organized, he might have just been annoyed I was moving his stuff.

"Where's the rune stone or enchanted parchment?" He closed the distance between us, hands reaching out and searching my sides for whatever he thought I was hiding.

"I don't freaking have either of those," I hissed, yanking my arms away from him. The magic started to overwhelm me as his hands moved toward me again, still searching for something he wouldn't find. "I just fucking told you I don't have an affinity. I can just move shit. You told me to show you, and I did. Now stop fucking touching me."

"There's no reason to cuss, Miss Calisto," he tried to lecture me, but the frustration of the day had finally caught up to me, too much to handle.

"Well, maybe if you had fucking listened and kept your grabby fucking hands to yourself, I wouldn't be!" I practically shouted, uncaring there was a class right outside the door or that he didn't deserve the brunt of all my anger. At that moment, I decided I was done with this fucking class, the professor, and all the unexplained things that had been happening since I arrived here. Overwhelmed and nearing a breaking point, I stomped out to the classroom and grabbed my bag, ignoring Caspian's questions as I hurried from the room.

No sooner did the classroom door shut behind me than Caspian threw it open and ran after me. When I refused to speak, he simply walked beside me, letting my anger run its course. I didn't speak until I made it all the way to the dorm and up the stairs to my tower.

"Alright, enough. What did he do to you?" Caspian demanded, his voice seething with anger. I took a deep breath, letting the last of my agitation fade.

"He asked what I could do, so I showed him. Then he pretty much called me a liar, and after all the shit today, on top of traveling for days on end, I was done. He assumed I had a rune stone or something on me." Now that my anger was fading, I felt I had overreacted. *Way to make an ass of yourself on day one.*

"What a fucking douche," Caspian bit out, shaking his head in disgust. "Don't let him make you feel like less because of what you can do or who you are. I happen to like who you are, Cupcake."

"Thanks, Caspian," I started, trying to come up with a way to turn the conversation to something else. "So, what's your affinity?" I started looking around at all the stuff I still needed to set up while I waited for him to answer. Caspian followed my lead and helped me push my bed in front of the big window before plopping down on top of it.

"Potions, though most see it barely above Mixtas," he said quietly, picking at a thread on his sleeve. When he finally looked up, I gave him another soft smile, knowing how it felt to be considered to be at the bottom. Not wanting to make him feel weird, I focused on finding my box of books and started to line them up on the shelves.

"Do you have a big family?" he asked, standing up and walking over to my curling iron, picking it up. He looked perplexed as he shifted it around in his hand.

A small smile crept across my face as I waited to see what he'd do with it. It was a human thing that most witches wouldn't understand. *I'm a weird witch in more than just my lack of affinity. I also can't help the obsession I have with everything to do with the human realm. It fascinates me.*

"My parents, my sister, and my two brothers are all I have, but I never *really* had them. They didn't like I was a Mixta and brought down their reputation," I said absently as I moved on to hanging my clothes in the wardrobe. I'd resigned myself to their opinion of me long ago.

"I get that. I come from a long line of Spell Casters, and here I am, a Potion Brewer," he sighed, finally putting down the curling iron without questioning it... much to my disappointment.

"Do you enjoy it?" I asked, turning around to gauge his reaction. I took a moment to study his ocean eyes as he got lost in his thoughts, his eyebrows furrowed as he thought it over. His hair was pushed out of his eyes, the brownish-red locks in that messy yet styled look boys could somehow pull off. The corner of his mouth finally quirked up into a small half-smile before he finally brought his gaze up to mine. Our eyes locked for a moment, and he finally relaxed.

"Yeah, I do like it," he admitted, lifting one shoulder in a shrug.

"Then fuck 'em," I replied in a cheerful tone, loving I finally found someone who understood how idiotic the ridiculous hierarchy witches loved to cling to was. He walked over to me, stopping when he was mere inches away. His hand moved to my face, tucking a strand of hair behind my ear, giving me a soft smile as heat bloomed in my chest.

"I'd like to fuck *you* instead," he said, the offer hanging in the air for a moment as he looked into my eyes. There was more than just innuendo within the deep blue depths. I could see a sense of acceptance in his eyes I'd never seen before. The warmth in my chest spread to the rest of my body, and my hands reached instinctively for his. The moment our hands touched, the warmth seemed to spread between us. A cool drop of water touched my face, startling me out of the moment. Above us, a small rain cloud was forming, the darkening gray swirling mass rumbling softly before a steady stream rained down on us—literally.

"Are you doing this?" I asked quietly, laughing as the rain poured down around us. I threw my hands up and danced in a circle, feeling an odd sense of magic flowing through me.

"I think *we* are doing this, Cupcake," he said, laughing at my antics. He grabbed my hands and pulled me to him when I turned back around, the movement causing my chest to crash into his, his arms circling around me, holding me close. He shook off the rain dripping from the ends of his hair. When his eyes locked onto mine, the world seemed to stop for a moment. It was just us and the new magic flowing between us, the strange magic amped up now that we were touching once more. Something changed within us at that moment, our emotions aligning under that rain cloud.

He leaned in slowly, the hesitation giving me a moment to pull away. I stretched up to reach him, closing the last inches between us and pressed my lips against his. The kiss started sweet, his soft lips barely touching against mine before he deepened it with a tentative brush of his tongue. My heart pounded in my chest, unable to deny something about this felt so right as if my body was calling to his. He must have felt it too, his hands moving from mine to run down my sides and lower, gripping my hips possessively. A soft moan escaped my lips as my hands ran down his chiseled chest, the thin material of his shirt clinging to him, thanks to the water cascading around us.

Caspian nipped at my bottom lip, his body shifting to

walk us to the bed shoved against the curved stone wall. When the back of my legs hit the side of the mattress, we fell back, not caring we were both dripping. My legs automatically opened, and he settled against me, his hard cock rubbing against my clit in the most delicious way. Tangling my hands into his russet hair, I held him against me as his hands hooked under me to grab my ass. Pulling up, he ground our bodies together as our tongues brushed against each other. Needing to feel his skin against mine, I gripped the hem of his shirt and broke the kiss, pulling it over his head. Before bringing his lips back to mine, he pushed my top up and off me, tossing it to join his on the floor.

His mouth moved to my neck, nipping at the sensitive flesh, pulling a moan from me. The magic pulsed through me, heightening with each new touch, kiss, and sensation, leaving me breathless and needing more. His hands moved from my ass up to the clasp of my bra, undoing and tossing it aside. He leaned back, his eyes taking me in before letting out a groan of appreciation.

"Cupcake, you're beautiful," he said, his voice husky. The rain was still falling steadily, but neither of us seemed to mind, more enraptured with each other than our surroundings. A small smile moved across my face at the compliment, loving the way he made me feel beautiful and sexy.

"You're pretty damn sexy yourself," I murmured, leaning forward to pepper his bare chest with kisses. Sucking at his skin, my hands fiddled with his belt buckle in a rush to feel the hardened bulge straining against his jeans. He moved on top of me, holding his weight on his arms as he rested them on either side of me, giving me the chance to take the lead. Once I got the belt unhooked, I unbuttoned his jeans and pushed them down, freeing his cock. *Thank God for going commando.* He let out a low groan as my hand circled him, his breath coming out in pants as I moved it up and down. My pussy throbbed with need as I explored his body, wanting his impressive length inside of me, despite never having done this before.

After only a few more minutes, he torqued our position, so I was on top, pushing the band of my skirt down to reveal my lacy pink underwear. I kicked off my skirt, wanting as few barriers between us as possible. I rocked my hips against him, my hands resting on his chest. Groaning, he pressed his head back into the bed as I continued to grind my lace-covered pussy over his length. I could feel myself soaking, each pass hitting just the right spot to stoke the flame growing in my core.

Needing more, I slid off Caspian and quickly shimmied out of my underwear. He propped himself up on his elbows, and the way his eyes raked over my body left a wave of shivers rolling down my spine. Now that I was standing here with him looking at me so intently, a shyness crept over me. As if sensing my dilemma, he sat up and reached for me, adjusting us, so I was underneath him again, his cock resting against my entrance. I wrapped my legs around him, urging him on as I pulled him in for a kiss. As he leaned into me, he pushed forward, entering me with little resistance thanks to how wet I was. I winced slightly as he rocked his hips, and his eyes widened at my reaction.

"Cupcake... are you... a virgin?"

I felt my cheeks burn as he was still inside, staring down at me with a surprised expression.

"Are you really asking that now?" I huffed, embarrassed. Still feeling fire burning within my veins, I shook my hips and nudged his with my legs.

"Are you sure you're okay with this?" His face reddened

as he started to pull away. Groaning, I cupped his face and yanked him back into me as I kissed him—hard.

"Stop talking, Caspian," I murmured against his lips, giving him a not-so-subtle hint to keep going as I wrapped my legs tighter, making him sink further into me.

That was all the nudge he needed before he started thrusting into me. Our eyes locked again, the magic now so thick in the air, the room seemed electrified. The more he moved inside of me, the more the power burned in my veins. My eyes rolled back, my moans turning to frantic cries as he pistoned in and out of me faster. As I neared that edge, Caspian captured my lips once more, silencing my cries as I fell into that pit of release.

As soon as the aftershocks subsided, he sat back, hooking his arms under my legs to position them on his shoulders. At the new angle, he hit deeper, my hands clawing the bed in response. His eyes closed and his head fell back as he lost himself in pleasure. The small, sexy noises he made as he fucked me only turned me on more. No matter how much he gave me, I felt like I *had* to have more of him.

"Fuck, Aris," he panted, shaking as he continued his relentless pace before finally finding his own release. But he didn't stop, and a few moments later, I found myself following him as my pussy tightened around his cock, milking him. When we both had our breathing and heart rate under control, I moved back from him, and we shifted, lying next to each other.

"So, Cupcake, you going to answer my question?"

"Ugh, yes, alright?" I ground out, my hands coming up to cover my quickly reddening cheeks. "Can you stop asking?"

"Why would I do that? I want to know everything about you," he added sweetly.

Glancing over at him through my fingers, I was met with a cute smile, his sapphire eyes lit up in happiness.

"Now, stop hiding that pretty face from me," he said gently, pulling my hands away and twining his fingers with mine.

A loud knock echoed through the room, startling us. The magic in the room seemed to disappear as we were pulled from our post-sex bubble. The loud banging continued as the boxes and furniture, including the bed we were on, dropped to the ground. Caspian's strong arms wrapped around me to stop me from pitching forward off it at the sudden movement.

"Oops," I giggled. "My bad." Rolling off, I grabbed the closest articles of clothing, which happened to be my wet skirt and shirt. I didn't stop to think about how my shirt was white, and now wet, shadowing the edge of my boobs since I didn't have a chance to throw on my bra. Opening the door, I came face-to-face with Professor Callahan and his narrowed seafoam-green eyes.

"Aris," he said, his voice strained. Even outside the classroom, his voice demanded all attention. His eyes hardened as his gaze dipped down to my chest. Grinding my teeth against a new wave of magic, my nerves fried from all the extra stimulation, I crossed my arms over my pebbling nipples as cold air rushed in from the hall. "Why are you soaking wet?"

"I took a shower," I blurted out the first thing that came to mind. He cocked a brow, looking extremely skeptical at my answer.

"In your tutu and shirt?" His question conveyed his disbelief.

I shrugged, unsure how to respond. A soft shuffling sounded behind me before Caspian's warm torso pressed into my back. I looked up at him as his arm propped up on the door frame as his other one curled around my shoulders possessively.

"Torryn," Caspian greeted coolly. Professor Callahan's jaw clenched at Caspian's disrespectful tone.

"Nice to see you're welcoming the new student in such a *personal* way, little brother," the teacher countered, looking pointedly at the scrap of pink lace lying in the middle of my bedroom floor. I didn't know whether to die of embarrassment or question how the fuck these two were related.

"Only for my Cupcake." Caspian flashed a challenging smile. "Is there something you need, or did you just come up here to yell some more? I know it's what you're good at and all, but we have shit to do, and I like my eardrums intact." It seemed like everything that came out of Caspian's mouth only put his brother more on edge.

I'm sure family holidays are a blast, I thought sarcastically, feeling awkward and out of place between the two feuding siblings.

"Yes, actually. Miss Calisto, you have mentoring with me Monday, Wednesday, and Friday afternoons after familiar training. Which you skipped today, by the way," he lectured. Glancing back to Caspian he continued, "Don't think I didn't notice you leaving class early, either. Be happy I'm not putting both of you in detention."

"You already put him in detention," I spouted before I realized what I said, my eyes widening at throwing Caspian under the bus. Professor Callahan's eyes brightened as his stony expression finally cracked the tiniest of smiles.

"That's right, I did. I guess I had two reasons for coming up here. I expect you to report to the Assistant Headmaster tomorrow morning before breakfast." Caspian's body trembled ever so slightly in anger.

"You never know, Tor, I could let it slip how you yelled at Aris enough to make her want to leave class." Caspian shrugged again, his smile triumphant as Professor Callahan's grin fell, his expression hardening.

"Miss Calisto, don't skip any more classes. I'll see you Wednesday. Caspian, stop acting up," he bit out, but before Caspian's brother left, his eyes fell to my discarded underwear once more before he turned and strode away. Pulling me back into the room, Caspian kicked the door shut, leaving us alone again.

"Sorry." I cringed. "I wasn't really thinking when I brought up the detention thing."

"It's okay, Cupcake. I know you just want me to play a bad boy," he smarted, throwing me a wink. Sobering, he curled me into his arms in a warm hug. "Don't worry about it, it's all good. I've been getting myself out of trouble from his wrath for a long time."

"So," I hummed, drawing out the word. "Brother?" I asked, looking up at him. He grimaced.

"Yeah, I don't really want to talk about Torryn right now after seeing him checking you out in a wet shirt." His expression went from angry to panicked as he turned to me with wide eyes. "What about birth control?"

I snorted at the sudden change in conversation.

"I've been spelled for birth control, so it's not an issue. Don't worry, no babies," I teased him, "but I do think we should talk about the fact that my fucking room is covered in water. It rained on us, Caspian."

"Are you sure you're not an elemental?" he asked, stepping away from me and looking around at the damage, seemingly transitioning from one major topic to another with ease. I'm just glad he was handling everything with a level head, not acting all freaking crazy or like a douche.

"I'm not, but I wish I was an air elemental so I could dry all of this," I mumbled, peeking into the boxes and hoping my stuff wasn't damaged. Thankfully, the water seemed to be contained, so only my bed and right around it were wet. I pulled a few towels out of my boxes and threw half to Caspian. Catching them easily, he started mopping up the water. When I walked closer, I felt that pulling sensation settle, and I couldn't resist asking him.

"Caspian, I know this seems crazy. But have you felt...?" I started to ask, trying to figure out how to describe the weird sensations that had been plaguing me all day.

"A pull?" he took over seamlessly. "A weird kind of vibe when I'm around you? Yes," he said definitively before his brows pulled low over his eyes. "But I'm not feeling it as much right now."

"Me either," I agreed with a nod. "Maybe it was just this weird magical fluke sort of thing?" I rambled with an exaggerated shrug.

"Maybe," he mumbled, not sounding convinced. "Maybe we can do some research during our study class, see if there's anything to it. I've never felt this kind of 'magical fluke thing,' as you so appropriately named it," he teased softly with finger quotes. Glancing around, he changed topics yet again, "So, with all this going on in here, do you want to warm my bed tonight?" he asked with an eyebrow wiggle.

"If we're just cuddling, hell yes. I don't think I can go another round," I murmured, shifting as an ache settled through me after our toss around in my bed.

"Don't worry, Cupcake. We can do that whenever you're ready, so if you just want cuddles, then cuddles it is," he agreed with a bright smile. "Grab what you need, and we can head down, hopefully, giving your room the night to dry."

Nodding, I wandered around the room, tossing a bunch of random things into my bag. I made sure to grab a dry pair of clothes for tomorrow, figuring I could change into my pajamas before leaving. When I was clothed in dry shorts and a shirt for bed, I made quick work of the windows scattered around the circular room, the cool air brushing over my face as I opened each one. *The breeze should dry at least some of this.*

Hopefully.

CHAPTER 4

September 2nd
Monday Night
Aris

Caspian took my bag from me and led the way downstairs, pausing for a moment so I could lock my door. The halls were empty now that it was getting late, only a few notes flying through the air instead of the hundreds that had flown overhead all day. My heart sped up a bit as I followed Caspian to his room. I shouldn't be nervous after everything we had been through today, but the thought of staying the night seemed so *big*. Once he opened the door and the lanterns overhead flared to life, I stood there awkwardly as I took it all in.

Caspian's room seemed fitting for what I knew of his personality so far. The bed was made, a simple blue comforter adorning the top. His wardrobe was closed, and the room tidy, the only mess on top of his desk where a few papers were strewn about. I was quickly drawn to a small table to the side. Jars and bags of ingredients lined the top and a hanging shelf above it. A stone mortar and pestle was set to the side, and several empty potion jars sat around a mini cauldron. My fingertips grazed over the jars as I read them, half of them things I hadn't heard of before. I was quiet as I wandered around his room, taking in his space while I mulled over what had happened upstairs.

"You're not getting shy on me now, are you?" Caspian teased as he slipped his shirt over his head. I turned abruptly on my heel to give him privacy, looking around for a place to drop my bag. Warm arms wrapped around me as I dropped the bag on a chair and stood there, waiting for him to finish. "You wore me out. You ready for some sleep?"

His voice was low and husky in my ear, sending a shiver down my spine. He pulled me with him to the bed, settling down and positioning me so my back rested against his chest. The awkwardness slipped away slowly as we laid there, relaxing bit by bit to the sound of his breathing evening out and the feel of his breath on the back of my neck.

Caspian slept peacefully behind me, but for some reason, my body refused to let me join him, despite how exhausted I was. After what felt like hours, my stomach went from a dull hunger to a near-constant growl. Sighing in defeat, I decided to get up and head to the dining hall for a snack.

"Where you going?" Caspian slurred sleepily as I gently moved his arm and tried to slip out of the bed.

"I'm hungry, I'm going to sneak over to the dining hall for a snack. Want anything?" I whispered back, half expecting him to fall back asleep and not answer.

"Get me a funkle cake with green furry unicorns," he mumbled into his pillow.

Well, no idea what a funkle cake is, so I'll just grab him whatever I find. Grabbing my slippers from my messenger bag, I smiled at the fuzzy bunny ears that flopped as I walked out of his room, grabbing his key on the way out.

The halls were empty and quiet, the only sound the shuffling of my steps on the stone flooring as I made my way down the main staircase and out into the courtyard. When I glanced up from walking down the path, I immediately stopped, completely enthralled by the crystal clock tower. The structure practically glowed in a radiant haze of light purples, blues, and iridescence as the moon's rays bounced through and off the multi-faceted crystals. Barely breathing, I didn't want to disturb the magic I felt flowing through the air as I walked closer. The pull that had been plaguing me all day when I was near Caspian flared, only this time it had a sense of peace and... rightness, almost filling me.

A loud, rumbling growl from my stomach broke the moment, startling me enough to jump slightly. Shaking my head to rid the odd sensations, I continued my trek to the dining hall, my hunger nearly all-consuming since I hadn't had dinner. I was pleasantly surprised to find the building and the dining hall doors unlocked. Since I hadn't had a chance to read through all the rule book, I wasn't sure what the hours or regulations surrounding late-night snacking were. The main space was empty, but a sliver of light peeked out from under a door I hadn't noticed before, catching my attention. When I drew closer, I saw a metal plaque saying 'Student Food and Drink' next to it. Humming softly, I opened the door and came face-to-face with my broody guide from this morning, Kyelerian, sitting on the counter, stuffing a handful of Sugary Sweet Hex Mix into his mouth.

We both froze for a moment, his handful of frosted treats stopping midair. His eyes slowly moved down my body, a slight quirk to his lips at the sight of my favorite slippers before looking back up. A blush bloomed across my cheeks, and I couldn't stop myself from blurting out something random. *Why do I do this?*

"Did you know that eye of newt explodes at six hundred degrees?" I blurted out, my blush deepening at my own ridiculousness.

"Huh," he hummed, looking at me like I was crazy as he shoved the bite into his mouth.

Well, now that I feel like a complete idiot... Trying to redeem myself, I switched tactics, putting my smile back in place.

"How was your day?" His eyes flickered back to mine at the question, giving a half-hearted shrug in response. Not one to give up easily, I continued. "Those look tasty, where did you find them?"

"I took the last one," he replied bluntly, not even looking sorry as he took another handful. A flash of humor swirled in his hickory depths as if he took pleasure in rattling me. My smile turned into a pout as my eyes roamed over the selection of sweet treats. Now that I knew I couldn't have the Hex Mix, nothing else sounded good, and an exaggerated sigh fell from my lips. His eyes narrowed on me, his hand slowing on the way to his mouth the longer he stared at my pout. My eyes drifted from the handful of sweetened cereal and nut mix to his face, putting extra curl to my lip.

"Ugh, fine," he ground out, holding out the bag. "Just don't eat all of it. I'm hungry too, you know."

I perked up and practically skipped over to him, hopping up to sit on the counter next to him. He scooted over slightly before I snatched the bag out of his hand and grabbed a handful. I offered the bag to him as I tipped my handful of sweets into my mouth, a moan of pure food happiness coming out before I could stop myself.

"Do you do anything like a normal person?" he asked, exasperation coloring his words. I just gave an unapologetic shrug as I reached for more. I loved that the school stocked my favorite treats.

"Do you ever give real smiles?" I shot back, raising an eyebrow.

"No," his answer was quick as he snatched the bag away from me while I was distracted. "Can't you go get some moon cookies or something?"

I narrowed my eyes, reaching for the bag again, but he extended it above his head, keeping it out of reach.

"That's just mean. Don't you feel sorry for me? It's my first day," I whined dramatically, poking out my bottom lip again.

"I feel sorry for *me*. I'm the one getting manipulated by a tiny pink witch," he said pointedly, bringing the bag back down to grab a handful, side-eyeing me the entire time, dodging my attempts to snatch it away.

When he popped another handful in, I successfully snatched the bag back, taking a few bites before tossing a piece at him. I couldn't help the boisterous laugh that bubbled out of me when the almond hit him square in the forehead.

"You seriously did not just throw that at me." He gaped as if trying to process I did, in fact, do just that. "You're wasting my late-night snack. Give it back."

He lunged toward me, his arm outstretched to take the half-empty bag away from me, but I laughed and spun off the counter until I stood on the other side of the little snack room. A hint of a smile played across his lips, and a tiny glimmer of playfulness lit up his hickory eyes as he stared me down. We both froze like little kids caught being naughty when the door swung open, and a guy stepped through.

Kyelerian froze, shutting down at the sight of him, a scowl moving back into place. My eyes slowly took in the new arrival. He was taller than Kyelerian but a bit shorter than Caspian at around six foot. He had shiny black hair, just long enough to fall into his eyes but perfectly styled. His eyes were a deep, rich brown, framed with long lashes, his face set in a serious gaze, not looking angry but definitely stoic.

"What's going on in here?" he asked, his deep voice echoing in the room. He had the kind of voice that could command the attention of a room without effort. Something stirred in me as I took him in, though I couldn't pinpoint if it was from my snack buddy, the newcomer, or my own nerves after today's events. "I didn't expect to see you in here playing around, Kyelerian."

"It's Kye," my brooding companion gritted out. His eyes flickered to my face, and I gave him a teasing smile, trying to brighten his mood. The way Kye was acting had me wondering who this guy was. *Whatever. We weren't doing anything wrong*, I thought, shrugging off his harsh tone and serious gaze.

"Hey! I'm Aris," I greeted, giving him a bright smile before heading back to the spot next to Kye. "Open up," I teased, holding up a pretzel. Kye's face was comical as he worked through the change in mood—a mixture of shock, disbelief, and amusement dancing across it. He opened his mouth obediently, much to my surprise, and I tossed the pretzel in. He gave a small grin as he closed his mouth and chewed it. *I did it! I made the broody boy smile!*

"Xanthius," the newcomer added. His tone, while still

commanding attention, held a hint of curiosity as his eyes darted between the two of us. Turning on his heel, he continued on his original path to the shelving unit filled to the brim with snacks and treats. Without hesitation, he grabbed a box of Cackling Crackers, my face scrunching up at the boring choice. *Who eats just plain crackers? Nope, he needs something better.*

"Open up!" I yelled, choosing one of the sugar-coated almonds and holding it up. He stood there for a moment, looking unsure before his eyebrows crinkled, and he opened his mouth, tilting his head ever so slightly. I took the opportunity to throw the treat, lacing my magic into the action, so it landed perfectly in his mouth. His mouth snapped closed, and he chewed, mumbling out a 'thanks' before abruptly turning and rushing out of the room. The moment the door clicked behind him, Kye burst out in laughter, big belly laughs that had tears streaming down his face.

"You... just threw... food at him. You have no clue who he is, do you?" he wheezed out. I gave a shrug, not really caring who he was.

"Nope, but that doesn't change the fact he needed something better than fucking plain crackers. I mean, seriously, who eats Cackling Crackers? *For fun.*" I shuddered.

"Why do I feel like you're going to cause chaos on this campus?" he asked, shaking his head as he tried to compose himself. He jumped gracefully off the counter, snatching the bag from me.

"Thank you," he sang out, walking toward the door. Stopping just inside the doorway, he turned to me, and looked me right in the eye as he shoved a huge handful of the stolen treat into his mouth. He tried to smirk with his chipmunk cheeks, which only made me laugh. The door closed behind him, leaving me alone to peruse the snacks and wonder about who exactly this Xanthius was while I made sure to grab a few different choices for Caspian. *Nope, no funkle cake with green furry unicorns here.* When my arms were completely full, I followed Kye's route and headed back to Caspian's room, my stomach and heart full from all the bewitching encounters today.

CHAPTER 5

September 3rd
Tuesday Morning
Aris

"Cupcake, it's time to get up," Caspian whispered, giving me a gentle shake. I peeked over at him before pulling the blanket over my head again. He laughed as I snuggled in deeper, starting to drift back off to sleep within seconds. The cover was ripped away moments later, forcing my eyes open so I could glare at him. "If you want breakfast, you have to get up and get ready."

"Eating is overrated," I mumbled as I scooted up to sit against the headboard.

"That's just the sleep talking. Get ready, and we can get coffee," he sang out, heading for his closet to grab fresh clothes and his shower caddy.

"Fine. I'll meet you back down here when I'm done showering," I mumbled, grabbing my stuff and heading for the girls' bathroom. The halls were still empty, so it must have been early. The prospect of a shower that wasn't overcrowded had me hurrying.

When I stepped inside, only one other girl was getting ready, combing her hair at the mirror. I recognized her as the girl Torryn called on the day before, so in an attempt to be friendly, I gave her a quick smile and wave before stepping into the closest shower stall.

The moment the hot water hit me, I knew Caspian would be waiting for a while. It felt too amazing, properly waking me up. A flash of the conversation I had with Torryn last night had me giggling to myself. *Oops, I mean Professor Callahan...* he's going to think I'm a crazy witch, showering with clothes on. Well... let's be honest, I doubt he believed me.

Once I rinsed out the last of my candied strawberry conditioner, I finally turned off the water. I half expected Caspian to be waiting not so patiently for me when I stepped out, but instead, it was filled with other girls waiting for their turn. Not wanting to hog the bathroom much longer, I quickly braided my hair to the side and put on my makeup.

By the time I made it back to Caspian, he had fallen asleep again, snuggled into the covers, looking way too peaceful for the guy who had forced me to get up early. Standing at the far wall, I put a mask of pure innocence on my face before using my powers to yank his cover away. He mumbled in his sleep but didn't fully wake up. Using my powers once more, I rolled him out of bed and onto the floor. The poor guy hit the stone with a thud and startled cry before jumping up and looking around for the culprit. His eyes locked on mine, narrowing slightly as a mischievous smile played on his oh so kissable lips.

"Payback's a witch, Cupcake," he warned, rubbing his ass where he hit the floor.

"How could you accuse me?" I gasped in mock offense, holding back my laughter. "I'm standing way over here, waiting on you to wake up," I reasoned, holding out my hands. He rolled his eyes and grabbed his school bag, ushering me out the door ahead of him.

"I need Witch's Bean. Now. It's too early to function without it," he mumbled, locking the door behind us, then grabbing my hand. A flush burned my cheeks as a smile curled my lips. Unable to stop the giddy feeling, I floated on cloud nine through breakfast and to my first class.

Who would have thought little me would have a friend already?

Too bad my parents couldn't be here to witness it.

I wandered through the stacks in the library, my fingers brushing lightly over the leather-bound spines of the manuscripts lined up on the research shelves, inhaling the intoxicating scent of parchment and leather. *There's nothing like the smell of a well-loved tome. Caspian had said research, so here I am, but what in the wing of bat am I looking for?* I spent the next little while pulling off random books I thought might have answers, but since I wasn't even sure what I was looking for, I came up empty-handed each time. The clock tower chiming throughout the building startled me out of my wandering and had me redirecting my steps toward the library front doors. Unfortunately, I turned the corner and ran straight into another student.

"Oh, my broomstick, I'm so sorry!" I squeaked, scrambling to pick up the strewn papers that fluttered from his arms.

"No worries," the guy's smooth voice came out, making him sound way too chill for someone who just got slammed into by a distracted witch.

"Here you go," I squeaked out, handing over the papers as I took in his bright hazel eyes. His mouth was pulled up in a lazy grin as he checked me out, his eyes roaming over me as he reached out to take back his fallen supplies. My mouth went dry as my eyes trailed over the corded muscles that teased me from underneath his Henley. Our fingers brushed as his hand wrapped around the papers, and the moment his skin touched mine, a gentle wave of magic flowed over me, light as it moved over my skin, like a soft summer breeze. My eyes widened and flickered up to his at the sensation, but the mossy depths didn't show any reaction.

"Be careful, wouldn't want you to hurt yourself," he warned lightly, tucking the papers under his arm, sauntering off, further into the library. With one last glance his way, I walked through the doors and off to lunch, trying not to think about yet another weird magical encounter.

Too many other things to deal with right now.

Lunch passed quickly, Caspian and I easily falling into our routine before we broke off from each other at the crystal clock tower with Caspian heading to his room since he had a free period while I veered toward the Summoning and Potions building.

Thanks to my interactions with Caspian, I no longer felt as timid and scared as I walked into new classrooms. He'd helped me to find my footing here even if it was all still new. With a deep breath, I walked in with my usual smile. The Potions classroom had an odd scent to it—a mix of plants, sulfur, and the odor of animal waste. I tried to discreetly wipe my nose to hide the wrinkle that scrunched my face, but it was no use. Thankfully, no one was paying attention to me as they were focused on pulling out their book and other ingredients at their designated cauldrons.

I took the chance to look around, taking in the high stone ceilings and huge windows. I could see why they chose this room—*though someone should probably open a few more of the windows to ventilate this smell*. Each workstation was essentially a long table with a cauldron and fire stone underneath and to the side, a row of sinks and several shelves piled with jars and baskets full of strange and intriguing things. I held back an excited noise at the prospect of doing new magic as I stood awkwardly to the side, waiting for the professor while more students filtered in.

"Ah, you must be Aris," a boisterous man proclaimed, his loud voice bouncing around the room, catching the eyes of several of my fellow witches. "Come now, dear, you can partner up with one of your classmates. Don't want to throw you right into the deep end, now do we? That would be awfully terrible of me." He flashed me a crooked smile, and despite his receding hairline and graying beard, his playful and open attitude reminded me of a lovable child. "Delilah, since you're one of our top students, why don't you assist Aris until she can safely handle all the dangerous ingredients we've been working with."

My eyes flickered over to Delilah to gauge her reaction. She had a small smile on her face as she gave the professor a nod. She didn't look upset, though honestly, she didn't seem to show a lot of emotion, seeming like the quiet and shy type, which should be interesting with my cheerful personality. As I walked around the tables to sit next to her, my eyes focused on her simple outfit. She had on a long, dark blue skirt with plain black shoes and a burnt orange sweater with the school's logo emblazoned on the front. Her short black hair was down, except for a small section she had tucked behind her ears. She was petite though she had a few inches of height on me, putting her at about five-foot-three. Her light blue eyes were taking me in as much as I was her. They were hard to read, but she seemed nice enough.

"Thanks for letting me sit with you," I said in a bright tone, taking the stool next to hers. Professor Brogan brought over a thick tome and sat it in front of me as Delilah flipped hers open.

"No problem," she said quietly as she found her spot. "We're on Chapter 12, Energy Elixirs."

"Awesome," I said quickly before flipping through my new book. Once I found the page, I started skimming it, hoping not to make too big of a mess of this class.

An hour later, I found myself packing up my bag, a tiny headache forming after attempting to absorb way more information than I thought it could handle. I gave Delilah a quick wave and checked my schedule, groaning at seeing mentoring next. The thought of sitting and being lectured by someone with an affinity or worse, being forced to perform all these stupid tests to make sure I was truly a Mixta didn't seem all that appealing. The mentoring classrooms were in the administrative building, so I stepped outside into the gentle sunshine. The fresh air was exactly what my head needed to clear, the headache slipping away and a smile spreading across my face.

Now that I was used to it, I didn't have any trouble jumping into the crowd of students who constantly bustled through the courtyard. I still got quite a few curious looks, but that could have been them just checking out my awesome pink hair.

The mentoring hall was full of tiny classrooms, separated to allow each pair to properly study without constant distractions. When I located the room number listed on my schedule, I opened the door and stepped in. I mentally groaned at the sight of the guy I almost took out in the library. *How do my embarrassing moments keep coming back to haunt me?*

"Nice to see you again," the guy said, a lazy smile spreading across his face as he leaned back in his chair. I took the chair on the opposite side of the table to face him.

"Sorry again about earlier," I mumbled, my cheeks heating. He waved me off before I could say more, clearly already over it.

"I told you not to worry about it," he reminded me, pulling a file out of his bag and setting it on the table in front of me. My name was scrawled across the front, and I could see my schedule on the top of the stack when he flipped it open. He thumbed through the papers for a moment before speaking again.

"So... Aris Calisto, daughter to an elementally affluent family, registered to Aether Academy earlier this year. Alright, that's all a bunch of shit," he exclaimed, slapping the folder closed and shoving it off the side of the table to where it fluttered to the ground. "Tell me about the Aris who's not in the file."

I felt my eyes narrow slightly, unsure whether he was

being serious or if he was going to pull a prank on me. My brother's friends loved to do that to me growing up—pretended they gave a shit, then proceeded to throw it in my face.

"I like pink," I stated, still cautious. When he gave me a small nod to continue, I started to ramble. "I like to draw, I collect strange things, my favorite thing to wear is tutus, and I've always wanted to learn how to fly a broomstick."

"You've never been on a broomstick?" he asked, his eyes showing emotion for the first time. I could see a bit of confusion and excitement in there. "We may just need to change that."

"That would be beyond amazing," I squealed, dancing in my chair, my eyes widening at the prospect of finally getting to fly. Seeing me so excited, he chuckled lightly.

"Let's work our way up to that. It never hurts to have a reward in mind," he said with a wink, folding his hands under his chin, leaning forward. "I'm sure every class, you've had to show if you can do magic, so why don't you just tell me what you've been working on, and we can go from there."

"I'm a Mixta, and I don't have a study or practice plan yet, so I've been stuck reading the rules and history books so far. Have an essay I have to write on it," I explained with a shrug; it's not like I had much to share with him.

"Cool. Since you don't have a plan yet, why don't we try to get ahead on that homework? I'm not going to sit here and try to make you go through all these random tests I'm sure you've done a hundred times by now," he stated, pulling out his own history textbook, the gold embossed 'History of Akasha 401' shining under the floating lantern above us. I couldn't stop the surprised expression that took over my face at the fact someone wasn't going to make me dance around like a spelled broom.

"So... that's it? Why do I have so many mentoring sessions then? I have some on Thursday, some with you...?" I trailed off, wanting to know if I was being singled out for some reason.

"It's something they do for first and second years. It helps them determine how strong their affinities, or lack of affinities, are and how to use them properly. You have one with a professor because you're a Mixta, and they want to figure out the best direction to take your education," he explained before looking down at his own work.

Despite having to read through my boring text and write up notes for the paper I had due, I felt a sense of calm happiness settle over me as we got to work. The silence around us wasn't stifling or oppressive, both of us able to focus without the feeling of a professor breathing down our necks. I flipped my book open to the first chapter and started reading.

> *Asteria is comprised of five major realms, each with their own unique style of government and landscape. Twice a year, the heads of government for each world meet in a five-day summit to keep the lines of communication and trade open. Each world is made of one major species. Aureus is the human world, Althaia home to the dragons, Altair home to the vampires, and Arcadia home to the Elves.*
>
> *Following that theory of five, Akasha's surface was made of five major areas that were later sectioned off into territories, each with their own unique landscape and council.*
>
> *Ignis is mainly comprised of deserts with a hot and arid climate. The academy of Ignis is comprised of Elementals and focused toward controlling the four major types of elemental*

powers—Fire, Air, Water, and Earth. The fifth power can be covered, but due to the rarity of the Spirit Elemental manipulation, it is not taught often.

The second territory is Caeli, where the winds are most notable behind the valleys and plains of the land. The academy is the first of two schools open to all types of magic, including Mixtas.

The third territory is Oceanum, where the majority of the landscape is made up of waterways, including marshes, rivers, streams, and lakes. The academy is exclusive to the two affinities of Scrying and Divination and Potions. It is one of the hardest to reach, only accessible through four bridges or by boat as it sits in the middle of Lake Tranquillo, the largest body of water in Akasha.

The fourth territory is Terra, where most of the land is comprised of cliffs and mountains. The Terra academy is built into the face of Altus Mountain with the interior of the school deep within the stone. It teaches Spell Casting and Summoning to help reduce any possible risk to the neighboring towns.

The final territory is Aether, which is abundant with forests and crystal caves. The academy here is open to all five affinities as well as Mixtas.

"Aris."

My mentor nudged my hand, and a wave of soft tingles brushed over my skin, radiating through me before he pulled his fingers back. "Class is up if you want to pack up your stuff."

Oh good, I was just starting to fall asleep from that boring as hell textbook passage. Sitting back from my hunched position, I stretched my tense muscles and shook out my hand after scribbling several pages of notes over the text I just deciphered.

"Thanks," I pepped up, practically jumping out of my seat when the clock tower rang.

"Oh, hey, Angel!" he hollered as I meshed into the crowd. Turning, I was bumped a few times but didn't move, waiting to hear whatever he had to say. "The name's Drayce! Also, try not to run into any more people!" Drayce flashed me a bright smile before I lost him in the wave of witches. *Did he just call me Angel?*

The encounter—and the cute nickname—had me smiling the entire way to Summoning class. This one, I was really excited about. The fact someone could use magic to summon creatures and objects had always impressed me. There were a few whispers I'd overheard of darker things that could be summoned, but those weren't something we'd learn about in class. *I just hope the professor lets us see some of it firsthand.*

The classroom had an ominous vibe—the way everyone turned and looked at me as I entered the room only amplified it. The room was dim, the lanterns overhead set with a low blue light that gave the room an ethereal glow. A raised circle was in the middle of the room with tables surrounding it. Runes were etched on the outer edge of the circle, currently dim since it wasn't in use. There wasn't a teacher's desk, so I stood to the side of the door and waited. A few moments later, she swept into the room. Her face was serious, but when her eyes landed on me, I could see kindness in her features.

"You must be this Aris I keep hearing about. Come join us," she said, her voice holding a musical quality. She seemed younger than most of my professors, closer to Torryn in age. Her black, long-sleeved robe was simple, but she made it look classy.

"Yes, ma'am," I confirmed as I followed behind her. She

led me to a row of hooks where similar black robes hung. She eyed me before searching through them, tossing one to me. I caught it easily and slipped it on, the hem hitting just above the floor.

"In order to keep yourselves grounded while summoning, you must form what we call a rune circle. You want to stand inside your circle as you form it, which keeps your summoned creature or object contained. There are five points within your rune circle, one for each element, which are the mandatory portions of your circle. Each circle is unique to the caster and the object they are conjuring. This is done to keep your magic focused, and as you know, is part of everything we as witches do. When you are finished summoning and want to release whatever you've conjured, draw the rune for dissipating the spell in the middle of your circle. You must follow these steps, and you must keep in mind the law of three. What you send magically into the world can come back three-fold. This is why dark magic is forbidden," she droned on, ending on the warning we'd all heard throughout our entire lives.

When the bell finally tolled, I was so drained, I practically sleepwalked through the halls. The moment I stepped into my room before dinner, I dropped my bag on the floor and face-planted on my bed, letting the exhaustion overtake me.

This will get easier... right?

CHAPTER 6

September 4th
Wednesday Morning
Aris

Something bumped into my face, waking me from a dreamless sleep. No matter how many times I swatted at it, it came right back. Eventually, I peeked open my eyes to see three paper airplanes flying around my room, dive-bombing me every few minutes. I snatched the first one out of the air and opened it up.

Hey! You want to hang out tonight?

That clearly had to have come in after I fell asleep; I barely remembered making it back before dinner last night. The next one came down, and I snatched it out of the air before it smacked me in the face.

Stopped by and could hear you snoring up a storm from all the way across the room and through your door, so I figured I'd let you sleep. See you tomorrow, Cupcake <3

I groaned as the third note continued to ram into the back of my head the entire time I was reading the first two. Instead of white like most I had seen around campus were, the note was attacking me was a brilliant red. *Guess whoever is really trying to make a statement.*

I'll see you tomorrow for our first mentoring session. Don't be late.
-Professor Callahan

I rolled my eyes at the formality of the note—as if I wasn't capable of remembering a simple schedule change. *I wrote it in my planner and everything.* Not wanting him to think I was ignoring him, I wrote a quick note back to Torryn on the spelled paper to let him know I'd be there. I muttered the activation incantation I had learned during my reading in Mixta Basics on Monday, the paper folding itself into a little paper airplane before it hovered in front of me. Tacking on Professor Callahan's name, I watched the message fly out of my room, slipping out under my door. Since I was already writing notes, I scribbled a quick reply to Caspian.

Excuse you, I do not snore, and if you keep that up, you'll never get to find out what it's like lying next to me, again!
Kisses,
Cupcake.

Once I finished getting ready, I headed out for a quick

breakfast, needing the fuel to get through another long day of classes.

Wanting to make sure Torryn wouldn't freak out at Caspian and me being late, I made sure to corral a still eating Caspian out of the dining hall and to our history classroom. Sinking into my seat, I placed my bag on the ground next to me. My and Caspian's desks were so close together, when he shifted to stretch out his legs, his left knee rested against my thigh under the table. I had to cover my cheeks as they flushed when he would nudge me every so often with a nearly inaudible chuckle. He slid a piece of paper onto my desk, which I recognized as my note from earlier. He winked over as I unfolded it.

You do, and it's the cutest snore in all of Akasha!

I folded the paper back up and threw it at him in indignation, but he just laughed and blew a kiss at me. *Ugh, he's incorrigible.*

Torryn strode out of his office and into the classroom right before the clock tower chimed, his gaze immediately falling on his younger brother and me, eyes dipping down to see where Caspian was playfully pushing my leg.

Did... he just grind his teeth? I mentally questioned with a furrowed brow. *No, you're imagining things*, I told myself.

"We have a guest speaker today. One of our students will be providing insight into the inner workings of the Council. As the son of a councilman, his experience and knowledge are unique, so pay attention. While we are learning the basics in class, I thought it would be beneficial to get a new viewpoint. Hold your questions until he asks for them, please," he said pointedly, glancing at me, then around the room. "Please welcome Xanthius Eideann."

A few students clapped awkwardly as the guy I met in the pantry walked in. He looked as stiff and stoic as I remembered him, his clothes perfectly starched and ironed, the pants still holding their crease. He had on a dark button-down shirt and kept fiddling with the hem as he made his way to the front of the room.

"Good afternoon. Thank you, Professor Callahan, for having me. Akasha is run by one main council headed by the prime minister, the Council of Akasha or CoA for short. The five council members are the head of each of their territories and oversee a smaller council, reporting back to the CoA. Each council oversees local laws and petty crimes. The CoA makes Akasha's laws and acts as the judge and jury for major crimes..." Xanthius continued to talk, but his words ran together in a haze of boring information I honestly didn't care about.

"Alright, thank you, Mr. Eideann," Torryn addressed the class before turning to me. "Miss Calisto," he called, stopping me from shoving my paper and pen into my bag.

Glancing up, I made eye contact, unable to push away the sensation of prickling tingles I always seemed to get when I was around him. *I really need to figure out what's going on with my magic and all these fucking encounters.*

Note to self—research!

"Don't forget, we have mentoring after your next class."

Torryn's statement pulled me from my thoughts to realize I had been staring at him. *Oops. It's not my fault he is sexy as hell.* He had a handsome, dignified style that drew me in. I didn't usually go for older men, but he was hard to resist.

"Aye, aye, captain!" I said, saluting with a teasing smile. I almost burst out into laughter at the warring emotions on his face—a mixture of wanting to laugh and 'oh shit, what have I gotten myself into.' *Good, he could use some humor in his life.*

"You ready, Cupcake?" Caspian called from the door, a hint of amusement in his voice. Torryn's face fell at his brother's nickname for me, irritation replacing the previous emotions. For a moment, his eyes held something else, a look resembling longing.

Longing? Okay, I'm definitely imagining things!

"Yup, let's go to familiar training!" I said with a squeal. This was one class I was really looking forward to. I didn't expect to get a familiar right away if ever. They were rare, but it was important for witches to understand how to properly care for familiars in case one chose you later in life. The bond between a familiar and a witch was a strong mental bond. If they let a familiar get hurt or sick, it could harm the witch. A witch felt what the animal felt, and that wasn't something any witch should be unprepared for.

The classes were split between twelve teachers by year but were all held in the familiar barn and clearing behind the library. Once we got there, I followed Caspian's instructions to find Professor Thane, who waiting with a small group in the fenced-off pasture attached to the huge familiar barn. Animals were roaming freely in the pasture, birds flying overhead and into the tower of the barn.

"Welcome, you must be Aris. I'm Professor Thane, but you can just call me Thane. Come meet Lulu," he called over to me as I made my way to the class. Lulu was not, in fact, a cute fluffy pet as I expected but actually, a rather large and grumpy alligator. Despite Thane's reassurance she was friendly, I wasn't too willing to stick my hand down there and touch her—the possibility of pulling back a bloody stump was none too appealing. The rest of the class was already at a safe distance, so I said a quick 'hello, pretty girl' and hurried to join them. Thane's smile grew as I greeted his intimidating pet.

Looking around at the class, only two others in my group had familiars. One was a tiny mouse burrowed into a girl's hair, only his white face and pink nose poking out. The second was a crow, sitting on a tall guy's shoulder, eyeing the poor mouse.

Thane rambled on about properly bathing and feeding your pet, handing out several guides on each animal type as he made his way around the group. The thought of a giant alligator choosing me had me shuddering. *No thanks!*

Another class walked by, heading for the back of the pasture. I noticed Kye right away, his face set in a scowl as he listened to a rather nasally teacher droning on.

"Kye!" I yelled, not thinking about the fact we were both in class. His eyes snapped over to me before a look of pure exasperation took over. He gave me a small nod to match my smartass smile and flirty little wave of my fingers. His teacher didn't even flinch, continuing to drone on while Kye shook his head at me.

"Who wants to feed Lulu?!" Thane asked excitedly, not seeming to care about my outburst. "Aris, you up for it?" he asked, his eyes full of naive excitement. There was no way he realized how terrified everyone was of her. I glanced over in Kye's direction, noticing he was barely suppressing his laughter while I faced off an alligator that could easily swallow me whole.

Turning back to Thane, I found him holding out a bucket full of gigantic, whole fish. Not willing to grab the slimy creatures inside the bin, I used my magic to pick out the biggest one. It floated out and alongside me as I stepped closer to Lulu. Crouching down, I floated her meal closer to her mouth, being sure to keep my hands and limbs far enough away from the food, in case she was a messy eater. Lulu crawled forward slightly before eating the fish from the air in a much gentler manner than I had anticipated. The not-so-little alligator proceeded to close the few steps between us, her head bumping into my leg.

"Awe, that's my sweet girl," I cooed, patting her head as she continued to nuzzle my calf. *She isn't so scary after all*

"And here I thought it was only marshmallows that won over her heart," Thane cheered, coming up and giving his sweet girl some scratches on her side. She rolled slightly to the side to give him better access, somehow making her look like the cutest creature around. A smug smile spread across Thane's face before he stood up and turned, shouting across the clearing to another group. "Hey, Callahan! I told you I'd eventually get a student to feed and love on my big girl!"

Callahan?! Of course, it was him!

Torryn and his class walked over, a shocked smile on his face as he clapped Thane on the back, clearly not noticing it was me. They joked back-and-forth about Lulu as I continued to show her love, hoping he wouldn't notice it was me.

"Of course, it was you, Miss Calisto," he said, his exasperation clear in his voice. When I looked up at him, a small smile played across his lips.

"What, Professor Callahan, you want a turn?" I challenged, raising an eyebrow and gesturing at my new friend. "Come on, girl, go show some love to Professor Callahan," I cooed to the alligator who rolled back onto her feet and started toward Torryn.

"Oh, hellsticks!" he shouted and jumped as the large

animal neared him, his class following his action and backing away.

"What's wrong?" I called out, cupping my hands around my mouth as I shouted toward his retreating form. "Scared of a sweet girl like Lulu? Come on back, baby, I'll pet you. I'm not afraid of you, sweetie." At my words, she stopped her pursuit and turned to come back to me, rolling sideways for belly rubs. I settled down on the ground next to Lulu, rubbing her belly and relaxing while I listened to Thane's explanation on how to care for big familiars and pets.

When class ended, both Torryn and Caspian approached, side-eyeing each other the entire way. I held back an eye roll at the obvious sibling rivalry. Caspian was the first to get to me, laughing as he took in me and my new bestie.

"I take it the first class went well?" he asked, crouching down beside me and slowly reaching a hand out. Lulu gave him a cute little grunt and a veiled glance but allowed him to pet her. Torryn slowed down as he got closer, keeping a safe distance away—*big baby*.

"It's time for mentoring, Miss Calisto. Ready?" he asked formally. I gave Lulu one last pet before walking away. The sad grunt she gave had me wanting to run back, but Thane intercepted with a huge bag of marshmallows. Following Torryn through the trees and back to the main part of campus, I wasn't sure where he was planning on holding mentoring until he led me back to his classroom. When we got there, he moved some of the desks out of the way to make more room in front before jumping right in.

"I know you can move things with your mind but let's see if any of the basic spells work for you. Whereas Elementals can manipulate the element itself, Casters are able to bring those elements about with magic. Only Advanced

Casters are able to bring it down to one word. Typically, Casters usually need long phrases to be able to manipulate things with magic. For instance," he explained before pointing to the floating lanterns overhead. "*Mergit in flamma,*" he muttered, the lights above us flickering out. With another phrase, they lit up again.

"So, you can bring fire about but couldn't manipulate it with just a phrase?" I clarified, trying to understand what he was explaining.

"Correct, and we can only light a fire where it's intended. A lantern is an object meant for fire, so we can light it, same with a candle. But I couldn't just go set fire to the pasture with a simple phrase. An elemental could do that if they wished. They would just need to say their activation word, which for fire would be *ignium.*"

His explanation made more sense now. Sure, they taught this stuff in school when we were growing up, but they never really broke it down in terms we could grasp as Torryn was. It was a welcome change, and I was excited I might actually learn something interesting, instead of being scolded for virtually everything I did. I was also glad Torryn and I seemed to be working so well together. After hearing Caspian talk about him, I hadn't exactly have high hopes.

"Alright, your turn," he said, extinguishing the flames so I could light them. "Focus on thoughts of fire and heat, picturing in your mind what you want to happen. Then say the spell-*ignem accende*-and push your magic forward," he finished, gesturing for me to give it a try.

Trying to mimic his actions, I focused on the lanterns overhead and thought of fire blazing to life in the closest one. When I muttered the incantation, a tiny flame flickered to life before sputtering out, the glow hardly big enough to even illuminate the space around us.

"Okay, fire isn't your thing. What about water?" he asked, showing me how to fill up a glass of water at the utterance of *implebis aqua*.

He showed me this one several times before I started to get annoyed. *I'm new to spell casting, not an idiot.* I couldn't help myself when I started to imagine copious amounts of water pouring on his head. I had started to giggle when a huge wave of water splashed over us both, leaving us drenched and him sputtering. Now I knew the incident in my room wasn't just a magical fluke.

What is happening to me?

"Oops?" I murmured with a tiny shrug. *What do you say after that kind of shit?*

The look he gave me at my words was one of shock, not anger as I expected. He whispered a few words, and a swirl of wind went through the room, drying the floor and us.

"I thought they tested you for elemental magic?" he asked though he seemed to be talking to himself. "You shouldn't be capable of that, especially without an activation word."

"They tested me for everything. I'm sure it was just a fluke or something," I muttered, trying to play it off like it was no big deal.

"Aris... that was hardly a fluke, that was a strong show of water elemental magic," he countered. "Is this what you were referring to when you said you just showered the other night?" I could almost see the wheels in his mind going a million miles a minute, trying to figure it all out, trying to figure me out.

"Uh... maybe?" I tried to divert my attention from his intense gaze, but he closed the distance between us, staring down at me from his over six-foot height. Being so close to him, I could see the similarities between him and Caspian, but I could also see what made Torryn... well, Torryn. His jaw had a shadow of red facial hair, and those seafoam-green of his eyes held specks of deep, rich blue, gold, even some brown. He smelled of pine and freshly cut grass, and I had to stop myself from taking a deep breath to sniff him. *I mean, that'd be weird, right?*

"Aris," he murmured, but even with his voice soft, it was still laced with a command that forced me to look at him. "Tell me the truth."

"Well," I started, scratching the side of my head in an attempt to distract myself from how close he was standing and the resulting waves of magic rolling over me at his proximity. "Hypothetically..." I trailed off, uncomfortable with explaining exactly how I got these powers. *Don't want to just blurt out I lost my V card to his brother. That's worse than smelling your teacher.*

"All right," he hummed with a skeptical eyebrow raise. "Hypothetically, what is going on?"

"What if someone—not me, obviously—but you know, a random witch," I emphasized with a wave of my hand. *Why am I this way?* "Was having weird feelings and vibes when around certain people and magically... ha,"—I chuckled in my nervousness—"somehow was to, I don't know, get powers they didn't have before?"

"I think we should bring this up to an Elemental teacher and get their take," he said firmly, starting to walk across the room.

"No!" I shouted, stopping him in his tracks. "Please, I just want to research it first. I'll be careful, and it's not harming anyone. No watery thoughts or even drinking or thinking of water until I know what it means," I pleaded, begging him to stop. His eyes narrowed as he looked at me, silent for several minutes. My anxiety flared, and I tried my best not to freak out while I waited, his eyes narrowing after a moment.

"What exactly were you thinking about, Miss Calisto?" *Oh shit, he used my last name. I'm in trouble.* My cheeks heated as I stuttered over my answer.

"I thought you were talking down to me like I was an idiot. Then I got irritated and maaaay have thought of water dumping all over you, but I didn't expect it to actually happen!" I rambled, feeling worse and worse by the second. I expected him to start yelling or get angry, but instead, he looked hurt. My heart ached at the dejected look he shot me.

"You know... I was only trying to help you, Aris. I'll see what I can find, but that's it for mentoring today. I'll see you Friday for History." He turned on his heel with no further words, walking into his office and closing the door. The click of the lock echoed in the empty classroom as a sinking feeling settled in my gut.

My mood dropped even further at the sight of pouring rain outside. *Man, I don't want to get soaking wet all over again,* I grumbled to myself as I walked outside into the downpour. Students were sliding in the grass and running outside, making the crowd even more chaotic than it had been before.

By the time I reached the door to the Administration building, I expected my feet to be squelching in my canvas shoes. Taking a tentative step, I froze, realizing I was, somehow, completely dry, not even my hair was dripping water. *What in the wing of bat is happening to me?!*

Nope, not freaking dealing with this today.

"Cupcake!" Caspian's overly happy mood was a stark contrast to my down in the bubbling cauldron mood. "How was mentoring?"

"I need Choco Bat Brownies and some soul cake as soon as freaking possible," I huffed, tucking under his arm that curled over my shoulder.

"Was my brother a douche?" He stopped, glancing down at me with a severe frown. I shook my head violently, not wanting him to blame Torryn for my fuck up.

"No, I promise it wasn't his fault, but I'm tired, and I just want sweets. Can we stockpile and go watch Boos and Brews? They're supposed to be making Spookhetti and Boo's signature Ghost Gin and Tonic." I poked out my bottom lip in a tiny pout, hoping he'd be willing to watch one of my favorite vegging out shows.

"Alright, Cupcake, but only because I happen to love Boos and Brews," he agreed readily without noticing that I was dry as dragon bones despite just coming in from the pouring rain. However, it didn't escape *my* notice, he was also dry in the sea of soaking witches who were squelching through the dining hall.

Not today, Satan, I'll save figuring that shit out for another time.

CHAPTER 7

September 5th
Thursday Midday
Aris

After checking in with Professor Embry for my study hall, I started looking through the tomes. This time, I specifically looked for books on Mixtas, hoping to discover if some found affinities later in their lives. A scrawling silver title caught my eye—*Mixtas Through the Years* seemed like exactly what I was looking for.

Claiming a comfy armchair, I threw my legs over the side and rested the book on my lap, flipping through the pages. It was a huge book, so I was stuck flipping pages for half of the study hour. Just as I was about to give up, a passage caught my eye.

"Though late bloomers are not unheard of, Mixtas rarely obtain affinities later in life. A few Mixtas develop a more diluted version of their affinity through rigorous training," I mumbled, reading the passage out loud. It was helpful, but it didn't really explain the craziness happening to me.

With a heavy sigh, I stood up and threw my bag over my shoulder before carrying the heavy tome back to its shelf. Just as I turned the corner, I ran into Drayce. This time, *my* book fell to the ground.

He chuckled, bending over to pick up. "We're going to have to stop meeting like this, Angel," he teased, making my cheeks flare again as I snatched it back from his outstretched hands.

"I'm so sorry," I said, hiding behind my book like a true weirdo.

Oh, my broomsticks, could I for once NOT make a fool out of myself?!

Drayce

I couldn't believe my luck—the cutest little witch ran into me for the second time in a week. I'd wanted to see her again before our next mentoring session, and I couldn't have planned a better reason to talk to her. Seeing that cute blush made it even better. She hid behind the book she had clutched in her hands before peeking enough of her face over the top just in time to see her blush deepen. I gently pulled it away since it really wasn't that serious.

"*Mixtas Through the Years*? What are you looking up?" I questioned, finally noticing what she had been reading, curious why her Mixta teacher would have her looking up the basics... that's kind of their job to teach her that.

"I just want to learn all I can about it," she shrugged, though a spark of panic in her eyes had my curiosity piqued. Not that she had to share everything with me, but something about her continued to pull me in and made me want to know everything about her, not just because she was cute either. Her odd sense of humor and clumsiness made her even more adorable. It didn't hurt she actually seemed genuine—what you saw from her didn't feel like a facade.

"Cool, cool, cool," I said, giving her a casual nod. Her stomach gave a loud rumble, and like clockwork, the chimes went off, indicating the end of the class. "You want to come have lunch with me?"

"I usually sit with my friend Caspian if you don't mind him joining us too?" Her face screwed up in concern as if she was afraid I'd make her go alone now.

"Sounds fun." I gave her a smile and took the book from her, walking over and resting it on the book return cart. "M'lady?" I asked, holding my arm out for her. She giggled and wound her arm through mine, letting me lead her safely through the crowd.

Goddess knows, if she'd left on her own, the entire crowd would go down like dominos.

Caspian

I couldn't stop the smile that seemed permanently affixed to my face when I knew I was about to see my Cupcake. I never thought things would have turned out this way, but I wasn't complaining. It wasn't that I didn't have friends—I had plenty of groups I could hang out with—but I always had that feeling of being an outsider. With her, it was different. We worked perfectly together, and she got me in a way no one else ever had.

I had no clue what was going on between us, but ever since that night, weird things had been happening. First the downpour on us, then the fact it was raining outside and not a drop got on me? Crazy. This morning in the shower, it took twice as long because the water seemed to move away from me every time I'd step under the warm spray. *Though I'm sure me constantly thinking about it, probably wasn't helping.*

Stepping into the dining hall, I scanned the space for Aris' signature pink hair. When I finally spotted her, I felt my eyes narrow slightly when I noticed another witch sitting with her. He was giving her flirty smiles, and when she wasn't looking, he stared at her shamelessly. *Son of a witch! Who the eye of newt is that guy?*

Taking a deep breath, I pushed back the jealous urge. *We aren't dating*, I reminded myself, but no matter how much I repeated the phrase, the tiniest sliver of jealousy wouldn't dissipate. I hurried through the line, grabbing several items in a rush to get to them as quickly as possible. A tiny self-satisfied smile curled my lip as I picked out a couple of Cupcake's favorite treats. *Ha, let's see you outdo that, random dude sitting with Aris.*

"Hey, Cupcake," I greeted, sinking into the seat next to her and flashing her a smile. *Hopefully, she doesn't see me being a jealous douche; I don't want to be like my brother.* I scooped up a bite of the soul cake I got for Aris and held it out for her. Her eyes sparkled as her dimples appeared on her blushing cheeks.

"Awe, Sprinkles," she chirped, leaning forward and taking the bite from my fork. Seeing her lips wrap around the fork had my thoughts wandering to places they shouldn't. I glanced over to the other guy, but he only had a small smile on his face as he watched us, no hints of possessiveness or jealousy, which helped calm me down. *If he's cool, I'm cool.*

"Caspian, meet Drayce. Drayce, meet Caspian," Aris said with a bright smile. "I keep running into Drayce... *literally*, and instead of being upset, he offered to walk me to lunch.

Well, the fact my stomach growled really loud helped," she explained, giving an awkward chuckle.

"Why doesn't it surprise me you ran into someone?" I teased, Drayce laughing with me as Cupcake ducked her reddening face behind her hands.

"That's exactly how I feel," Drayce nodded in agreement, throwing his hand up and over the table for me to shake. "It's nice to meet you, Sprinkles."

"Nice to meet you too," I replied, chuckling as I shook his hand. Drayce gave me a wink as he pulled his hand away, and it caught me off guard. *Is this guy flirting with me?* "So, other than bulldozing people, Cupcake, how's your day been going?"

"Not bad," she stated with a shrug. "Just worked on that essay for Mixta Basics that's due tomorrow. Did some research into that weird magical... urge to learn everything," she stumbled over her words, realizing we weren't alone. "Didn't find anything super interesting. Mixta history is boooring. What about you guys? How was your day?" she asked, trying to deflect attention from her.

"Not terrible, just boring. I had study period, so I focused on my Potions conversions," I said with a shrug as I took a huge bite of my sandwich.

"Had summoning this morning, which wasn't anything special since we weren't doing too much. Then study hall where I was doing some research for my magical agriculture elective. Well... before I got ran over by this cute pink witch." Drayce flashed Aris another smile. My lips thinned, but I kept hold of my jealous urge to snap at Drayce as he looked over at me. "And here I sit with an equally cute Potions Brewer."

I choked on my bite of sandwich at the blatant flirting. Aris' tiny fist pounded on my back as I coughed roughly.

"Awe, Sprinkles, you have a fan!" Cupcake squealed happily. I didn't know how to feel about him hitting on me, so I just gave a choked laugh and shoved my moon cookie into my mouth, hoping Cupcake would change the subject.

Well, at least she's happy about this.

Aris

As I walked to mentoring, I had to keep shoving my nerves back down. My mentoring with Drayce went well, but that didn't mean the next student mentor they paired me with would. *Why couldn't Drayce be my mentor on both Tuesdays and Thursdays?* Pushing into the hallway where the mentoring rooms were, I scanned the hall, trying to figure out who my Thursday after lunch mentor was going to be. Suddenly, another wave of odd sensations crept over me. Sighing, I glanced around for Caspian, Kye, Torryn, or Drayce since it seemed to only happen with those weirdos, but I didn't see any of them. *So, who the hell is making my magic act up?* I grouched, turning back to the dwindling crowd. I knew as soon as I saw him.

Xanthius, the boring guy who ate boring crackers as a snack.

I mean, who does that?

"You're Aris Calisto, correct?" he asked, his deep voice stiff as if he were approaching a business client instead of me.

"That's me.... How could you forget with hair like this?" I said cheerfully, holding out some of my hair as I gave him my brightest smile and an awkward wave, trying to bring a smile out of him. *Why am I like this?! You're just embarrassing yourself... again!*

"Ah, yes. The girl who disliked my snack choice and

threw food at me. How could I forget?" he deadpanned, gesturing to a nearby table for us to sit down.

Blushing at the reminder of throwing food at him, I joined him. *Did I seriously do that? Yup, sounds like something I'd do.*

"My affinity is Spell Casting, so my job as your mentor is to explain the basics and see if we can coax some magic out of you," he started, but it felt like the perfect opportunity to bring up my issue.

"Wait... it's still possible to learn new magic as a Mixta? Does that include getting affinities? Does that happen often?" I asked in a rush. He sputtered for a second at my verbal onslaught before contemplating my words. *He definitely doesn't seem to have my runaway mouth problem.*

"It can happen, but it doesn't very often. It's not full affinities either, usually just small bursts of magic," he explained.

"So, for those with affinities, or even Mixtas, do they ever form magical bonds?" I asked bluntly, not sure how to word my way around it. His eyebrows pulled down as he thought over what I had said.

"I've not heard of anything like that. Where did you hear about that?" he asked, rubbing his chin. My cheeks heated, a telltale sign I was about to spout off a lie.

"Oh, I don't remember anymore, someone was just talking about it in passing, and I love a good mystery, so I've been trying to research it. I just haven't had any luck," I explained quickly, hoping he'd buy into the random curiosity angle.

"Well, it never hurts to learn new things. I'm intrigued as well, so I may see what I can find in the library during study hall," he said, giving me a formal smile. "Now. We are here to talk about Spell Casting..." He started droning on about his affinity, but my mind was a million miles away. I pretended to listen as I waited for the glorious sound of the bell.

It can't happen soon enough.

September 6th
Friday Midday
Aris

I sank into my desk for history, my mind a mushy mess from the monotony of the last day. Spell Casting 101 was interesting, but it wasn't anything I hadn't gone over with Torryn during our mentoring on Wednesday. Although Professor Nesrin wasn't super boring, it was boring material. Scrying and Divination was very much the same—good teacher but basics on the information. I think at this point in the week, my brain had reached capacity.

Today dragged so far, just turning in my essay for Mixta Basics and reading the chapter in Magic 101 with Caspian because they still hadn't given me a textbook. Now though, my anxiety was through the roof as I waited for Torryn to come into the room. A sense of sadness filled me, remembering his hurt expression two days ago, and the fact I hadn't gotten a chance yet to properly apologize. *Hopefully, he's not too upset with me.*

"Class," Torryn greeted us, his eyes darting everywhere but at me. "Today we're going to be discussing the five territories of Akasha. Who can tell me the names of the five territories?" I raised my hand, probably a bit more enthusiastically than I needed to. *But I actually know the answer to something in this freaking school, and I'm excited, damn it!*

"Miss Thana," he called on Delilah with a wave of his hand.

"Ignis, Aether, Terra, Oceanum, and Caeli," she explained quietly. Torryn gave her a small but proud smile, and I felt the urge to nibble on my lip. The painful sting of him avoiding my gaze built the longer class went on. I understood I was a bit of an asshole during our mentoring, but he had been talking down to me at the time. *And in my defense, I didn't know that would be the outcome.* I couldn't lie though—it was kind of satisfying to see the water move at just a mere thought.

Torryn continued his lecture, pulling me out of my rambling thoughts. My hand shot up at the next question, and once again, he picked Delilah to answer. This time, I didn't stop my bottom lip from finding its way between my teeth as I nibbled it. The pattern continued until I finally gave up raising my hand.

By the time class was over, I was thoroughly agitated and, for whatever reason, abnormally jealous. *What is wrong with me?* I tried to physically shake the strange prickling sensation running over my skin and the rock in my stomach as I got up from my desk. I turned to walk over to Torryn's desk but was greeted with the sound of his office door slamming. *How the hell am I supposed to apologize if he won't stand still long enough?*

At least, he can't avoid me during our mentoring session.

You have got to be kidding me, I growled, glaring at the red paper airplane I had just unfolded. Torryn had canceled our mentoring session for the afternoon with plans to resume on Monday.

Now, who's being a childish little brat?

"What's wrong, Cupcake?" Caspian called, propping up

on his elbow from where he had collapsed on the ground of the familiar pasture. Lulu's snout nudged me, reminding me I had stopped petting her. It was really cute how she waddled to me when she saw me across the field. My mood lifted as I bent down and rubbed her sides. *Who knew alligators were so lovable!*

"Your brother is avoiding me!" I snapped as I threw him the paper, turning my head away so he wouldn't see how upset it was making me. I rested my cheek against my knee, my attention focused on giving the sweet alligator all the love she wanted. I pulled out another marshmallow from the pocket of my sweatshirt and put it in front of her mouth. She made a cute noise of appreciation before rolling over for belly rubs.

"Why would he be avoiding you?" he asked, tucking a stray strand of my pink hair behind my ear.

"Because I may or may not have conjured a bunch of water to fall on his head because he was talking down to me," I mumbled, feeding Lulu another treat to avoid looking at him.

"I would have paid good money to see that," he said before letting out a loud belly laugh.

"Not funny," I grumbled, throwing a marshmallow at his head. He took a breath and calmed his laughter, swiping a tear away before looking at me again.

"Sorry, go on," he said with an apologetic smile though I could tell his laughter was barely suppressed.

"He was purposefully not picking me in class, and now he's canceled mentoring? That's not a coincidence," I defended.

"So, apologize," he hedged, trailing his fingers along my back to soothe me. I took a breath and relaxed a little at the calming motion.

"I tried, but he won't freaking stay still long enough for me to talk to him," I said, throwing my hands up in frustration. "At this rate, I'm going to have to bribe him with something for him to forgive me." At that thought, an idea sparked. "Oh! Come on, we have to plan," I exclaimed, patting Lulu before jumping up and dragging a whining Caspian behind me.

"I don't like the sound of that," he mumbled.

"Too bad, you're helping me, Sprinkles, and that's that!"

"You're lucky you're so damn cute."

I smiled brightly as we made our way up to my room.

"You know you love me," I spouted over my shoulder. He grumbled unintelligibly behind me in response.

I'm going to take that as a yes.

CHAPTER 8

September 6th
Friday Night
Aris

𝓐 few hours later, Caspian and I found ourselves standing in the dark, empty kitchen. It was a bit intimidating looking around at the giant silver appliances. They had more knobs than normal ovens. *This might get interesting.* I tried to play it cool as if this was the sort of thing I did all the time.

"Alright, we need flour, eggs, butter, sugar, and chocolate," I started reading down the list as Caspian walked over to the fridge. He started pulling items out before letting out an excited laugh.

"You know what else we need? This!" he yelled over, holding up a bottle of Witches Brew. I'd had that stuff before, a mixture of different hard alcohol and probably a spell or two that would get you sloppy drunk before you realized it. *Baking and drinking? What could go wrong? What the hellsticks, let's do it!*

"There isn't enough chocolate in this pantry. Let's go check the student one," I said, closing the pantry and turning to Caspian, who was already pouring shots for both of us.

"Shots first, pantry after," he cheered, holding a shot out for me. I took it and sucked a deep breath, clinking my glass to his before swallowing the fiery liquid in one big gulp. A shudder tore through my body as I made a ridiculous noise and scrunched my face. *Note to self—get a chaser before the next one.* Caspian laughed at the display, but I didn't miss his slight shudder.

"Come on, chocolate," I piped in, hooking an arm through his. We made our way out of the kitchen and into the dining hall, only to run into Drayce.

Again.

At least it wasn't just me this time.

"Angel," he laughed, steadying me and Caspian as we teetered from the collision. "What are you two up to?"

"Brownies!" Caspian practically shouted. I shushed him, trying to not draw too much attention. Drinking was allowed since we were of legal age, but that didn't mean I wanted it advertised to the entire freaking school.

"Brownies, you say?" Drayce's brow quirked. "Got room for one more?" It might have been the warmth spreading through my body from the Witches Brew, but there *definitely* seemed to be innuendo in his question.

"Sure, dude, let's go!" Caspian smiled brightly, hooking his arm through Drayce's, practically dragging him over to the pantry.

The moment I pulled the door open, I spotted Kye sitting in the same spot as the last time, eating out of a bag of chocolate chips. Seeing my first friend holding the object I was searching for, I let out an excited squeak and ran for my designated spot next to him, trying to jump but missing slightly and half landing in his lap. He let out a startled yelp, his arm coming around me to keep me from pitching forward off the counter.

"Hells bells and tarot tells, Aris!" he grunted, holding me to him as I half-hugged and half-scrambled for the chocolate. "Why are you always stealing my snacks?! Are you drunk?" he questioned with wide eyes, his face crowding mine as he scanned my face. I couldn't help but get lost in the pretty gold flecks that danced in his eyes until his talking brought me back to reality. "You've totally been drinking."

"Want some? We have more, and we're baking brownies, and we're out of chocolate, and my favorite-ist Rune Drawer happens to have more. You *have* to come help," I pouted, leaning into him and batting my eyelashes. He ground his teeth and sighed.

"Fine, but only 'cause someone has to freaking watch you, so you don't end up blowing up the kitchen or something," he bit out, sliding from his spot.

I couldn't stop my jaw dropping as he turned and helped me off the stainless-steel counter. Based on his wide eyes and surprised expression, he didn't realize what he was doing either.

"Come on, you two!" Caspian hopped up and down, his arm still looped through Drayce's, who laughed at his excitement. We made our way back into the kitchen, Caspian immediately darting to the open bottle on the counter before grabbing two more shot glasses and pouring four shots.

"How many shots have you guys had?" Kye asked, eyeing Caspian's behavior warily.

"One! But it's Witches Brew!" I cheered, holding out the other glasses to them. They each took them from my hands, Drayce looking amused and Kye looking torn between amused and exasperated, cautiously sniffing the liquid in question.

"Cheersssss," Caspian slurred, taking his shot and letting out a loud whoop. I danced over to the refrigerator and grabbed a bottle of Sorcery Soda, then hurried back to join the others. Kye and Drayce both took theirs with no signs of disgust and turned their eyes to me. Kye raised an eyebrow and smirked, gesturing for me to take mine now. Popping open the top of my soda can, I took a drink before slamming down the shot and ending with the chaser, the shudder almost nonexistent this time.

"So, we're making brownies?" Drayce questioned as he looked over all the ingredients. "Any particular reason?"

"You need a reason for brownies?" Kye muttered under his breath.

Based on his casual glance around the kitchen, I don't think he intended for anyone to hear him. But I did, and I chuckled, running over to him. Wrapping my arm around his trim waist, I squeezed.

"You speak my kind of language, Honey," I squeaked out as I smashed him to me before turning my attention to the others in the room.

"Caspian, grab the flour and start mixing the dry ingredients," I ordered, sliding the recipe card his way. I giggled as he struggled to measure the ingredients out precisely when his eyes couldn't fully focus. Eventually, Drayce walked up behind him and pressed into Caspian, moving his hands over his to help steady him and finish measuring. My mouth went dry at the sight of Drayce wrapped around Caspian, part of me wishing they were naked so I could join in. Heat flooded me, and I nearly tackled them when Drayce looked over at me and winked. Glancing over at Kye, I almost laughed at his raised eyebrow and surprised expression.

"Thanks," Caspian said in a husky voice as Drayce leaned back before a grin spread across his face. He dipped his hand into the bag of flour and flicked it, covering Drayce in the white powder. We all stood still in shock and anticipation of what Drayce would do at this sudden turn of events.

"Oh, that's how it's going to be?" Drayce challenged with a cocky smirk and narrowed eyes. "Alright then, it's on," he challenged confidently, reaching around Caspian and grabbing a handful. Caspian tried—and failed—to jump away from the onslaught of the baking ingredient as it rained down on him, both men now covered in a light dusting of flour.

"You have some crazy friends, Sweets," Kye mumbled.

"Aww!" I was practically brimming with happiness and tingling magic as it continued to run over my skin with the closeness of the three men in the room. "They're pretty great, aren't they? But you're pretty awesome yourself," I teased, poking him in the stomach. "Ow." I shook my hand out, having poked him too hard in his ab muscles, hurting my finger. "You have some serious muscle hiding under that shirt." Not sure what came over me, I reached out without hesitation and pulled his shirt up enough to see the six-pack. *Holy hells bells.* "Yup, definitely some muscle. Hot damn, Honey." Kye quickly brushed my hands away so his shirt would drop back down, his cheeks reddening slightly at my appreciation. So modest!

"No more shots for you, Sweets," he murmured, stepping out of arm's reach and moving over to help Drayce and Caspian, who were still fighting with food.

"Never send anyone else to do what I need done," I hummed at the chaos, skipping up to the counter. Picking up one of the measuring cups, I looked it over. "Is this the right one? I'm going with it." I started to sing under my breath as I threw random ingredients into the bowl. Once the brownie was turned into a proper looking batter, I poured it in the pan and put it in the oven.

"Well done!" Caspian cheered, gathering up the dishes and swaying over to the sink. Drayce followed suit, grabbing my arm and pulling me with him, almost as if he had a magnetic pull to Caspian. Drayce started washing the dishes, ordering Caspian to dry and me to put them away. The first measuring cup that clattered to the ground was all it took for Drayce to laugh, grab Caspian by the hips, and guide him to the counter. In a show of strength, he picked him up easily and placed him on the countertop.

"I feel like you're safer here," Drayce said with laughter in his voice as he patted Caspian on the thigh. "Angel, you sober enough to dry?" he asked, turning to me. I gave an overly enthusiastic nod and bounced on my toes in excitement. Drayce came over to me, curling me under his arm and into his warm chest. "Good, then you keep your pretty ass over here. Otherwise, I'll have to come over and spank it," he whispered the last bit in my ear, making my cheeks flair in a bright pink blush.

"You got it, Babe" I mumbled, too distracted by the surge of desire uncurling in my belly to say much else.

"Good," he murmured against my cheek as he held me tightly before moving toward the dishes. "Kye, come help me."

"Why?" Kye countered, his arms crossed. "I didn't ask to come here." Drayce cocked a brow and glanced at him.

"Because your girl wanted to bake brownies, and you're

going to help her clean it up. Just like the rest of us... well, except for lightweight over there," Drayce countered with a tiny chuckle, looking over at Caspian who was slouched against the wall in a drunken stupor. Kye grumbled but didn't argue as he came over to us.

"Thank you," I chimed in, looking up at Kye, his hickory and gold eyes glancing down at me. "I appreciate your help. Yours too, Drayce."

"You're welcome, Angel," Drayce responded, leaning forward to look at me from around Kye.

"You're welcome," Kye grumbled but couldn't hide the hint of laughter in his eyes as he turned back to the dishes. It took a bit, but the dishes were clean before the brownies finished baking, and the Witches Brew was safely back in the fridge. Drayce took them out and placed them on a plate before reaching for one.

"Only one!" I squeaked, taking the plate from him. "I need these for an apology."

"Did you run into someone?" Drayce asked me with a grin. I shook my head quickly.

"No, I was a meanie pants, and I haven't been able to apologize properly, so I figured what's a better apology than baked treats!" I held up the plate as emphasis with a bright smile. "Come on now, I got to deliver these while they're fresh!"

"Oh, yay, time to go see my douche brother," Caspian huffed sarcastically, stumbling off the counter. I pouted looking at him, not appreciating his negativity. Realizing I was upset, he perked up and threw an arm over my shoulder. "Sorry, Cupcake. Let's go give Torryn these brownies. Come on, Buttercup," he hooked his other arm around Drayce's shoulders to pull him along.

"Gladly, Sprinkles." Drayce looked over at Kye. "Come

on, dude, Aris wants you to come along too, right, Angel?" I nodded brightly.

"Pleaseee, Honey?" I begged with a pout. Kye sighed but moved to my other side, mumbling under his breath.

"That damn pout will be the death of me," he grumbled.

"You think it's cute," I challenged with a proud smile. He balked, realizing I could hear him.

"Maybe a little," he teased quietly, quickly looking away. He slowed his steps, so he hung just behind us as we walked. I think the cheerfulness was starting to get to him. We stumbled all the way to Torryn's classroom, stopping just outside of the door.

"You guys wait here, please," I whispered, clutching the plate to my chest and opening the door. The classroom was empty and dark as I stepped in. The lack of light was a bit much for my drunken haze, making me wish I could manage that fire spell he'd tried to teach me. A noise from his office had me stopping in my tracks. *Holy shit! I didn't think he'd be here this time of night!*

There goes my plan of leaving a note and brownies as a surprise for him.

Torryn

I was sitting at my desk, the words in front of me crossing as I read the same sentence for the hundredth time since familiar training had finished. *Why the hell can't I focus?* Despite asking, I knew the answer.

A petite, pink-haired witch with the cutest dimples and fire in her steel eyes.

I groaned, shoving the book away and finally giving up on attempting to read. *This is going to be a long year if I don't get my shit straight.* I had just started to get up from my chair when I heard a shuffling in my classroom. *What the...* I strode out of the room, readying myself to reprimand the witch who came into my classroom after hours, only to discover Aris standing with wide eyes and a plate of brownies. The urge I got every time she was around was nearly enough to bring me to my knees. *I know it's inappropriate, yet nothing has ever felt so right. Gods... she's perfect. No, you need to stop.*

"Uh," she started. "Hi?" she stated with the tiniest tilt at the end, making it sound more like a question.

"Aris." I couldn't stop my voice from lowering as a surge of magic filled me—something about her pulled to me. *Seriously, stop it, she's a student, and you're a teacher... her* teacher. With that sobering thought, I crossed my arms, and my stern look had her smile faltering. She took a tentative step forward, a slight wobble to her walk.

"Look, I tried to apologize, but you kept leaving before I could. So, I made you brownies as a way to say I'm sorry for pouring water on you, but then you were here, so I couldn't just leave them..." she trailed off. I noticed she had a tendency to ramble when she was nervous. Only then did it occur to me she said she had made me brownies.

"Wait, what?" I said stupidly, my brows furrowing as I stared at her. *She made me brownies?* "Why?"

She huffed and glared at me like I was an idiot.

"Because I was a meanie pants, and you got mad at me—rightly so—but I felt bad because I don't like when you're mad at me, Torryn. So, I decided to bake you brownies since you wouldn't freaking stand still long enough for me to apologize today, then you canceled familiar training and yeah. So, here are your brownies!" she said cheerfully, taking a step forward and holding them out—except she swayed as she stepped and nearly fell into me. I caught the brownies with one hand and steadied her with the other. Now that she was closer, I could smell alcohol mixed in with the sweet strawberry scent that followed her, teasing me relentlessly.

"Have you been drinking?" I asked, surprised. She gave a guilty smile and nodded slowly before her eyes widened. My annoyance gave way to worry, and I knew, despite my best efforts to remain professionally aloof, I was fully on my way to being a lost cause.

"Your eyes are so pretty!" she squealed, stepping forward and stumbling into me. As her face smashed into my chest, she took a long inhale.

"Did you just fucking smell me?" I asked in shock, unable to stop the surge of blood rushing to my cock at the feeling of her in my arms. Her gray eyes pulled me in as I felt her breasts pushing against my side. *Focus on something else.* I forced my eyes to stay on her face despite wanting desperately to look at where she had molded herself to me.

"Yes, you smell like pine and freshly cut grass. I had to stop myself from sniffing you on Wednesday. I mean, that'd be really weird," she rambled, more to herself than to me as her head tilted back-and-forth, the succulent strawberry scent making it harder to focus on the fact I was a teacher and shouldn't be enjoying her in my arms. "But totally wouldn't have been as weird as telling you I lost my virginity to your brother because that totally crossed my mind too. I mean, hell, I didn't even know you two were related, but I guess that makes sense. I see the similarities now, although your facial hair makes you look very rugged while Caspian has a cute, slightly babyface," she continued to ramble until I cut her off.

"You lost your virginity to Caspian?" I enunciated very slowly, anger building at the fact he would take that from someone on their first day... take that from *Aris* on her first day here. Her eyes grew comically wide, realizing she said all her internal thoughts out loud. She pulled her bottom lip into her mouth and holy hellsticks if I didn't want to do the same.

"Uh... I mean... I'm just going to go." She stumbled back, her face turning beet red in embarrassment. I dropped the plate of brownies on the closest desk and wrapped my arms around her tiny waist to keep her from falling on her face in her poor attempt to run away.

"Aris," I urged as she struggled against me. "Please stop. I'm not going to yell at you. Just tell me the truth?" She deflated in my arms, giving up all pretense of running away, her arms falling to her sides.

"Yes, but it wasn't like it wasn't wanted. He didn't try to make me do anything, so don't yell at him or whatever you would do. Please," she sniffled.

Oh, fucking hellsticks, nice job making her cry, ass.

"Look at me," I commanded softly, and when she didn't, I hooked her chin with a finger until she made eye contact with me. "I'm not. I just want to make sure you're safe, and drinking and being around kitchen appliances probably isn't the best thing, but thank you for the brownies." She perked up slightly.

"You forgive me for being a meanie pants?" she questioned with such hope, my chest squeezed.

She stepped into me, her hopeful eyes meeting mine as her candied strawberry scent filled my senses. A flow of magic I had noticed around her started to intensify the longer we held our gaze. A small smile blossomed on her lips, and I sighed, having no choice but to return the smile. I was finding it harder and harder to resist her the longer she was in my arms.

"Yes. Just next time, try not to douse us in water, alright?" She bobbed her head eagerly, her tears drying as she became her happy, bubbly self again.

"Promise! I'm happy you liked the brownies we made!" she chirped out, turning and stepping away again as if she suddenly remembered she had somewhere to be. *We? What in the witch's wart?*

"Who is 'we'?" I questioned casually, trying not to let jealousy tint my words, but I couldn't stop the acid burning in my gut at the word.

"My friends!" she called over her shoulder, already fumbling with the doorknob. I followed her over to the door, gently pulling her back and opening it for her so she could stumble out to the hallway. *Let's see who these friends are.*

Her friends turned out to be my very drunk younger brother, being held up by Drayce Nodin while Kyelerian Tanan sat against the wall, looking like he'd rather be anywhere else. My eyes zeroed in on the way Drayce was holding Caspian, almost a little too close for only friends. *Caspian better not fucking hurt Aris with whatever he had going on with Drayce.*

"Oh! Hi, Professor Callahan!" Drayce greeted happily, finally realizing I stood at the door, Aris slowly leaning more and more into me in such a way, I actively had to ignore the tight feeling in my trousers. "Wait," Drayce murmured, looking over at Caspian who was leaning into his chest. "Brother? Professor Callahan is your brother?" The witch turned his eyes back to me before glancing back at Caspian, and after a few more times of his gaze darting back-and-forth, he responded, "Yeah, I can see it."

"So, why were you four drinking and cooking in the kitchen?" I questioned, looking between the three of them with narrowed eyes. "Whose idea was it to drink?"

"Oh, Caspian and I found some Witches Brew, and the other two just kind of joined in as we stumbled across them," Aris answered, looking up at me, her pink hair bright against my black button-up shirt. My brows shot up.

"Hellsticks, you've been drinking Witches Brew?" I bit out. She bobbed her head against my chest, a long yawn escaping her lips, making it hard to stay mad at them for being reckless. "Alright, Mr. Nodin and Mr. Tanan, can you assist my younger brother back to his room? I feel it'll take both of you to get him there safely," I requested, glancing at Caspian with a frown.

"What about Sweets?" Kyelerian challenged, shifting from his seated position. "Who is going to help her to her room?" I didn't hear any type of innuendo in his statement, but it still irked me he called her Sweets, so I moved us forward, shutting the classroom door behind us.

"I will," I bit out. Leaning down, I wrapped her arm around my shoulder as I steadied her increasingly swaying body. With a small glare from both Drayce and Kyelerian at the way she leaned into me, they moved to help a barely conscious Caspian down the hall toward the student dorms.

"Come on, Gorgeous, let's get you to your room," I mumbled softly as I scooped her up in my arms as another yawn flew from her mouth with a shiver of her body, alerting me she was quickly reaching the point of passing out. *Witches Brew will get you every time.* A smile played across her lips at the nickname which made my heart warm. I made it about a hundred feet down the hall before I realized I didn't even know where to find her key, and I wasn't about to check her pockets. Sighing, I turned and carried her back to my office, placing her gently on the couch. Grabbing a throw blanket off the back, I covered her and dimmed the lanterns overhead. She made a small, sleepy noise before her breaths evened out as she fell asleep.

Trying to ignore the magic still floating between us, I moved back to my desk. Knowing I would get no work done now, I slid my book and notes away before grabbing a piece of parchment and quickly jotted a quick plane to Caspian, letting him know where Aris was so he didn't worry. *Not that he would care,* I grumbled, sending the little red note zipping through the air. As soon as it left my hand, I rested my head on my arms before peering over at the small pink witch who was determined to make my life complicated. But damn if I didn't want her, more than I'd ever wanted anyone.

This is going to be difficult to fight.

CHAPTER 9

September 7th
Saturday Morning
Aris

This isn't my bed. Shifting, the smooth leather of the couch I was on brushed against my fingers. My eyes popped open, memories of last night coming in all at once, a flood of ridiculous moments. I let out a groan, putting my hand on my forehead as I scolded myself. *Way to make yourself look like a crazy witch, Aris!*

"Sleep well, Aris?"

Torryn's smooth voice echoed loudly in the room, the sudden noise making me wince, my head hurting slightly with the aftereffects of Witches Brew.

"Like a rock," I deadpanned. When I risked a glance at him, amusement danced in his eyes though his rumpled shirt and dark circles under his eyes told me he had slept at his desk. "I'm sorry, Tor, I didn't mean for you to have to babysit me," I huffed. His eyebrow quirked as his lips curled into a tiny smile.

"Tor, huh?" he questioned, a hint of joy coloring his words.

I groaned, adjusting to get comfortable enough so my headache would ease, but it didn't do any good.

"Well, I thought I should get to call you something since you called me Gorgeous last night, but I figured it wouldn't be 'proper' to call you Handsome, *Sir*," I mumbled, tossing my arm over my eyes as the sun peeked out from behind a cloud as it filtered through the window. "But I would if you wanted me to." I balked, realizing I said that last portion out loud. *I might still be a bit drunk.* Shooting up, I ignored the throbbing in my skull as I popped off the couch. "Alrighty, time for me to go before I die of embarrassment. Bye!" I attempted to scurry out of his office, but Torryn was faster, wrapping me in his arms before I could avoid dealing with what I had said.

"Hmm," he hummed, his muscled chest and soft dress shirt molding to my back, my heart rate picking up as he held me intimately against him. "If that nickname comes from your pretty lips, I would definitely want you to say it," he whispered, his breath caressing my neck as he dipped his head and buried his nose into my hair. "You're not the only one who struggles with not getting too close. You smell pretty damn delicious, Aris."

Warmth flooded me at the feel of him pressed against me. His obvious flirting caught me off guard, but I loved it.

"That can be arranged," I teased back, twisting in his arms, my hands resting on his chiseled chest. He was hiding more muscles under his shirt than I had anticipated. His eyes darkened as he leaned down, one of his hands going to rest on my hip. His face moved lower, making my heart beat furiously in my chest. Before his lips could touch mine, a loud thud of the classroom door closing had us both jumping away. The door was open, so I hurried to straighten out my sleep-wrinkled clothes and stepped out of the room first. Torryn's face was pale, his eyes wide in fear as he froze in his spot.

"Thanks for answering that question, Professor Callahan. I was struggling with it. I'll see you in class on Monday," I said cheerfully, turning to see Delilah walking up to the office. Her eyebrows furrowed as she studied us, obviously not expecting him to have visitors. I gave her a cheerful smile as I passed, turning and winking at a very relieved Torryn while her back was turned. Pushing the door open with my back, I blew him an air kiss when he glanced at me one last time. The heated glint in his seafoam-green eyes warmed me from the inside out as I made my way to my room.

I need some fresh freaking air before I self-combust.

An hour later, after showering and dressing in another tutu and plain shirt, I found myself walking on the main road from the academy to the nearest town, Crystal Borough.

Going for walks was one of the ways I kept myself sane back home, so needing some time to myself, this felt like the perfect opportunity to learn my new territory. The birds chirped as the breeze rustled the leaves of the trees lining the road. It was peaceful out here, the crisp autumn air soothing my hangover and giving me a new outlook on the day.

My smile widened as I got my first glimpse of Crystal Borough from the top of a small hill. Nestled into the valley at the bottom, the tiny town bustled despite its small size. Most of the homes were simple and small, save for one that loomed over the rest. In the center of town was an open-air market where carts were set up for everyone to browse the wares. The smell of something delicious had my feet moving a bit quicker, my stomach rumbling loudly as I bounded down the road.

I quickly found the source of the smell, my nose leading the way. The bazaar was full of street food vendors mixed among the merchants, showcasing everything from tacos to soul cakes to 'poison' toffee apples. Reaching into my purse, I hurried toward the one selling the toffee apples. *I haven't had one of these in ages! Mom always made us eat healthy at home.*

The first bite of the delicious treat was heavenly, the flavors exploding across my taste buds as I closed my eyes and savored it. It almost made me miss the guys for a moment, thinking about how they'd love it here. I made a mental note to bring them the next time we all needed to get away.

When I finished my food, I tossed the stick in the trash and started to browse the different hanging items. A gorgeous dream catcher woven in pastel blues and pinks caught my eye, causing me to trip over a rock and bump into another witch.

"Oh, my broomsticks! I'm so sorry!" I yelped, catching myself before I could fall. I didn't recognize the girl, but she was clearly around my age, so she must have been from Aether Academy too.

"Watch yourself, *Mixta*," she sneered, brushing off her shirt like I'd soiled her with my lack of an affinity.

"Witch, please. You aren't going to catch Mixta, it's not a

freaking disease," I scoffed, thrown off by the rude comment. It had been so good here so far.

"Don't think you're special because Caspian is hanging out with you. He can do so much better than a Spellbeggar. Don't drag him down," she said again, this time making sure her friends heard, so they could laugh along with her. My cheeks burned, and I had to take a breath to calm my emotions. Bringing Cas into it made it hurt even more... I mean, I didn't even know what we were. Were we just friends? Were we more? Could we be more if I had feelings for other guys at the same time? *Should* we be? These questions continued to swirl in my mind despite the cocky grin I plastered on my face.

"I mean, he chose me, so I'd say that makes me pretty special. Man... witches be petty," I stage whispered the last portion, starting to walk away. Their dumb comments ruined the appeal of the market, so I turned and walked down one of the side streets, hoping to get away for a moment before looping back to the main road. I turned around to see if they were following, letting out a sigh of relief when I found myself alone. Turning to head down the street, I almost ran into someone again.

"Whoa, there," Kye said, catching me when I started to stumble. I jumped a bit, not expecting someone to be there. His hands dropped to his sides after I had moved out of arm's reach, and his hickory golden-brown eyes dimmed a little when he took in my tiny frown and hunched shoulders.

"Oh, hey, Kye," I said, trying to give a small grin, but based on his growing scowl, it came out more of a grimace.

"You okay, Sweets?" he asked, his demeanor changing from worried to pensive to apprehensive. His voice said he wanted to know what was wrong, but his body language said he was struggling to find the words to communicate.

"Yeah, Honey. I'm fine. I'm just going to do some shopping," I muttered, giving a small wave as I continued on, not wanting any company at the moment. "See you later, Kye."

Without turning back, I kept walking down the street. A small shop with a bright red sign caught my eye, *Gertie's Trinkets*, the enchanted letters sparkling in the sunlight. It seemed like the perfect distraction, so I hurried inside.

"Welcome to Gertie's!" A little old witch hobbled to the front of the store to greet me. "I'm not used to visitors on market days. I'm glad you stopped by." Her cheerfulness brought out my smile, and I relaxed a little.

"Oh, I bet the market makes it hard to sell on these days," I said, glancing around at the beautiful, but empty shop.

"My daughter takes a cart up to the square, so we don't miss out," she explained as she moved behind the counter, sitting down on a stool with a relieved sigh.

"Oh. I spotted a beautiful dreamcatcher out there. One of yours?" I asked, pointing to a display.

"It must have been. We are the only one in town who makes them. Which one caught your eye?" she asked, her eyes sparkling with excitement now that she knew I appreciated her work.

"It was pink and blue with ribbons hanging down. I loved it, but I couldn't stay in the square," I mumbled the last part, suddenly reminded why I was so down.

"Why don't you leave your name, and I'll send word if it doesn't sell." She slid a piece of paper and a pen over, giving me a sympathetic smile. She had clearly picked up on my mood change and didn't question me further.

"Oh, that would be amazing! Thank you," I gushed,

genuinely excited she was willing to do that for me. After writing my name down, I started to browse the shelves. She had several human trinkets on the back shelf, the Magic 8-Ball catching my eye. I'd read about these once in a human book. They told your fortune when you shook them. To make it even better, this one was pink! I snatched it off the shelf with a squeal, my mood quickly changing back to excited. With one last walk around the shop, I walked to the front and handed her the treasure. She smiled excitedly at the sight of it.

"You like human items from Aureus, too? I find them so intriguing. I get new shipments on the third Friday of the month, so you'll have to come check them out when they come in," she said, happy to find someone with similar tastes. I handed her the proper amount of coin for the little piece of the human world I had found before responding.

"I definitely will come back. Thanks for the help," I said, exchanging a quick goodbye and heading out of the shop, my new treasure clutched in my arms.

At least something good came out of this trip.

Kyelerian

I'd never seen Aris so serious; something must have really been bothering her. I wanted to ask her if something was wrong, but I didn't want to make it worse. *Nothing is worse than making a girl cry. And let's face it, I'm not the best at talking to her when she's in a good mood.* My mental conflict went back-and-forth as I walked toward the market. Shoving my hands in my pockets, I turned the corner and stepped up to one of the food vendors. I ordered quickly, craving something sweet after spotting a cotton candy pink foaming fizzle popper. *Damn tiny pink witch getting under my skin*, I half-assed grumbled as I took a bite of my treat, letting the airy confection fizzle and pop in my mouth, invading my senses —just like Aris.

As I walked away from the vendor, I heard a high-pitched girly laugh that grated against on my eardrum. A wave of matching cackling followed, pulling my attention from the sugary deliciousness I had clutched in my hands. I spotted Amber, Tasha, and Esmerelda standing a few feet away. They were known throughout the school as gossips, so I was sure they had found a new target to chat about. I rolled my eyes and tried to walk away until I heard them joking about the annoying witch with the ridiculous pink hair. I froze in place, anger flooding me at the knowledge they were targeting Aris. I guess that explained why Sweets was so down. Instinctively, I took a step forward before stopping myself, though I did send a glare their way. *I can't fight her battles for her. Even if they got to her this time, Sweets doesn't strike me as the type who stays down for very long. But that doesn't mean I can't defend her when she's not around to defend herself.*

"What?" Esmerelda snarked at me, having seen my steely stare.

"Sorry, I couldn't help but overhear the utter bullshit spewing from your mouths. Why don't you guys stop spending so much time focused on other people and work on yourselves?" I shot back, turning and stomping away. They didn't even bother to retaliate—bullies rarely do when called out. *They can talk about me all they want, I don't give a fuck.*

Knowing something was going on and not knowing what to say was eating at me, but I let my anger simmer and started back toward Aether. *I need to talk to Caspian—he'll know how to cheer her up.* Just as I walked into the dormitory, I spotted his russet hair heading for the stairs.

"Caspian!" My loud voice had several people stopping to see what was going on, including Caspian. He looked confused but turned and walked over to where I was waiting.

"What's up?" Caspian asked in his cheerful tone. He was almost as bad as Aris with how damn happy he was all the time.

"I just got back from Crystal Borough. Aris was getting picked on. When I said hi to her, she didn't even smile. Go check on your girl," I said, my tone more aggressive than I meant it to be, but I knew I wasn't the man for this job. *I've already almost hit my quota for social interaction for today.*

Caspian's brows drew down at my words, worry clear on his features. "Should I just ask about it? See how she's doing?" he trailed off, clearly starting to panic.

"I don't know. She's your girlfriend, shouldn't you know the answer?" I spouted with a wave of my hand. His eyes widened with surprise, a tiny grin spreading across his face.

"Girlfriend?" he asked, confusing me. What kind of dumb question was that?

"Uh, yes," I hedged, the word stretched out as I eyed him.

"Well, that makes me feel better. I don't know what the hell we are, but it's nice to hear that." He looked too smug, and I couldn't help but roll my eyes.

"Just go check on her," I ordered, shaking my head and waving him off. He gave one last grin before hurrying out the door.

She doesn't have a boyfriend? Hmm... For once, I let my mind wander with the possibilities of what I could do with a certain tiny pink witch.

Caspian may have a little competition.

September 9th
Monday Afternoon
Aris

I felt refreshed and ready for the day when I got up the morning after spending Saturday night and all of Sunday relaxing, eating junk food, and binge-watching Boos and Brews with Caspian. He'd tried talking to me about my less-than-cheerful mood when I got back to campus, but I kept brushing it off. Thankfully, he didn't push after I finally told him I didn't want to talk about it.

The morning passed quickly, and I hadn't run into the witchy trio from the market, so that made it even better. My usual chipper attitude was back as I took a pit stop to the student pantry and shoved my pockets full of marshmallows for Lulu. Usually, Caspian would have caught up with me by now, but he must have been running late. I started off without him, making my way to the familiar training barn and pasture.

The animals and students were already grouping, the recognizable sound of chattering and animal noises filling the area. *This place always has a way of cheering me up.* I wove around the groups until I managed to reach the pasture. Before I could even join my class, a nasally voice reached my ears.

"Oh, look, it's the new girl. Did you charm your hair pink just for attention?" Tasha sneered, stopping me in my tracks.

Oh great, there goes my good mood. Witches be bitches.

"Oh, look, it's the girl who needs to mind her own business. I'll charm my hair whatever color I want," I said cheerfully, giving an exaggerated flip of my hair before continuing on my way.

"Oh, really, then uncharm this, *Mixta*," Amber called after me before a wave of magic hit me. I stopped walking as everyone around me gasped. A soft breeze blew through the pasture, ruffling my hair and bringing it in front of my eyes. My mouth dropped open as the deep green locks fluttered in my view.

"Thanks, it was about time for a change," I called over my shoulder with a happy grin before continuing on. I refused to show how much it bothered me, but on the inside, I was throwing a witchy fit, kicking and screaming that they would dare mess with my hair like that.

Don't let them win, Aris, take it with a smile. You've dealt with worse.

Caspian finally came into view just as Thane and Lulu joined the class. He cocked his head to the side, but couldn't interrupt us, so I just gave him a bright but strained smile and turned my attention to Thane. Lulu ambled over, nudging her nose against my pockets as soon as she could reach. I smiled down at my cute and scaly companion before plopping down on the grass and feeding her a handful of marshmallows.

"When caring for your familiar, you need to make sure you're listening to their needs. They'll let you know what they like and dislike, so it's best to keep them happy. Happy familiar means stronger bond and stronger magical contribution," Thane droned on. My heart wasn't in class today, despite the fact I wanted a familiar so badly, I was determined to learn all I could.

Class passed quickly since I spent my time focusing on feeding Lulu and daydreaming. As soon as the bell chimed, Caspian and Torryn both stormed over to me.

"What happened to your hair?" Torryn hissed, narrowing his eyes at me.

"Who did that to you?" Caspian demanded at the same time. They glanced at each other with a slight glare but didn't bother to argue, turning back on me in demand for answers.

Is hell freezing over? Did they just pass up an opportunity to argue?

"Don't worry about it, I'll rock it," I explained confidently, gathering up my bag and tossing one last marshmallow at Lulu before shooing Torryn off to our mentoring session. "Come on, we have mentoring."

"I'll see you at dinner," Caspian said, his voice holding an inflection of hurt because I didn't confide in him. He had clearly caught on that something was happening, but I couldn't bring myself to talk about it—not yet, anyway. It was too soon, and I wasn't totally sure how to react with people *actually* giving a shit about me. I ignored the twist of pain in my chest at his slightly downturned lip. *Damn it all to hex.* I made a mental note to talk to him tonight. *It was hard work making real friends. I've got to try though; friendship or whatever we are is a two-way street.*

Torryn didn't press me further as we walked to campus. He passed the student dorms and veered to the left by the creek. We walked further into the forest and eventually passed the staff housing with no sign of stopping. As we walked, I noticed small crystals sprouting out of the ground here and there. They caught my eye, sparkling in the sunlight that streamed through the trees.

"Why are crystals growing out here?" I inquired, but Torryn just chuckled and kept walking. The sound caught me off guard. For once, he didn't seem so gruff, the sound light and carefree.

"You'll see," he teased, looking over his shoulder and winking.

He stopped walking abruptly, making me slam into his toned back. *What the heck? There's nothing here,* I thought as I glanced around. He chuckled at my confusion before pushing aside a cluster of vines to reveal an entrance to a cave. My excitement ramped up as I peered in, the grin on my face now matching his. He turned and continued his journey, leading me further into the cave, an odd, iridescent glow of purples, blues, and pinks filling the space. The sight only had my confusion growing until the tunnel gave way to a large cavern filled with crystals of every color and size.

"Wow," I breathed out, my voice low as I gaped at the beautiful sight. The sun filtered in from somewhere above us, reflecting through the crystals and bouncing the rays around the room in an opal kaleidoscope of colors. "What is this place? Why are we here?"

"I've seen the sparks of magic in you, and nothing fuels magic quite like crystals. I thought this would be the perfect training grounds, and it's far enough away from the school so nobody gets hurt," he teased lightly before taking my hand and leading me to the center of the space.

My heart thudded in my chest at the contact, the feeling of his hand in mine enough to distract me from the beauty around us. Magic danced between our intertwined fingers, tingling against my skin, but I didn't let go... it felt... amazing.

"It's beautiful here," I said, finally breaking the silence and getting myself out of my own thoughts. Overthinking feelings with Torryn was a bad idea.

"Look up," he commanded lightly, looking down at me to make sure I followed through. I smirked at him before following his orders. What I had thought was a simple cave opening was actually a long tunnel heading upward. The tunnel walls were crystal, not stone, before ending in the flat surface of a clear crystal. The colors of the walls were the same colors as the school's center fixture, cluing me into what I was seeing.

"The clock tower?" I asked, not bothering to look over at him but saw him nod in my periphery before I continued on. "It's beautiful."

"You are," he breathed, his voice so low, I didn't think I was meant to hear it... I peeked over at him, finding his eyes focused on my face. A blush colored my cheeks at his soft gaze before he reached over and brushed his fingers along my cheek in a caress that had the magic jumping between us until I felt like it was buzzing through my veins.

"Thank you," I said, unsure of what else to say before I looked back up. It took everything I had to peel my eyes away from his, but I knew it was for the best. I could see the internal war in his eyes, and despite what I wanted, I didn't want to make his life any harder. *Besides, you have Caspian, who cares about you.* The tension in my chest squeezed harder as I remembered Torryn's younger brother.

Torryn cleared his throat as he stepped away, finally releasing my hand.

"Alright, let's see if you can do a basic spell," he said, his voice holding a husky quality. He gently grabbed my shoulders and turned me, this time to position me. When he seemed satisfied with where I was standing, his eyes met mine. A visible spark lit up between us, causing both of us to jump. It grew brighter for a moment, a mix of pale pink and green before fizzling out.

He shook it off quickly, but from the quirk to his eyebrow, he was just as surprised as I was. Finally letting go and stepping away, he walked away and turned to face me.

Only when he walked away did I glance down and notice he had positioned me in the center of a rune circle perfectly aligned with the center of the clock tower.

"Now, I need you to say *ignem accende* while you focus on the light," he commanded, waving his hand for me to begin.

I closed my eyes for a moment, reveling in the charged energy of the crystals around me, letting them bolster my own magic. I focused on the light filtering in, picturing it growing bigger and brighter as I chanted the words. A wave of power built within my chest, the swell radiating toward my arms and legs before I could feel the power tingling within my fingertips as if I had been shocked by a giant static charge. I yelped, and my eyes popped open in time to see a bright set of the pink and green sparkles arcing between my fingers and Torryn's.

"Fucking hellsticks, ow!" he shouted, suddenly hopping as he shook his hand vigorously. "How the hex did you do that?"

"Me? I'm a Mixta, *you're* the one with powers," I accused, rubbing my palm to ease the ache.

"I'm a Spell Caster, and you're hardly a Mixta... you're more of an anomaly," he said quickly. I rolled my eyes at the accusations.

"We aren't going to get very far in these lessons if you keep throwing around accusations and ending class early," I challenged, crossing my arms in front of my chest. He huffed but didn't really argue.

"I end class when things amp up, and I need to do research. It has nothing to do with not trusting your magic. Mentoring you comes with some challenges I didn't expect, and I wouldn't be much of a mentor if I went into this blind. For now, it's dinner time, and we have quite the walk back. In the meantime, I'll be researching these arcing powers between us and try to find a source," he explained, looking offended he had to explain himself.

"Fine, dinner it is," I agreed, grabbing my bag from the entrance of the room and starting off down the long, winding tunnel.

Of course, I'm an anomaly—Mixta just wasn't good enough for me.

CHAPTER 10

September 12th
Thursday Early Morning
Aris

Sleep eluded me until I finally gave up and tried to find anything to distract me, waiting out the clock until it was late enough for me to go to breakfast. Eyeing the boxes of stuff I had yet to finish putting away, I grimaced. That was *so* not what I wanted to do right now. I groaned and turned back to the front of my room before heading out, my focus on finding Caspian, his hurt gaze from yesterday burning in my mind. It only took a few moments until I was standing outside what I thought was Caspian's room. *Although it's been a week and a half, so I could be wrong, but I* was *pretty sure this was where his room was.* I took a deep breath and knocked.

"Can I help you?" the boy with wide-frame glasses asked

when he opened the door, his eyes narrowed in confusion. I flashed an awkward smile; definitely not Caspian's room.

"Do you by any chance know where Caspian is? I knew his room was around here, but I can't remember exactly," I rushed through my explanation, trying not to let the nerves get to me. His scrunched face smoothed over in understanding before widening into a bright smile.

"He's right next door," he explained, tossing a thumb toward the door he pointed out. I thanked him quickly before taking the few steps to Caspian's door and knocking.

"It's open," he called, his words muffled through the wood of his closed door. I opened it and stepped inside, my eyes falling on Caspian's long body lying on his unmade bed. His gaze flickered over me, and before he could speak, everything just came tumbling out.

"I'm sorry I haven't talked to you about everything lately. It's just really hard because I haven't had anyone who actually cares about me, and I'm just so used to being alone, ya know?" I rambled quickly, my hands fiddling with the tulle of my tutu as I explained. "There's just been a couple of girls who have been saying some mean things the last few days because I'm a Mixta. Which really isn't that much different from back home, so I just keep going on with my day. I didn't mean to make you think I didn't trust you or something, and I didn't mean to hurt you. So, I'm sorry that I did..." I mumbled, trailing off awkwardly as I looked at him. "Are you mad at me?"

Caspian rolled off the bed, his long legs closing the distance between us in three quick steps. His blue eyes were soft as he looked at me, his hands coming to cup my face.

"Of course, I'm not mad, Cupcake," he reassured quietly, his thumbs brushing against my cheeks. "I just want to make sure you're okay, and that you're happy. I don't like it when people are mean to my Cupcake, but I understand not being ready to explain it. If there's anything you want to talk about at any time, ever, I promise you can come talk to me. Now," he murmured, pulling me closer, "come here." I couldn't stop the smile spreading across my face as I stepped into his waiting arms.

As soon as I was cocooned in his embrace, I felt such an intense wave of relief I wasn't expecting, not having realized just how much I cared about how Caspian felt. It had always been only me, so I didn't know how to connect with others, but Caspian made it so easy. We had meshed right from the beginning. Without a second thought, I popped up onto my toes and kissed him.

His arms tightened around me, holding me tightly to his lean muscles as he kissed back. Tangling my fingers in his hair, I deepened the kiss, sucking his bottom lip between my teeth. He moaned, deep within his chest as I nipped his lip, his hands shifting lower to cup my ass. Taking a step forward, he pressed me back against his door as he lifted me. Surprise flooded me as I instinctively wrapped my legs around his trim hips. His deep blue eyes lit up with a hint of laughter at my gasp and wide eyes, but he didn't tease me before peppering my neck in a string of kisses as he made his way back up to my mouth.

A small rumbling startled us, and our eyes pulled to look up at another forming storm cloud. *I really don't want to get rained on. I would like water-free sex this go-around since we aren't in the shower.* As soon as the thought popped in my head, the cloud started to dissipate, the gray floof thinning but not fully disappearing.

"Cas, think about not wanting to get rained on," I murmured, afraid if I spoke too loudly the storm would intensify and pour down on us. Caspian gave me a quirked brow but did as I suggested, and the impending storm evaporated, not a drop on us or his room. "Holy shit that's so cool." I whispered. "But we can talk about that later. I would rather have you right now instead of talking about weird magical phenomenons, so kiss me like you mean it." I smiled as his eyes heated, his grip on my ass tightening as I spoke.

"You got it, Cupcake." Caspian did exactly as I asked, peppering me in dominating kisses and teasing bites as his lips moved with fervor against mine. Grinding his hips up, the rough material of his jeans and hard cock confined underneath rubbed against my thin underwear. A pulse of desire shot straight through me to my core as he moved his attention from my lips to my jaw and neck as his cock rolled over my sensitive clit.

Pulling me away from the door, he walked us over to his bed, dropping on top of me with a cocky smile. He pushed my shirt up, nipping my stomach and chest until he finally reached my breasts. A hand wrapped around my back, unclipping my bra to bare my chest to his hungry gaze. I gasped as he cupped one before sucking the pebbled peak into his mouth, his teeth barely grazing the sensitive skin as his other hand cupped between my legs.

"So wet," he murmured, his eyes and smirk centered on me as he kissed his way to my other breast. My eyes fluttered shut as I clutched at Cas's sheets, his fingers circling before barely dipping into me, teasing me in the most torturously delicious way. A breathy moan escaped me as he sank two fingers into me, curling slightly to hit the perfect spot. My core tightened, my body buzzing with an impending orgasm, but before I could reach my release, Caspian pulled his fingers away, taking my underwear with him. Prying my eyes open, I watched him shuck his shirt and unbutton his pants, pulling them down just enough to let his hard cock free from behind the dark fabric of his jeans.

Without much fanfare, he crawled back over me, the head of his cock pressing into me before slipping in slowly. Both of us groaned, needing... craving this connection without magic fueling our actions. When he was fully sheathed inside me, I whimpered, feeling so deliciously full. And when he started to fuck me in earnest? I was completely lost in a sea of pure desire. I was a puddle of need, melting in his arms as he moved slowly, quickly picking up his pace until the only sounds surrounding us were our moans and his hips crashing into mine.

"Caspian," I cried out as I finally reached my release, my eyes squeezing shut as I clamped around him. Frantic kisses swallowed my moans as he kissed me like he was drowning, and I was the only thing to save him, his hips continuing to pound into me before he followed me into a satisfying release. Our panting filled the space as Cas pressed a sweaty forehead into my shoulder, neither of us wanting to move as we came down from the post-sex high.

"Boos and Brews, now?" Caspian asked softly, looking down at me with such softness, I felt my heart nearly burst with warmth. I nodded, a happy laugh bubbling out as he pulled out, flopping next to me to cuddle.

"Are you going to give me back my underwear?" I asked as he curled himself into my back, already pulling out his Witches Glass and scrolling through the magical tech, mumbling the incantation until our favorite cooking show materialized in the middle of the room.

"Nope, they're mine now," he teased with a tiny kiss on my cheek. "Now shush, Cupcake, they're making my favorite food."

I shook my head but couldn't argue when there was a

small portion of me that liked knowing he'd have that piece of me to remind him of our fun.

September 12th
Thursday Afternoon
Aris

My day had once again been filled with taunts from the Curse Crew, despite my continued attempts to ignore them. I even turned down a few offers to change my hair back because I wanted to show them I could rock whatever they threw at me, so today, I was rocking makeup in browns and earthy tones, my outfit coordinating nicely. *And I look amazing if I do say so myself.* I tried to brush off my hurt feelings while I made my way to mentoring.

"Hey, there," Drayce's smooth voice pulled me out of my inner musings, his smiling face helping to wash away the sour mood that was forming.

"Fancy meeting you here," I teased, pulling my bag further up on my shoulder. "What brings you to this side of campus?"

"I also have mentoring, though my first year isn't as adorable as you," he said with a wink. "Oh, hey, he's right over there." He pointed to a burly witch who looked like he'd just rolled out of bed, his grungy clothes wrinkled and a grumpy look on his face. *Ouch.*

"I'd like to think I'm a bit more cheerful than that," I snorted, knowing it was a vast understatement.

"And a whole lot sexier," he said, his eyes roaming slowly over my body. Despite the fun I'd just had with Caspian, my body was already perking up at his flirting.

"Not as much as Caspian though," I joked, hiding my grin as I turned my eyes back to the path in front of us.

"As hot as Caspian is, he's got nothing on you," he murmured, starting to walk away from me as we reached the mentoring hallway. His lips curled in a tiny smirk, and he winked. "See you later, Angel."

Giving him a tiny wave, I couldn't stop the blood from rushing to my face in a flush or the surge of wetness that now coated my underwear. I took a deep breath, trying to push dirty thoughts away as I started toward the room I knew we would be in. Xanthius was pacing outside the door when I got closer, his hands in his pocket as he waited for me.

"Hey, Xan!" I called cheerfully, hoping he wasn't upset I shortened his name. It felt too formal to call him Xanthius. He looked surprised for a moment before eyeing my hair and looking even more shocked.

"Green?" he asked pointedly, staring at my hair in confusion before shaking his head and continuing. "Either way, I found some information on that question you asked last week. Essentially, there is a possibility of a Mixta gaining powers from a magical bonding, but they would be minimal at best. And though powers can be suppressed by certain charms, the magic would still wear off or be overpowered by the Mixta's latent powers. So, in summary, no, it's not possible for a Mixta to gain strength or even normal powers later in life." His words were punctuated by that annoying sympathy.

I think the fact I dumped a waterfall on Torryn would dispute your claims, Mr. Know-it-all.

"The only other thing it mentioned was a slight boost of magic could be awoken within partners if the physical bond was strong enough. It didn't get too far into the details, but from what I understood, their magic has to align and be aided by the physical bond for it to make a difference. I'm unsure how reliable it is though since it was centuries old, and it's the only mention I've found," he explained, looking frustrated at being bested by my query.

"Thanks for looking, Xan. I'll add that to my essay for Mixta Basics," I said cheerfully, stepping around him into our mentoring room. I dropped into my chair with a sigh, slightly disappointed he hadn't found anything more worthwhile. Knowing my recent luck, it was probably just another odd quirk that would be unexplainable to every expert in the field.

A loud knock resounded through the tiny room, Xan's mouth curling down in a frown at the interruption. He stood and walked to the door, opening it to reveal... Headmaster Tallis and my parents? My pulse pounded in my head, and my vision tunneled for a moment at the sight of them. When I said I wanted them to see me flourishing, I didn't mean literally!

Note to self—be careful what you witch for.

"Aris!" my mother called out, pushing past the headmaster and my father, arms outstretched toward me. To an untrained eye, it would look like she was going to hug me, but I knew better. *She might catch Mixta that way.* In true Mother fashion, she stopped just out of reach and air-kissed each cheek before pulling away.

"What is this hair color? It looks positively dreadful on you!"

My cheeks heated, and I purposely avoided Xan, not wanting him to see how much she got to me.

"Aris has been a delight to have in school. She's always cheerful and helps out her fellow students. She's been showing promise with her mentors as well," Headmaster Tallis boasted, giving me a proud smile though a hint of a threat was there, challenging me not to prove him a liar. I put on a fake smile as I turned to them, still refusing to say anything.

"I'm glad to hear that. Calistos are known for their leadership, even Calistos who are a bit... different," my father said, saying different as if it were distasteful. By different, he meant I was a disgrace to his family and his name. *Dick.*

"Good job, honey!" Mom said brightly, the saccharine sweet smile making me want to vomit. She loved to put on a show for anyone willing to listen. "I can't wait to see the school, it's beautiful. Of course, it's not quite as prestigious as the one in Ignis, but it's lovely, nonetheless." Nothing like giving an insult mixed with a shitty compliment. *My mom, always the classy one.*

"Shall we take a tour of the campus?" the headmaster asked with a slight hint of ice in his tone. I doubt they'd notice, but I could see how offended he was about them insulting his institution.

"Come, Aris, show us around," Father demanded, gesturing for me to go with them, a clear command to his tone. I nodded and grabbed my bag, following him out of the room.

Tallis started the tour, giving bits of history and what I'm sure was a gripping recount of the finer points of Aether. I tuned it out, following along dutifully like the good daughter. I was always taught to fade to the background, not make myself stand out. That way, people were more likely to miss me during conversations with my parents, not asking about their secret shame... me.

At one point, they closed a door in my face, completely forgetting I was tagging along. The longer I spent with them, the lower my mood seemed to drop. Nothing killed a mood quite like being treated like a shameful little secret. Our procession garnered quite a few curious stares, which I continued to ignore. I was itching to ask why they were here in the first place, but nobody would shut up long enough for me to ask.

By the time the dinner bell rang, I was hangry and annoyed, just wanting to slip away. For the first time since I'd arrived, the usual crowd of students hung back and walked slowly behind our group, showing respect to the headmaster and his guests. Which, of course, only spotlighted the weird drop-in even more.

"I think I'd like to have a meeting with you, Headmaster Tallis, if that's alright?" Father asked the headmaster, making it clear no wasn't an option.

"Of course," Tallis said with a strained smile. His annoyance made me feel a bit better, at least.

"Aris, honey, we'll catch up with you after dinner," Mother said quickly, literally shooing me away, waving her hands at me. I held back my eye roll and turned when I ran headfirst into a furious looking Caspian surrounded by Drayce, Kye, and Xan. None of us said anything as we watched them walk away toward the administrative side of the building.

"Why are you guys all together?" I asked finally, breaking what was sure to be a long stretch of awkward silence.

"Xanthius came and found me, saying you were upset, then I got the others because I'm not equipped to handle that. Your parents are assholes, Sweets," Kye answered, shaking his head.

"Are... are you alright?" Xanthius asked as his eyebrows creased. It was adorable how sweet he was about everything. He could have just walked away, but instead, he did all this.

"Thank you, Xan, that was really sweet of you," I said quickly, leaning up and kissing him on the cheek. As my lips made contact with his cheek, a spark of electricity shocked me, making me pull away quickly. *Weird... that was like the first time Kye touched me. Maybe it has something to do with how much I care about them?* The guys had slowly wormed their way into my heart, and here Xan was, making my heart melt with his kindness.

"I'm okay, they're just not my favorite people. Nobody else seems to know how to knock my confidence down quite like my family," I deadpanned, turning away from their pitying stares, heading into the dining hall. Instead of standing in the food line, I went straight for the desserts, piling my plate with a few different forms of chocolate. Drayce raised his eyebrows at my choice but didn't say anything. I grabbed my milk and hurried off to the spot we had claimed as ours.

"That bad, huh?" Drayce asked as he plopped down on the chair next to mine. "Their loss, they're missing out on an amazing little witch." My cheeks warmed at the compliment, and his sweet words made me feel a bit better.

Now that I was looking down at the sweet confections, my stomach rolled. The guys were talking about the latest spell warrior competition, so I just poked at my food and wondered why the hell my parents had shown up here, in the first place, and what the hell they needed to speak to the headmaster about. *Father may be a big deal on the Ignis council, but that hardly makes him anything here.*

"Aris, honey," my mother's voice interrupted my internal musings, making me drop my fork and cringe.

No, why are they in here?! I looked up reluctantly to find them walking toward me, the headmaster already looking worn out. *I get it, buddy, they do the same to me.*

"We are on our way to speak with your mentor, and you are coming as well," my father commanded, looking down his nose at me. The cold, calculating gaze bothered me even if it was the only kind of gaze he ever bothered to give me.

Keep smiling, Aris, don't let him win. I stood, meeting each guys' eyes briefly, noting the anger and worry that marred their faces. I gave them all a tight smile before I turned and followed my parents. *If only they knew how grateful I am for them.*

"Are you eating cupcakes for dinner? That's not going to help you marry a man worthy of the Calisto family name, dear," Mother chastised, poking me in my nonexistent love handles. Someone made an angry noise behind me, but I couldn't bear to look back.

When we reached the last table, I heard snickering and comments about the new girl getting special privileges and how the Mixta needed her mommy. I took a deep breath and kept walking, my head held high. They kept walking, not even stopping at the barrier between the student and faculty dining sections, but when I tried to join them, the impact sent me backward, landing on my butt. The urge to angry cry was pressing on me as I stood and waited, a look of realization hitting the headmaster. He hurried back through, giving me an apologetic smile.

"I'm sorry, Miss Calisto, I forgot it was spelled against students," he said, waving a hand over the walkway for a moment, separating it, and ushering me through. This time, I slipped through easily, both of my parents looking down at me disapprovingly like I'd done it to myself.

"Professor Callahan is your daughter's mentor, so he will be able to answer any of your questions. Right this way." He ushered them to an empty table before waving a confused Torryn over. I didn't bother to look up at him, focusing on a spot on the table as they introduced themselves.

"We were told you could tell us how Aris has been doing

with her magic. Any improvements? We were hoping with your expertise at this school, she wouldn't have to live as a... *Mixta* for the rest of her life. Is she showing signs of any affinities?" my father demanded. Torryn's eyebrows rose in shock at the way he said Mixta like it was a dirty disease.

"Well, Mr. Calisto," Torryn started, but was rudely interrupted by my father again.

"It's Councilman Calisto," he scoffed as if everyone in the entire realm should know who he was.

"My apologies, Councilman Calisto," Torryn said quickly, his voice cold and hard. "Your daughter has been extremely attentive in class. We've had some success with her telekinesis, but her affinities are all at the level we expected." My shoulders relaxed when he kept the water a secret. No doubt they'd cling to that, and frankly, I didn't want to tell anyone yet, especially not these vultures, who would swoop in at any sign I could be a "respectable" member of the Calisto family.

"That's not what I wanted to hear," he shot back, giving me and Torryn a disapproving look.

"Some students are simply Mixtas. It's not uncommon, and it's not a bad thing," Torryn said in a calming tone. My father's face reddened at his words, his cold eyes turning positively icy as he glared him down.

"Not in my family," he sneered, crossing his arms and turning his glare to the headmaster. "This is the faculty you have to offer? A man who thinks a Mixta is worthwhile?"

"She must have latent ability. We've not had a Mixta in the family... ever. You need to work her harder. Less time for cupcakes never hurts a girl," Mother said as she looked me up and down, clearly not happy with what she saw. I felt myself shrink under their scrutiny, hating myself even more for not fighting back or causing a scene, but I knew what little good it would do. *They'll never change. I let that dream go long ago.*

"I assure you, my faculty is held to the highest standards," Headmaster Tallis grit out, looking like he wanted to punch both of them in the face.

I'd pay good money to see that.

"I think we've seen enough. Let's hope, by the end of the semester, there is more to see," Father said, walking toward the barrier and stepping through.

"I'm positive there will be. Now, Aris, I presume you can show your parents out?" Headmaster Tallis said quickly, offering a half-hearted goodbye and hurrying off like his ass was on fire. *Lucky.*

"Well, Aris, why don't you introduce us to your friends before we go?" Mother asked, already heading that way. I held in my groan and hurried after her, hoping the guys would see my expression and realize they were about to be ambushed. Caspian caught my eye first, and his face remained blank, but I knew him well enough, I saw the strain around his eyes and his sly motion to notify the rest of the guys.

"Mother," I started politely, trying extremely hard not to sound irritated or defeated, both of which were weighing down my shoulders. "These are my friends." I named each of them as I pointed.

"What are your affinities?" she questioned with a smile, but her eyes hardened as she sized them up. I ground my teeth at the rude question but didn't argue as the guys rattled off what they were.

"No elementals?" my father bit out gruffly.

I closed my eyes. *Please don't be doing that right now.*

"How are you supposed to learn how to be a true Calisto if you're not associating with other elementals?"

And he went there, damn it all to hex.

"I will be sure to do that, Father," I piped up, my voice strained and an octave higher than normal as the urge to angry cry grew.

"Good. It would do a councilman well to have a daughter who follows the family line." I didn't have to look at him to know he was glaring, his gray eyes throwing icicles at me.

"I knew you looked familiar, sir," Xan started formally as he stood. He walked toward my father with his hand out. My father looked at it as if it was contaminated, no intention of shaking it. "I'm Xanthius Eideann." As soon as Xan said his last name, it was almost comical the way my father changed. *Well, it would be comical if he wasn't such a dick.*

"Ah, Councilman Eideann's son. It's wonderful to make your acquaintance," my father boasted in faux joy.

I rolled my eyes, unable to keep it contained. Unfortunately, my mother saw and pinched the back of my arm sharply in retaliation. I ground my teeth and held back the curse I wanted to scream. *That fucking hurt, Mother.*

They continued to talk for a few moments, Xan looking every part a councilman's son, but I saw the tension in his body as he stood stick straight. *Poor Xan. At least I typically blend into the background. He just got chucked into the fire.* Finally, their obligated pleasantries ended, and my parents commanded me to follow them.

Great, time to practice my nonexistent powers for hours on end.

CHAPTER 11

September 13th
Friday Morning
Aris

As I led my parents to the main part of campus, I had to fight to keep my grumbling comments to myself. This was day two of not sleeping well, and I was definitely feeling it. It didn't help that my parents had made me practice elemental spells—which I had no hope of actually getting right—all freaking night. I'd never been more ready for two people to leave than I was right now.

"We'll check on your progress in a few weeks," my father said as his form of goodbye, but of course, it sounded more like a threat.

Yeah, let me just pull my nonexistent powers out of my cauldron to please you.

"Remember to eat right and find new elemental friends. They'll take you farther in life than those friends of yours,"

Mother chided, giving me a small wiggle of her fingers before linking arms with my father and stalking off, the clicking of her heels echoing in the empty and silent courtyard.

At least the Curse Crew wasn't here to witness this encounter.

Not bothering to even give them a backward glance, I stomped back to the dorm, mumbling about asshole parents the entire way. Things were going so well here, minus the random bullying, then they had to show up and make it worse.

Once I was safely in my room, the grumbling continued. I slammed boxes and items around as I gathered my school stuff for the day, putting more aggression into it than necessary. A soft knock on my door stopped me from slamming another box down, and I hurried over to answer it, surprised to find Torryn there.

"Uh, hey," I stuttered out, still struggling to form coherent thoughts in my agitation. I attempted to flash him a smile, but I was pretty sure it looked forced and awkward. *What else is new?* His gaze hardened as he looked at me, obviously able to see past the facade.

"So... your parents are assholes. I came to check on you, and you *clearly* are not okay," he said, opening his arms. "Come here."

Tears fell at his sweet gesture, everything from the past two days crashing down on me all at once. He didn't hesitate to pull me in and hold me tight, letting me fall apart in his arms. After a few minutes, my sniffling died down, and I stepped back to look up at him, my cheeks heating in embarrassment.

"Sorry," I mumbled, feeling even more awkward now. "And yes, they are assholes."

"I wanted to punch your dad in the face yesterday," he deadpanned, making me giggle.

"Is it wrong to say I wish you had?" I shot back, picking up my school bag and drying off my face.

Torryn's eyes were soft as they roamed my features, his head inching forward ever so slowly before he quickly collected himself, stepping back and clearing his throat.

"I have to meet the headmaster before class, so I'll see you in history. Keep your head up. You're worth way more than they will ever be," he said, giving me a wink before turning and jogging down the stairs and out of sight.

I took a deep, steadying breath and followed, mentally preparing myself for the day.

Hopefully, this goes quick.

Definitely not quick. I groaned as I slipped into my seat for Magic 101. Nerves radiated through my body as I fidgeted, my eyes scanning for Caspian. I had been itching to tell him what Xan had found about bonding, half of me excited while the other half was nervous about how he would feel being bonded to someone like me. *No, knock that shit off right now, Aris. Remember what Torryn said.* Finally, right before class was about to begin, Caspian came barreling into the room, followed closely by Professor Ruslan.

"Hey, Cupcake," he whispered breathlessly as he sank into the chair next to me with a quick smile. Once again, I found myself giving him a weird-ass smile. His eyes narrowed slightly at my grimace, but Professor Ruslan's instructions for our newest essay prevented Caspian from asking about it. I pulled out a spare scrap of paper and scribbled across it, shoving it over to his half of the table before the nerves could become too much.

So, talked to Xanthius about what could be happening to us.

Caspian's brows raised before he jotted a quick reply and slid it back over, his eyes focusing back on his book, so he didn't get yelled at by Professor Ruslan.

Oh, yeah? What'd he find?

I took a deep breath, swallowing the acid that had started to burn in my throat.

We're bonded, you know, like forever.

My leg bounced anxiously the longer he stared at the paper. *Come on, Sprinkles, hurry the hex up and respond already.*

"Like... forever, forever?" he whispered under his breath. I nodded, unable to look at him in fear of what I would find in his deep ocean eyes.

"Hey, wicked whisperers. Stop talking," Professor Ruslan hollered out from his desk, his harsh gaze centered on us. I shrank down in my seat as eyes from around the room landed on us. Turning my eyes back to my book, I freaked out silently while I waited for some sort of response. A paper slid into view a moment later, and I had to take a calming breath before opening it.

If I had to be bonded to someone for my entire life, at least I got my Cupcake. Don't worry, we're going to make an awesome team. Plus, remember, everything I brew, I brew it for you.

P.S. We'll make adorable babies!

Relief flooded me at his response, and I couldn't stop the giggle that erupted from me at the bottom line. Caspian's eyes lit up before he threw me a saucy wink.

"Seriously, are you two deaf?"

I snapped back to the front of the room when I heard the question.

"No, sir," Caspian hollered back with an apologetic raise of his hand. "We'll be quiet."

"Good, or I'll separate you two like children."

With that, we focused on our reading, but inside, I couldn't stop the girly squealing.

I'm the luckiest witch in all of Akasha.

Thoughts of Caspian and his response to the bonding still had me practically floating down the hallway as we headed to lunch. Just as I turned to finally say something to him, something slammed into me, sending me flying backward. My head hit sharply on the stone floor, and bats danced in front of my eyes for a second, the dazed feeling passing slowly.

"Oh, Aris! I didn't see you there, I'm so sorry!" Delilah squeaked out, shoving something back into her bag before handing me the book that had fallen out of my hands. I rubbed the back of my head and gave her an attempt at a smile.

"You alright there, Cupcake?" Caspian asked, helping me stand up as he gently ran his fingers over the back of my head. I winced as he touched the tender spot before Delilah grabbed our attention again.

"Definitely my fault, I should have been paying attention," she mumbled, fixing her bag over her shoulder and giving me one last apologetic smile before hurrying off.

"Come on, let's get some food." Caspian directed me toward the dining hall, his arm slung over my shoulder. As per usual, my tray ended up being stacked way higher than his, including at least four different kinds of desserts.

"So," he started hesitantly, once we sat down. "Does this bonding thing mean we're... you know..."

My brows scrunched in confusion. What the what now?

"We're what?" I prompted, taking a bite of my pizza. Caspian's gaze darted around, finally landing on Drayce, who was still making his way through the line. When it seemed Caspian found what he was looking for, he turned back to me.

"You know... together... like,"—he hesitated with an unsure shoulder shrug—"boyfriend-girlfriend?" He looked up at me from under his lashes, shy and slightly awkward as he talked.

"Do you want to date me?" I asked, unable to keep the hope from my words. He tilted his head, and his lips thinned like he couldn't believe I just asked that question.

"Cupcake, I've wanted to since the first day. I don't just sleep with anyone, especially not the first day I meet them," he reminded me. My face burned bright red in reminder we had done that only a few hours after meeting. "So, is that a yes?"

I bounced in my seat with a joyous, 'Yes.'

"Yes!" he cheered, leaning over the table. "Now give your boyfriend a kiss, Cupcake."

I shot forward and did just that, my face hurting from how wide my smile was.

"Do I get one?" Drayce asked as he sank down next to me. Caspian cocked a brow as he took a bite of his lunch.

"From her or from me?" he teased, but Drayce's lips curled in a smug smile as he leaned forward.

"Both," he challenged, looking between us.

I bit my lip and crossed my legs under the table at the thought and based on the way Drayce's eyes heated up, he saw what I'd done.

Wait, you're with Caspian now, you can't think like that.

"If that's what Cupcake wants," Caspian responded, unfazed by my inner turmoil.

"Maybe later. I have to get to history early, so I need to be quick," Drayce winked at us, slowly eating his pasta off his fork.

Hell's bells and tarot tells, I think I need a cold shower.

Thanks to Caspian and Drayce, I was completely unfocused through history and familiar training, almost losing a few fingers to a hungry Lulu when I wasn't fast enough with the marshmallows. By the time I got to mentoring, I was exhausted. It'd been a few days of ups and downs, and I was really feeling it by then.

"You look chipper and ready to go," Torryn teased as he took in my appearance. Clearly, I wasn't the only one who thought I looked like a walking zombie.

"Yeah," I mumbled incoherently, causing his brows to quirk down in concern. He set down the book he was holding and walked over to me.

"Why don't we call it a day and start fresh on Monday? Try not to do any magic and let yourself rest up. Tell my brother to pamper you or some shit, get a back rub out of him," he joked, a hint of jealousy in his eyes for a second before he fixed his expression.

"Don't be jealous, you can give me a back rub any time

you want." I blurted out, too tired to properly filter my thoughts

His eyes darkened at my answer, but he didn't say anything more on the subject though I could tell he wanted to.

Weekend goal—find my filter again.

"Go get some food and go to bed," he ordered.

I simply nodded, turning and walking out without further response. I barely remembered the walk back to my room, completely lost in my sleep-deprived daze. After dropping my bag on the floor, I face-planted on my bed, asleep within seconds.

It felt like I'd only been asleep for a few moments when an incessant knocking woke me up. I stumbled over to the door and opened it slowly, only to find Torryn on the other side. He wavered for a moment before a sloppy smile lit up his face. Barreling into the room without a word, he plopped down on my bed, staring over at me.

"You alright?" I asked, eyeing him in concern.

"Oh, yeah. I'm fine. I came to check on you since I didn't see you at dinner, even after I told you to get something to eat, so I came here," he rambled. "You know what? I love your pink hair much better. Hold still."

I barely heard what he had said when a wave of magic flowed over me, and my green hair shifted around my face, going from a pea soup green back to its normal bubblegum pink.

"Yes, there, much better. I mean, not that you don't look beautiful with green hair, but pink is definitely more you, Gorgeous."

"Thank you," I mumbled, confused at where all of this was coming from. "Torryn, are you—"

"Say it again," he commanded, getting up.

"Say what?" I hadn't even finished my question yet.

"My name," he whispered, closing the distance between us. "Say it again."

"Torryn," I murmured, unable to move as he stood before me. That indescribable pull filled me, urging me to touch him, but knowing he wasn't comfortable with that, I kept my hands at my sides. His eyes closed, a deep rumble softly filling the room. My brows shot up at his weird behavior, but that incessant need for him slowly overpowered my drive to figure out what the hex was wrong with him.

"I love when you say my name. I love your candied strawberry scent that fucking teases me any time you get close to me," he groaned, his hands coming up to cup my face. His eyes burned as he looked down at me intensely. "I haven't been able to get you out of my head since you first showed up here, Aris. You were always so close, but not close enough. Now, here you are, right in my arms." Without any hesitation, he dipped his head and pressed his lips to mine.

My mind blanked, my body moving as if it had a mind of its own, leaning into Torryn's warm and solid body. Power swelled in my chest, and a feeling of being grounded surrounded me. All the uncertainty of the last few days disappeared as I kissed back, my mouth opening against his tongue as it brushed against my lips. Wrapping my arms around his shoulders, I let that solid feeling grow as I clutched his broad shoulders. When he smirked, it reminded me of Cas, and it was like a cold bucket of water had been thrown over me as I remembered Caspian, my boyfriend... Torryn's *brother*. *Damn it all to hex.*

"Torryn," I pulled back, placing my hands on his chest. "We can't." He nipped at my bottom lip before giving me a sinful smile.

"Why not? No one is here to stop us," he countered.

I rolled my eyes, purposely ignoring the surge of heat between my thighs. Stepping away, I crossed my arms and gave him a hard stare.

"Because you're a teacher, and I'm a student, *your* student. I'm dating your brother. A whole lot of reasons why we can't," I argued, and instead of him sobering like I thought he would, he laughed. "What is so funny?"

"I don't care about any of those things. I just want you, Gorgeous," he insisted, trying to reach for me, almost throwing himself off balance.

It was then I knew something was wrong. Looking closer, now that I wasn't overpowered by magic and his tempting kisses, I saw his eyes were glazed, and his cheeks were flushed.

"Are you drunk?"

"Nope," he shook his head, his red hair flopping at the sharp movement.

Yup, something is definitely wrong. Time to call in reinforcements.

"Alright, sit down." I directed him to my bed, hurrying over to my desk after he sat down for me. I scribbled notes to everyone I could think of, hoping between Caspian, Kye, Drayce, and Xan... someone would come. As I started to fold them and send them off, hands circled my waist, and Torryn started peppering kisses down my neck. With more willpower than should have been necessary, I finally managed to send them out, praying the guys would be quick.

"I don't want to sit. I want you, Gorgeous," he murmured into my skin, his hands starting to roam before I forced him to sit back down.

"Did someone give you something to eat or drink?" I

asked, holding him at arm's length. He shook his head as he continued to fight, not bothering with words. "Torryn, we..." My words died off as I looked behind him to witness the effects of our kissing. Just like with Caspian, it had resulted in new magic surfacing. Vines grew through the cracks around my windows and up my walls before meeting at the ceiling. Pretty pink flowers blossomed here and there, adding to its beauty. This was much more pleasant than being soaked in water.

"Torryn, look." He finally turned at my command, smiling at the sight above and around us.

"Pink, like you," he pointed out, standing up and walking over to the lowest vine, plucking a flower. Another flower grew back in its place as quickly as he picked it. He strode over, his sultry smile still in place as he tucked it behind my ear and lowered his face to mine again.

"Cupcake?"

"Angel?"

"Sweets?"

My three friends burst into the room, Xan following a few moments later. I was still trying to pry Torryn off me when they ran in, and they thankfully caught on quickly, helping to pull him off me and sitting him in my desk chair. Kye looked around, mumbling about something to tie him up with as Torryn still struggled with the others. A thought popped into my head, and I visualized vines growing around him, securing him in place. *Hey, it's worth a try.* Despite the intense moment, I couldn't help but let out a squeal as I watched vines grow in through the window to secure him in place, starting small, snaking along the wall and floors before wrapping around him.

"What the hell is going on?" Kye asked, all four of them looking as confused as I felt.

"The vines were all me, but I have no idea what's up. Something's wrong, but he says he isn't drunk. Could it be magic?" I asked, walking toward Torryn who continued to struggle against his leafy hold.

"Gorgeous," he pleaded, his forehead shining with sweat as he started to pant. "Please."

His broken cry hurt my heart as I watched him struggle with whatever was affecting him. I wanted it, but I couldn't, not when he was like this, and not when I was with Caspian.

"*Gorgeous?*" Caspian cut in, his voice tight. I grimaced, looking over at him but unable to keep eye contact. He didn't look hurt, more angry and confused as he crossed his arms. "Is he in here hitting on my girlfriend? My own brother?"

"Girlfriend?" Kye interrupted, "I thought you said she wasn't your girlfriend."

I rubbed my forehead as everyone started talking at once. *This is so not helping.*

"Guys!" I finally shouted. "Can we focus, please?" I huffed, waving a hand at Torryn, who was looking worse by the minute.

"Wait, did you just fucking grow vines?" Kye accused, finally cluing into the new magic. Caspian gasped as he looked above and around him, taking in the new decorations in my room.

"Uh, yeah," I mumbled, watching Xan as he circled Torryn, studying him.

"He's been hexed. There's always a drain after a hex wears off, and Professor Callahan is looking haggard now. This one had to have been darker than usual. I've never seen one leave a drain quite this bad," Xan explained in his calming, deep tone. The gravity of the situation settled on us all, making them forget for a moment about the vines and focus on Torryn.

"Is there anything we can do?" I asked, grabbing a towel from my hook and wiping at Torryn's sweaty brow. *Who would do this to him?!*

"At this point, there's not much we can do besides wait it out. Someone grab some water, so we can rehydrate him," Xan commanded, ushering me to remove the vines. I let them fall back slowly, and the guys led Torryn to the bed and settled him down, his movements more feeble as the fight drained out of him. I sat next to him, letting him pull me close and lay his head in my lap. He finally closed his eyes a few moments later, his soft snores the only noise in the room as silence fell over the rest of us.

"Now, back to my question. How are you using Earth magic?" Kye asked, raising an eyebrow. "That's Earth Elemental magic, not Mixta magic."

"Well... you see. I sort of bonded with Torryn, and just like last time, I seem to have gained another power," I explained tentatively, ducking my head at his glare.

"What do you mean 'another'?" Drayce asked, his tone a bit less biting than Kye's.

"When I bonded with Caspian, I was able to manipulate water," I answered, just now looking over at my boyfriend.

"Of all the people you had to bond with, why did it have to be Torryn? This means we're stuck with him too, doesn't it?" he groaned playfully, coming over and taking my hand, giving it a reassuring squeeze. I could tell he wasn't happy about it but didn't want me to feel bad.

"Wait. Bonding? Is this why you asked me about Mixta powers?" Xan asked, his eyes narrowing like I'd used him.

"Yes. I couldn't exactly tell you what was happening," I

said defensively. Torryn mumbled and pulled me in tighter at my raised voice.

"So, you've bonded with two people and unlocked new powers?" Xan asked, this time losing the accusing note.

"Yes, and I'm not sure what triggers it. With Caspian, it was a sense of acceptance. With Torryn, it was more of a sense of safety and grounding like he was keeping me from getting overwhelmed with emotion," I explained, unsure how to put into words the emotions and feelings of the situation.

"I'm going to look into it some more, but that's something I've never heard of before," Xan said as he studied Torryn. "I think the hex has passed, so he'll sleep it off until morning. Just keep water nearby because he's going to feel awful tomorrow. I'm going to the library now that you're safe," he said, turning to walk away before I stopped him.

"Wait. With Torryn I didn't have a... uh... physical connection. It doesn't fully work if you aren't intimate, right?" I fumbled around my words. Kye made an upset noise from his spot by the window, and Caspian choked out a shocked laugh. Xan didn't even flinch, scratching his chin thoughtfully as he turned his eyes to me.

"No, bonds don't work like that. It's more of an aligning on a mental capacity. The physical intimacy is more like consummating the marriage and solidifying that bond. I doubt your bond just disappears because there's no physical intimacy... It will likely be weaker than Caspian's though," he added, finally walking out and leaving us in awkward silence.

"I've heard of something like this before," Drayce finally spoke up, stepping away from the desk and coming over to us. "If it's what I think it is, it's rare. I'm going to go with Xan and see what we can find. Don't worry, Angel. We'll figure this out. You aren't alone. Someone should stay with her tonight," he said, giving me a kiss on the forehead before hurrying after Xan.

"Call me if you need me," Kye said, his usually stoic face back in place, making me miss my joking Kye. I couldn't really say anything to make this better, but I managed a feeble apology. "No worries, I'll talk to you guys later." He strode out of the room without looking back, leaving me with Caspian.

"I'm so sorry," I started before he held a hand up to stop me.

"Don't even try to apologize. There was magic involved with our bond, feeding off our attraction. I felt that pull too, Cupcake. I doubt this was any different," he said, pulling me from Torryn's loosening grip into his arms. "This changes nothing."

"It's not that I think you're mad, it's that it's your brother this time," I explained quietly. He gave a long sigh, nodding lightly.

"It sucks, I won't lie. Torryn and I don't exactly see eye-to-eye... we never have. I'll try to make it work... what choice do I have?" he said, a bit of sadness in his eyes, "I don't blame you. I just can't stand him."

"He didn't have any more say than any of us did," I pointed out, hating that I couldn't fix this. I knew he wasn't mad at me, but I hated we had so much tension this early on.

"We'll make it work, Cupcake. I promise, I still feel the same," he said, giving me a soft, sweet kiss that had butterflies dancing in my stomach.

Let's hope he feels the same way tomorrow because if this magic I feel with all of them has anything to say about the situation, I doubt it's done.

CHAPTER 12

September 15th
Sunday Morning
Aris

We parted ways after breakfast, each of us having different things to do. I hurried up to my room and grabbed my school bag and folder before heading to the library. With everything going on, I wanted to actually finish my Mixta project and look a bit more into this bond thing. We hadn't heard back yet from Xan and Drayce, both too preoccupied with whatever research they'd done to actually explain it to us. Kye was a bit distant, which was really bothering me. It seemed like we'd taken baby steps in a better direction, and now, that was slipping away. Once I was done, I planned to find him and see if he was alright.

The library was still empty when I entered, most students either sleeping in or still eating. I chose a table by the window, hoping the sunshine would keep me from getting sleepy—something about a comfy library made me want to doze off. Shuffling through my bag, I tried to find my notes on the bond, but nothing was there. *Weird, I know I put them in here yesterday.*

I continued to search, but knowing me, I had probably dropped them somewhere. Ever since the first bonding, my brain had felt frazzled. Trying not to panic at the thought my bonding notes could be in the wrong hands, I focused on my Mixta studies paper, trying to get something accomplished.

An hour later, I had a good chunk finished, but thoughts of Kye's frown continued to play through my head. Finally giving up, I packed my remaining papers in my bag and left the library. Just as I entered the dorms, I was cornered by the Curse Crew.

Just what I need right now.

"Oh, look, it's the little Mixta who thinks she can have the *real* witch men," Esmerelda said with a hollow laugh.

"You're useless, I don't see why you keep coming to school here. Oh wait, it's because your rich daddy paid your way in, isn't it? I saw them dragging you all over campus," Amber added in.

"The real question is, how did such powerful parents have such a failure for a child? I bet you're the family's dirty little secret, dragging down their reputation by existing," Tasha said, cackling at the redness tinting my cheeks.

"I thought the puke green actually fit you better," Esmerelda taunted, pulling on a chunk of my hair.

"Good thing I don't give a flying bat what you think of me. I'm three times the woman you'll ever be. Don't be assholes because the hot guys in school want to hang out with me."

"Don't think you'll ever be good enough for them or anyone else. Mixtas need to learn their place," Tasha bit out, shoving me into the wall behind me. It took everything in me not to hit back. I doubted the headmaster would feel very charitable toward me after my parents were such assholes. *And we all know the Mixta would be blamed.*

"What the fuck do you think you're doing?!" Kye's biting tone interrupted them, looks of shock taking over all three of their faces. "How dare you talk to anyone that way!"

"Oh, Kye, we were just teasing her. Why do you care?" Esmerelda asked, her tone light but strained.

"Because she's my fucking friend," he bit out, bumping them aside as he reached for me, pulling me away from them and down the hall. He didn't look at me or say anything as he led me to what I assumed was his room. When the door was shut behind us, he finally let go, pacing for a few minutes before I bothered to speak up.

"Um, Kye?" I asked tentatively, almost afraid he'd snap at me. He looked angry as he stomped back-and-forth across the dark room. From the blankets on the bed to the huge tapestry of stars that hung on the wall, it seemed fitting for his broody side. His voice pulled me from my thoughts, his tone hard as he bit out his words.

"Why did you just take it? Why didn't you fight back?"

I thought over his words for a second, thinking of how to explain to him the way Mixtas were usually treated. Sometimes, it was subtle and easy to miss, like little punishments that weren't as fair, but often enough, others' behaviors took on the aggressive, insulting tactics the Curse Crew liked best.

"Because I didn't want to be punished for fighting. She could have easily told the headmaster I confronted her and had two more to back it up. I've lived as a Mixta my entire life, and I know the headmaster would have taken them for their word," I said frankly, not wanting him to think I was being rude but wanting him to see the truth in it. "I've been punished or blamed for a lot for things other witches did. When you're a Mixta, you're seen as unworthy, less intelligent, and sometimes, even less of a person when you are below someone in status."

He studied me for a second before letting out a sigh and flopping on his bed.

"I don't like when people are mean to you. You're too nice for this school," he mumbled, placing his arm over his eyes, blocking everything out.

"Maybe I'm not as nice as you think," I challenged, glaring down at him, trying to show him my inner strength. He finally sat up and stared back, his eyes narrowing at mine.

"Maybe I'm not as mean as people think I am," he shot back, a slight vulnerability showing in the brown and gold depths of his eyes.

"I know that. I've known that since I first met you," I said softly. "We all wear a mask from time to time. My chipper personality combats all the hate I've seen. Yours is your broodiness, though personally, I find it pretty hot."

"Shut up," he said, shaking his head at me like I was ridiculous. A hint of a smile played on his lips, and I really wanted to see it brighten.

"No, I mean it. The whole glowering, dark clothes, and stomping around really does it for me. Sometimes, I can barely control myself," I joked, fanning my face like he had set me ablaze. "See, I'm all hot and bothered over here."

This time his laugh bubbled out, and the deep rumble behind his softer voice was music to my ears. This was the

Kye I liked, the Kye who showed how he really felt and didn't shove it away.

"You're ridiculous," he said with a shake of his head. I gave an unapologetic shrug and smiled back at him, plopping on the bed next to him, tucking my legs under me. "I'm glad the hair is back," he said softly, tucking a strand behind my ear.

"I like this smile on you. It feels special because you don't just give them away," I said quietly, brushing my thumb over his lip. We both had a way of hiding behind our exteriors, not easily revealing what we really felt to anyone.

"Well, you see, this cute little witch came into my life with her pink hair and her bubbly personality and pulled me right in," he joked, bringing his hickory eyes to meet mine. A spark of magic danced between us as our eyes locked, his hand reaching for mine and holding it tight. The tingling sensation moved over me, dancing along my skin and seeming to pull me closer. Before I realized what was happening, we were leaning in, our lips meeting in a harsh kiss. The primal pull to touch him, to taste him was overwhelming. We were a rush of movement as we pulled our clothes free, my hands trailing over his heated skin as soon as it was bared to me. He was much calmer than I was, his fingertips grazing softly over my pale skin.

"You're just as beautiful as I imagined," he said reverently, leaning me back onto the bed as his lips moved to mine. He kept murmuring sweet words as he kissed over my body, his soft lips gently roaming over me, setting my entire body on fire.

The magic refused to let me sit back and take it, needing to make him feel just as good. Sitting up, I pushed him back until I could move out from under him. Lowering to the floor, I pushed his legs further apart as I scooted closer. His thick erection jutted up, begging me to wrap my lips around him. He groaned as I licked up his cock before sliding my mouth over him. His fingers tangled in my hair as I focused on what I was doing to him, his pants of pleasure, sending a wave of heat through me. Bobbing my head over his soft skin, I swirled my tongue around him, moving my hands to his thighs.

"Sweets, you have to stop," he moaned, gently pushing me away as a shudder of pleasure raced through him. He pulled me up from the ground for another searing kiss, not caring if he tasted himself on my tongue. "My turn to torture you, I think," he said, tugging me onto the bed and leaning me back, so I was lying on his dark sheets, my pale skin nearly glowing in contrast. He licked his tongue down my chest, swirling over each nipple torturously slow, grazing his teeth softly over the peaks as he dipped a hand between my thighs.

A jolt of pleasure pulled a moan from my lips as he slid a finger over my folds before flicking his thumb over my already throbbing clit. My hips bucked into his hand as he dipped a finger inside me, making me beg him for more. Bringing his mouth back to mine, he continued to swirl his fingers over my sensitive bud, teasing and pleasing me until I was shaking with my impending orgasm. When I let out a whimper, he didn't stop, picking up his pace until my body gave into him, shaking as my orgasm pulsed through me, his name bursting from my lips. He didn't stop pumping his fingers into me as my body pulsed around him, only pulling away as it subsided.

He didn't give me time to recover before his cock replaced his fingers, sliding the head over me, gathering my wetness before slowly sliding inside. He was thick, stretching me deliciously as he pushed further in. Not as patient, I wrapped my legs behind his back, forcing him to bury himself fully.

"Fuck, Sweets," he moaned, slowly thrusting his hips. His eyes locked onto mine as he fucked me, being gentler than I had anticipated. My body sang for him as each movement awakened even more waves of desire until I was a whimpering mess. I gasped as the room descended into shadows, a beautiful mix of colors sweeping through the darkness, illuminating the room in their vibrant glow. A mixture of blues, greens, pinks, and purples bathed us in their light, giving the entire situation an ethereal glow. The colors pulsed as he shifted us, sliding his hand between us to tease me again, sending me crashing over that edge once more. This time, my body coaxed him to follow, his orgasm pulling a low, sexy groan from his lips as he stiffened under my touch, his muscles flexing deliciously above me—a glorious sight to behold.

Pulling out of me, he laid down, tucking me into his side. We watched the lights dancing above us as our breathing slowed back to normal, the pull of magic starting to slowly fade and letting my mind settle back down. And that was the moment reality smacked me in the face.

You bonded with another guy... again! Who does this? Aris, you've never even managed to keep ONE boyfriend before, now you've got three guys for eternity!

"Shit, what the fuck was that?" he asked, his voice still husky with lust. I took a deep breath, bracing myself for what I was sure would be an intense reaction.

"Uh, I think we're bonded. Welcome to the club?" I said slowly, peeking up at him as he processed my words. He sat bolt upright, dropping me down on the mattress with a soft bounce before standing up to pace. "Hey!"

"What do you mean, 'bonded'?!" he asked, a slight panic in his eyes he was really trying hard to suppress.

"I don't know, it's not exactly something I can pinpoint or even help. It's a magical pull that seems to happen when our thoughts or spirits or whatever align. With you, it felt like we had a mutual empathy for each other nobody else would understand. It's been a completely different feeling with each bond. Either way, the magic overwhelms us, and apparently, makes us seek a deeper connection... hence the sex," I explained, scooting off the bed and pulling my clothes back on. I had a feeling he was about to freak out and kick me out, or I would get frustrated and leave on my own. I hoped desperately he would prove me wrong. I didn't want to feel used or tossed aside.

"So, this bond is... *permanent*?" he asked quietly, sitting back down, resting his hands on his knees. His eyes pleaded with me to prove him wrong, but I couldn't. That wasn't how this worked, how it was supposed to go.

I didn't ask for this any more than he did, but it always feels like it's somehow my fault.

"Yes," I answered, my voice cracking. He nodded slowly before standing again and pulling on his pants.

"I need a minute," he said, his tone oddly clipped. I nodded slowly as a tear fell from my eye.

"I'm sorry," I said, bolting for the door and slamming it behind me, tears falling as I hurried up to my room.

What if he blames me?
What if he won't forgive me?

September 15th
Sunday Evening
Kyelerian

I paced my room for what felt like the hundredth time. After how I reacted, it was likely she'd never talk to me again. *Fuck. Way to go, asshole.* I wasn't one for pretty, flowery words. I didn't date or talk to girls for exactly this fucking reason—I sucked at it.

The fact it was *her* I hurt bothered me even more. I couldn't shake the image of her tear-filled eyes that clearly reflected every ounce of pain. I grunted as my fist made contact with the stone walls, hating myself more than ever.

The truth? I wasn't even mad, not at her, anyway. There was something about the pink-haired witch that had called to me from the first time I met her. I tried and tried to push her away, but she always came barreling in with her smiles and sunshine, making it so I could never forget her. The other night when I heard Caspian was her boyfriend, I was angry. *I wanted that.* That, more than anything, was what bothered me. If she was dating Caspian, where did that leave the rest of us? I didn't want to go all-in if I was only going to be left disappointed and depressed in the end.

Fuck, what do I do to fix this?

Do I want to fix it?

Knowing the answer already, I pulled on my shirt and walked out, locking the door behind me. I fought myself the entire way up to Aris' room, part of me wanting to talk this out, the other demanding I run away and take no part in the chaos. I paused outside her door, my hand raised to knock but unable to bring myself to do it. *Fuck, man up and knock, you fool!* My hand finally made contact with her door, the sound echoing beyond the door. *No turning back now, just talk to her.*

"Kye?" she asked, her voice raspy and hollow. In fact, her whole appearance was disheveled, all the way up to her puffy eyes.

Man, I'm such a dick.

"I'm sorry, Sweets. Can we talk?" I asked timidly, hoping desperately she wouldn't slam the door in my face.

"Sure," she said, turning and heading back into the room, sitting on her bed and waiting for me to talk.

"I'm sorry I reacted that way, I shouldn't have freaked out. I just... after finding out you were dating Caspian, I didn't want to be the deadweight left behind. What does this make us?" I asked bluntly, desperately needing to hear her answer.

"Cupcake?!" Caspian's voice echoed from the door as his fists slammed against it. She gave me a relieved look as she hurried to the door, dodging the answer. Caspian burst in as soon as she pulled it open, taking one look at her tear-stained face before he was in front of me, our noses practically touching.

"What the fuck did you do?" he shouted, but there were no words I could use to defend myself. He was right, I fucking made her cry.

"Hold on, Caspian, it's complicated," Aris said, rushing forward and pulling him toward the bed until he was sitting. Once she had him under control, she looked at me expectantly.

Fuck. Well, I guess this conversation is happening with the three of us now.

Unable to look either of them in the eye while talking about something that made me feel vulnerable, I focused on a spot on the wall.

"We bonded and had sex under its magic. And now, I wanted to know what happens from here... what I am to her. She's crying because I freaked out at first and said I needed a minute," I explained. "After she left, I realized how much of a dick I'd sounded like."

Caspian stood back up at my words, his eyes narrowing as he moved forward. A dark and rumbling storm cloud formed above them, swirling angrily, Caspian's frustration clear as he approached. My eyes narrowed at him as the shadows from Aris' room shifted and moved around him, pushing against the impending storm. The moment Caspian pushed me, she dove between us and pulled us apart. The shadows and storm clouds disappeared as we focused back on her.

"No, you don't get to fight in my room! I don't want all my shit wet again, and I don't want to see either of you hurt. It's my fault we all keep fucking bonding. I'm sorry, Caspian, I didn't mean for it to happen, it just did. I'm such a shitty girlfriend," she said, her tears spilling over again, deflating our anger.

"Cupcake, you're *not* a shitty girlfriend. I've bonded with you, remember? I know the magic isn't exactly something you can ignore. I don't necessarily like that you bonded with him, but I get it. I think I'd also like the answer to his question, though. Our party is up to four now, and honestly, I'm still wrapping my head around the fact my brother is one of them," Caspian said with a sigh, plopping down on the bed.

"It's not only up to me. I'd be lying if I said I didn't have feelings for Kye and Torryn, the same feelings I have for you. And that hint of magic I felt with you guys before we bonded... I've noticed it with Drayce and Xan too. You five are the only ones who've ever triggered that feeling or magical pull, so you should know about them too," she rushed through the words, collapsing on her rug, pulling her knees into her chest as she curled her arms around them like they were the only things holding her together through all the chaos.

"If you like them too, I think you should date them. It

would be a super shitty existence to be bonded to someone and not be with them," Caspian said quietly. Relief flooded me at his words, not even realizing how much I wanted him to say it. Even though it seemed like I was fine with being alone, I was starting to feel like that wasn't truly what I needed.

"I can share. I mean, it seems we have little choice, anyway. I'd rather have this with you than be without you," I admitted, feeling relief at the revelation. I never considered myself a guy who would share a woman, but something about this just felt right.

"Really?" she asked, her voice wavering as her shoulders sagged in relief. Caspian swooped in and scooped her up, snuggling her in his lap for a moment before speaking.

"I just want you, and I want you to be happy. It'd be selfish of me to keep you to myself in this situation. We were all clearly meant to be a group, so we'll be a group," he said simply like that was that. I couldn't argue with him. Something about the situation felt right—even if I still wished I could have her to myself.

"Let's go grab something to eat," I said, reaching down to help them stand. Her stomach rumbled on cue at the mention of food, erasing the last bit of tension that hung in the air.

Now we just need to talk to the last two.
Maybe this will actually work out.

CHAPTER 13

September 16th
Monday Afternoon
Aris

"Hey, Angel," Drayce's smooth voice reached me, his denim-clad legs coming into view as he stepped up next to my seated form. Looking up, I saw him giving me a cute smile that lit up his face. "How's it going?" he asked, sinking to sit on the grass next to me.

"It's alright," I said with a half-hearted shrug, deflated. "It's been a long few days."

"Aww, I'm sorry." His arm curled around my shoulders and pulled me into his side, the warmth from his body seeping into my drained one.

While Caspian and Kye had worked everything out, and our semi-group date went amazingly well, the fact none of us really knew what was going on with the bondings or our new powers was stressful and wearing on me. *Also, can't forget that my notes are still missing even though I've looked everywhere.*

"Want to know some good news? You've got me for mentoring today since Professor Callahan is still recovering from the last bit of the effects from that hex."

At the mention of Tor, uneasiness settled in my stomach. I knew I should probably send him a note or go see him, but I was still worried he wouldn't react well. *Holy hellsticks, what if he doesn't even remember the bond?!*

"We can make it an easy session," he teased, bringing me out of my inner worries, putting a tentative smile on my lips. It was hard to stay upset with Drayce around.

"Really? You're willing to help this little witch out?" I perked up, realizing I'd barely seen him since Friday.

"Oh, I am definitely willing to help you out," he murmured, his words laced with heat as he tossed a wink my way with a tiny curl of his lips.

"I don't think that's the kind of mentoring they were thinking," I teased, but his lighthearted playfulness helped ease the stress of the last few days. "Do you have anywhere, in particular, you would like to work?"

"Is there somewhere you guys have been doing your sessions? I don't want to throw off too much of your progress by changing it up." We both stood, grabbing our bags off the ground as we did so. "Hold on, Angel, you've got some grass on your skirt."

My face heated as his hand brushed gently down the back of my skirt. *Is he... purposely cupping my ass? No, Aris, you're being ridiculous after all that extra attention this weekend.*

"Alright, show me where you usually practice."

Feeling a swell of confidence, I grabbed his hand and started down the path between the buildings toward the crystal cave. I wasn't sure if Torryn would be okay with us going there, but he didn't say it was off-limits. Not to mention, if the vibes between Drayce and me were potential bonds, I didn't want whatever chaos that came next happening inside.

"Um, Angel? This is where Professor Callahan takes you? Why are we going into the woods?" His voice was still light, but he sounded confused.

"You'll see," I sang, pulling him along behind me. I remembered Tor mentioning not a lot of people used the cave, so I was hoping it would be a surprise for Drayce. We finished the walk in silence, the warm glow of the setting sun illuminating our path and giving the forest an extra vibe of peacefulness. It took me a moment to spot the entrance. Drayce gave a noise of surprise when I tugged him inside.

It was just as breathtaking as it was the first time I saw it if not more so. The setting sun reflected down into the room, giving the crystal light an even more vibrant hue. I turned toward Drayce, smiling to myself as he twirled in a circle, taking in all the sights.

"It's amazing! I can feel the power. No wonder he brought you here. If you had latent powers, it would definitely bring them out!" he exclaimed, his hazel eyes dancing with his enthusiasm.

"I was completely mesmerized when I saw it for the first time," I told him, eyeing the space once more, feeling like I was witnessing it for the first time all over again.

Drayce turned back to me, holding his hands out as he spoke. "I know you're a Mixta, but I also know you feel the power coursing through this place. That power is inside of you too. It's not just in those with affinities. This is why he brought you here—to bring that out."

"I do feel it, but that doesn't mean I can start

summoning dragons or anything," I teased, knowing what he was saying was true to some extent but still feeling shy about acknowledging it. I felt that building swell within my chest as he talked, knowing it was power and not just in my head.

"Don't be cheeky, come here," he ordered, holding both of his hands out for mine. The sparks that usually danced between us were practically fireworks at this point, and my eyes widened at the intense feeling.

"Do you feel that?" I asked, knowing very well he couldn't miss it. "Is that your magic or this place?"

"I told you, my stubborn girl, that's your magic too. Let it fill you to the point, you feel it in your bones all the way to your very soul. Believe in it, Angel, and use it," he ordered, his eyes full of determination that fueled my own.

Without a real plan in place, I closed my eyes and let the new power course through me. It took a moment before I was actually able to handle the sensation, but when I did, it made me feel like anything was possible, that I was *actually* able to do it. So, I unleashed all the power that had built, pushing it out around me, letting it have a mind of its own. When the power inside of me had settled, I opened my eyes. The hazel irises that stared at me were filled with a spark of awe at what I'd accomplished.

"I told you, you could do it, Angel," he murmured, leaning forward and pressing his lips lightly to mine. The kiss was short and sweet, but I felt the passion behind it.

Finally taking a moment to look around, I looked at what I had done. A thin veil of glittering shadows hung in the air while a slight mist of water was falling, giving the lights even more surfaces to dance off until the room took on an even more magical appearance. A soft bed of grass had sprouted at our feet, giving us a cushion for the crystal and stone floor. Apparently, I had activated all my new powers at once.

"Oh, my broomsticks," I breathed out, looking back at him in shock, a surprised giggle bubbling out of me. "I fucking did it."

"Yes, you did," he agreed. This time when our eyes met, it was a look of mutual pride and understanding, knowing we each had power, even though I was a Mixta, and he was one of the major five. It just took the encouragement of someone who cared to bring it out of me. I couldn't have taken my gaze from his if I tried. We were locked into the familiar feeling, the pull ramping up until it was overwhelming.

Drayce was the first to make a move, stepping forward and grabbing me around the waist, then spinning me around so my tutu flared around me and happy laughter filled the room. A moment later, his excitement died down, and a startled noise escaped him as he looked down. Confused, I looked down only to see we were floating a good four feet off the ground, too occupied with each other to notice it. This time, it was my turn to lose my cool, a girlish scream escaping me as I dove into his arms.

I told him I wanted to fly, but fuck this, I want my feet firmly on the ground.

"Is this what I think it is?" he questioned, holding me tightly.

Worry wormed its way into my chest after how Kye had responded, so staring directly at his Henley, I nodded slightly, unable to speak.

"So, you're mine now, too?"

"Uh, yes..." I hedged, my anxiety making my voice come out in a squeak.

"That's pretty cool," he added, tilting his head to catch

my eye. When I finally looked at him, his eyes were twinkling, and he was smiling. "Who else is part of our gang? Caspian and Torryn?"

"And Kye," I murmured, but Drayce surprised me yet again and just nodded.

"Cool," he stated simply. His voice was soft and didn't hold anger or irritation, seemingly unfazed by the magnitude of the fact we were now connected for life.

His laid-back attitude slowly eased my panic, helping me enjoy the moment, making that physical urge flare, and I found myself leaning into him.

"Angel?" he asked softly as I pressed my forehead against his jaw.

"Yeah?" My voice was breathy, need slowly building the longer I felt his heated, sepia skin pressing against mine.

"I want you right now, and I know you're feeling the same pull I am, but I want our first time to be when *you* want it, not the magic."

I felt my heart clench, not from pain or rejection but from warmth and feeling cared for. Our feet slowly hit the floor as the moment deflated slightly, the pull still there, but the need slowing down a fraction.

"I understand," I agreed, not wanting him to feel guilty for saying no. I respected that he chose to wait.

"I don't want us to feel pressured to do something we aren't ready for, and I'm not sure if this pull will stop until we get further away from each other. I'm going to head back to the dorms, so we can both clear our minds a bit. Send me a plane when you get back to campus?" he asked, looking vulnerable for the first time since I'd met him.

"Of course," I nodded, shooing him away with a smile. He leaned in and gave me a quick kiss. The passion was still strong behind it, but he pulled away far too soon. Before I could even open my eyes, he was gone, his footsteps echoing behind him. I lowered myself to the ground for a moment, giving him a head start and myself a moment to calm down.

Being in the cave alone brought my thoughts to Torryn. He'd been quiet since the hex, not quite his usual confident self. I could see the dark circles under his eyes and the miniscule disheveledness to him. Clearly, the effects were still an issue. Deciding it had been long enough, and my own worries were not as important, I gathered my bag and hurried off to find him. *It's time for us to talk about everything, face-to-face.*

Once I got out of the cave, I hesitated. I had no clue where his room was, but if the energy levels he'd had during history class today were any indication, he had likely passed out in his office shortly after. Now that I had a destination, I hurried toward campus and through the building to his office.

Not bothering to knock, I turned the knob on his office door and slowly pushed it open. My suspicions were right. He was sprawled out on his couch, soft snores coming from his direction. With a soft chuckle, I walked over, sinking onto the sliver of couch that was free, running my hand gently over his cheek.

"Handsome, you with me?" I said softly, trying not to startle him too much. His eyes popped open, his gaze darting around before settling on my face.

"Aris?" he asked, blinking his eyes a few times before pulling himself up to sit.

"You alright? I noticed how rough you looked earlier and wanted to check on you."

"I'm getting there. That hex wasn't fun," he mumbled,

taking a deep, shaky breath. "I need a week's worth of sleep and a stiff drink."

"I can't help you there, but if you need me to grab you some food or something, I can handle that." His eyes widened at my words and darted to his desk. I followed his gaze to the brownie container still sitting there, only one bite taken. "Hey! They couldn't have been that bad," I pouted, and his lips finally quirked up into a smile.

"Can you just recap for me? I feel like my brain is all muddled. What happened?" he asked, serious again.

"Well, uh…" I trailed off, unsure how to tell him he had bonded to a student for… life. Now seemed like a good time for a drink, so I walked over to his bookshelf and poked around until I saw the brown bottle hiding behind a stack of books. Pulling it out, I uncorked it and took a swig, handing it over with a grimace.

"Just spit it out, it can't be that bad," he urged, but his face told me he was bracing for the worst.

"Well, we have no idea who hexed you since no gossip has spread or anything. You lost some of your inhibitions, it seemed and ended up in my room. I called for the other guys I knew would help, and they came over. We restrained you because you were being a bit… handsy." His eyes widened at that, and he opened and closed his mouth like he couldn't figure out what to say. "Then we, uh, bonded, which means, uh, you'restuckwithmeforlife," I finished, rushing the words together, then snatching back the bottle for another swig of encouragement.

"Bonded?" he hedged like he couldn't quite grasp the concept. I stood in front of him awkwardly, not sure what to do other than take another drink. He eyed me as I took a swig, snatching the bottle the moment I pulled it from my lips. "That's enough for you."

"Well?" I finally blurted out, wanting to face the freak-out now rather than later. "You're stuck with me for life, so are you telling me how you feel about it, or are you going to make me wait because of those elemental powers? Yeah, that's because of that bond. I somehow magically tied myself to another witch and boom, elemental powers."

"So, Caspian and I are both tied to you?" he asked slowly. I could practically see the gears turning as he thought it over.

"And Drayce and Kye... and I'm assuming Xan if the magic that dances between us means anything like it did for all of you," I said, gritting my teeth as everything kept pouring out of my mouth.

"What the fuck," he mumbled, blinking his eyes rapidly as if it would make all of this go away.

I started pacing, unable to stay still in all this tension.

"I swear I didn't ask for this crazy shit, but it seems to be following me. Am I being tested? Or punished for something? I can't take this! I feel like everyone is just going to keep getting mad at me. How the hell am I going to handle being connected to all of them?" I hissed the statements under my breath, not meaning for him to overhear as I worked myself into a panic.

"Uh, Gorgeous? Why are you floating?" Torryn's voice cut through the haze of panic overtaking me, and my eyes snapped down to the ground, which was further down than I anticipated.

"Gah! I hate heights," I whined, stomping my foot down on the invisible cloud under me.

"Okay. First, come here," he commanded firmly, standing up and coming over to me. He reached up and grabbed my waist, bringing me back to solid ground. With a hand on either side of my face, he forced me to still and look up at him.

"I'm not mad, I've felt it too. Panicked because you're my student? Yes. Panicked about spending the rest of my life with someone as gorgeous, smart, and sassy as you? No. There was a reason we were all brought together, and until we figure that out, we have to figure out how to make this work. It will be fine," he reassured me.

He looked down at me softly, moving toward me like he couldn't believe I was here, in front of him. The moment didn't last long before he smirked and pulled me to him, pressing his lips to mine. My worries melted away as his lips moved against mine, butterflies dancing in my stomach as he pulled me even closer. When he pulled away, he wavered slightly on his feet.

"No more of this, mister!" I chastised, guiding him back to the couch and settling him down on the fluffy cushions. He smiled softly at me as I spread the blanket over him and kissed his forehead. "You get some rest. I'm going to go grab some food and bring it back for you," I promised, slipping from the room.

The halls were empty since dinner was long over, and everyone had moved out of the building. My footsteps echoed off the stone walls as I hurried down to the dining hall. An uneasy feeling settled over me, encouraging me to walk faster, my eyes darting from side-to-side.

The feeling only grew as I moved further through the halls until a soft peal of laughter broke the silence. My heart pounded in my chest as I stopped in my tracks, my head swiveling side-to-side as I searched for anything out of the ordinary. *Shake it off, Aris, it's probably nothing.*

Shadows started to dance on the wall around me, panic swelling up as they grew, closing in on me. A door nearby opened as someone came into the building, their timing impeccable. The shadows hissed and receded as someone ran off down the opposite hall. *What the hell?*

"What are you doing, Mixta weirdo?" Esmerelda's voice cut into my freak-out.

"Who just hangs out in the dark halls?" Tasha sneered, scoffing at the weird expression I was sure had taken over my face.

"Come on, I just want to grab my textbook from my locker. We have better things to do than hang out with this sorry excuse for a witch," Amber bit out, pulling them with her, each one bumping me on the shoulder as they passed. I took it with a smile on my face, knowing they had saved me from something far worse than bullying.

I ran into the pantry at top speed, grabbing Torryn whatever I could stuff in my arms, along with an energy drink and water before running back through the halls. I burst into his classroom, slamming the door behind me when I came face-to-face with a cloaked figure. It had to be a student since its stature was just barely bigger than mine. The items in my hands dropped all at once, clattering to the floor. I tried to see who was under the shadow of the cloak while bringing my magic forward so I could defend myself if needed.

"Aris?" Torryn's voice drifted out as his office door opened. The next moment, I was shoved aside as the figure hurried from the room, knocking me to the floor. Torryn rushed forward, but his energy was still depleted, making him pant before he even reached me.

"It's alright, Tor. I'm fine," I said wearily, gathering up the supplies I had dropped, urging him back to his office. I lined up the supplies on the desk before turning to him to see how he was.

"You're staying here tonight," he said firmly, directing me to the couch as he locked the door and started a fire. I kicked off my shoes, settling beside him when he joined me on the couch. I knew there would be an impending investigation tomorrow when he had enough energy to process what had happened, but for now, I tried to hide how freaked out I was.

Now if I can just shake off the creepy feeling hanging over me.

CHAPTER 14

September 17th
Tuesday Morning
Aris

I felt refreshed the next morning as I changed. After getting up early enough to avoid prying eyes and leaving a still-sleeping Tor a note, I headed back to my room. The weather was a bit chilly this morning, the crisp Fall air blowing through the leaves that had started to change colors in the last few days, so when I got to my tower room and started changing, I decided to forgo my usual skirt in exchange for a pair of mint-colored skinny jeans and a black and white polka-dotted sweater. Thanks to the storm late last night, the ground was covered in puddles and mud, and while I knew I could keep myself dry, I didn't want to risk getting my pink Converse dirty, so I put on a pair of boots, the tops folded outward, showing off the cute skull patterned fabric that lined the inside.

"Where did I put that?" I mumbled, shuffling through my bag in search for one of my notebooks. It wasn't one of any importance, just a list of random facts I wanted to remember for my classes just in case, but for the life of me, I couldn't find it in my bag or room. "Did I leave it somewhere?" Groaning, I gave up, knowing it was probably lost forever now because it wasn't anywhere I would have normally put it.

As I made my way to Mixta Basics, I ignored the stares I was getting from my fellow witches, their eyes falling on my bright pastel pants. Thankfully, I didn't run into any of my bullies, and by the time I reached my desk, my mood had picked up even more, and I forgot about my misplaced notes. The teacher came into the room with an extravagant whoosh that made me want to roll my eyes. *So dramatic.*

"Alright, class," she started cheerfully, her arms waving wildly as she talked. "Since it's Tuesday, we will be working on our practical exercises to see if we've made any progress!"

I ground my teeth in irritation. The rest of my classes were awesome, and I was actually learning a lot of stuff, like how to brew very basic potions or how to take care of different types of animals. But this class? I wanted to scream every time I had it. Unfortunately, that was every day of the week, save for Wednesdays when I had my progress tests. We either went over some of the most basic information on Mixtas and powers or did our 'practical work' from our learning plan. *Pssh, learning plan my cauldron.* It was a shitty set of exercises that attempted to stuff us into one of the major five affinities even though it was impossible. There was nothing wrong with us just because we had powers that weren't within society's stupid classifications.

Not wanting to cause an issue, I spent the hour going through my exercises, taking care not to let any of my new elemental abilities show. I wasn't sure why I didn't want to show that I did, in fact, make progress, but something deep in my gut urged it would be a bad idea. Half of me also didn't want to make it worse for the other Mixtas—like if I could do it, they could too. *Wing of bat! The witches in charge don't need any more reason to make us feel less than.*

The clock tower chimed at the end of class, and I walked across the campus to the library for study period, enjoying the sound of my boots sloshing in the puddles. Heading to the desk where Professor Embry was seated with the sign-in sheet, I scribbled my name down, along with the date and time before dropping my bag onto my regular chair and heading toward the archives and research section.

"Oof," I exclaimed when I turned the corner and ran face-first into a muscled, Henley-covered chest. Warm hands caught me before I could fall to the floor, and when I saw who I had run into, I laughed.

"We really need to get you to look where you're going, Angel," Drayce teased with a happy smile. "Are you over here looking into the same thing I am?"

"About... us?" I whispered softly, not wanting to have anyone overhear. He nodded, nudging me to follow him down the aisle. "Then, yes, but I have no idea where to even start. So, want some help?"

"From you? Always," he said, flashing me a cheeky grin. "Just start scanning these few books here. I've already gone through the bottom two shelves."

"Alright, I can do that." I had just gotten up on my tiptoes to grab the book when the briefest touch ran down my back, barely tracing over the curve of my ass.

"I love these jeans on you," Drayce whispered, his breath tickling my cheek as he leaned into me. I couldn't stop the tiny giggle that bubbled up, my cheeks burning at the heated glimmer in his hazel eyes.

"Thanks. You'll be seeing them a lot more now that it's getting cold. My body isn't used to super cold."

"Why's that?" Drayce asked, his brow drew low. "The weather is usually like this, this time of year."

"I'm from Ignis."

He stood silently, staring down at me intensely as I opened the first book.

"I don't think I know anything about you, Aris, or Caspian and the other guys," he explained with a start.

"Well," I started with a hum, my brain coming up with an idea. "Instead of eating in the dining hall after classes, maybe all of us can get together and go out for food down in town. Give us a chance to really learn more about each other. That's half the fun of dating, right?"

"Angel, are you asking me on a group date? Does that mean we're *officially* dating?" he teased softly, wrapping his arms around my waist. I giggled again and flashed him a tiny smirk. "I would love to do that, but first let's research and see if we can dig up what exactly is going on with all of us. Work first, play later."

I pouted playfully, and the warm and smooth sound of his laughter surrounded me as he kissed my cheek lightly.

"Yes, we are," I said with a confident smile. His answering grin had my heart fluttering, but I couldn't argue with his statement. "Alright, fine. Work now, play later," I agreed, finally turning my attention back to the book in my hand.

Hopefully, this goes quickly.

I could have easily sent a plane to the guys, but I didn't want to give them the chance to say no. Drayce had met me after class, so we were waiting outside of the Administration building to catch the others... and make it much harder for them to turn me down. *Hey, might as well cash in on the cuteness when I can.*

Drayce spotted Cas, calling him over in true Drayce fashion.

"Hey, hot stuff." He let out a shrill whistle and an overexaggerated wink that had Caspian blushing and shaking his head as he joined us.

"What's going on?" he asked, confused why we were waiting outside, instead of at our usual spot.

"Group date night!" I cheered, giving an excited squeal and grabbing Kye's arm as he tried to slip by us unnoticed. From the look on his face, I knew he'd heard me explain. "Nope, you're part of it too, Honey!"

"Where are we going? It better involve food," he mumbled as he gave me a small smile.

"It definitely will involve food," Drayce agreed, ushering us to the main road. I noticed Xan walking near the clock tower and decided to drag him along.

"Xan!" Leaving the group after giving Kye strict orders not to run away, I hurried toward him. "We're going out for dinner and fun, and you're coming!"

"Uh, I don't think that sounds like my kind of thing," he hedged, trying to keep walking as I blocked his path.

"Fun isn't your thing? I would never have guessed," I deadpanned, rolling my eyes and linking an arm through his. "Come on, you won't regret it!" I dragged him over to the group, but something was missing. My eyes scanned the crowd for my favorite burly professor, spotting him walking out of the dining hall heading for the back of campus. *Perfect!*

"Professor Callahan," I called, eyeing the nearby students and hating having to call him by his professional title.

"Miss Calisto, how can I help you?" he asked in his professor voice. I wrinkled my nose at the tone, which made him smile slightly before pulling me away from the crowd.

"We're going into town to have dinner and do something fun. Want to come?" I asked hopefully, really wanting us all to be together. There was just something about having us together that felt right.

"Oh, Aris," he murmured with a soft smile, "I would love to spend time with you guys, but I can't. At least, not this time. I'm still a professor, and you're still a student, but if you want, you can stop by tonight afterward."

"Now that's an offer I can't refuse, but I'll miss you," I pouted, giving him a wave that only left me wanting to do more, even though I knew I couldn't. I joined the others, a hangry Kye glaring at me until I linked my arm through his as we hurried toward Crystal Borough. *Maybe this time, I can actually enjoy it.*

"Anyone have any ideas?" Caspian asked as we walked, giving Drayce the side-eye as he moved closer to me again. *I need to pull him aside and explain what happened.*

"Food," Kye grumbled. "They have a really good diner on the edge of town. It's out of the tourist area, which means it's not as busy. Fewer people make it my kind of place."

"Food makes it your kind of place," I teased, trying to lighten his mood, but he just shrugged.

By the time we made it to the diner, you would have thought the guys hadn't eaten in years, the whining and dramatics at a ridiculous level. *And people say girls are dramatic.* The nice witch behind the counter ushered us in, letting us pick our table. Of course, I chose the corner booth, sliding in, so I was in the middle. Drayce and Cas slid in one side, Xan and Kye taking the other. As soon as the waitress came over, I ordered two servings of their garlic bat bites.

The diner was fast, the appetizer coming out before I could even pick my food, eventually picking a burger and fries before digging into the deliciousness waiting for me. Conversation lagged for a bit as we stuffed our faces, Kye's frown finally turning into a relaxed expression. *Note to self— never let Kye get too hungry.*

"Any ideas about what to do after this?" I asked the others. They were all probably a bit more familiar with the town than I was.

"We could do a bit of shopping," Drayce started but was immediately interrupted by Kye.

"Hell, no. I was promised fun," he said, flat out vetoing that option.

"Um, okay, how about mini-golf? There's a course off the main square that's run by Professor Ruslan's family," Drayce countered, clearly refusing to let the first rejection bother him.

"Ah, competition, I can handle that," Kye said, his eyes lighting up at the prospect.

"I've always wanted to play! Did you know the humans have this same game?" I asked excitedly, loving this idea.

"You've never played?" Caspian asked in shock.

"I haven't either," Xan added with a small shrug.

He's so quiet I sometimes forget he's there. I'll have to change that.

"Well, my parents are assholes. Did you really think we had family outings like this?" I asked, shaking my head at the idea of family fun. *Maybe if the media was involved or something.*

"Well, then tonight will be awesome," Drayce said, not letting me get down. "Why don't we up the ante a bit. Whoever wins gets to take Aris on a date."

"Challenge accepted," Xan said, shocking us all. His lips turned up in the tiniest of smirks. Thankfully, our food's arrival interrupted us before the bets could get any higher. We practically shoveled our food into our faces until we all lounged in the booth with stuffed stomachs and pained groans.

"Ugh," I moaned dramatically. "So full... Someone is going to have to roll me to mini-golf."

Drayce snorted and threw me a smirk as I slouched against Caspian's shoulder.

"I may or may not fall asleep with just mini-golf, so why don't we up the ante a bit more?" Kye added in a soft mumble, his eyes half-open as he glanced at us.

"How?" I questioned with a brow raise.

"I'm not sure. Someone come up with an idea, I'm too full." He waved a hand as he talked.

"We could ask questions during the game. Whoever does the best each round gets to ask a question, no matter how embarrassing," Caspian suggested.

"That would be a good way to get to know each other, seeing as how we're all stuck together," Drayce added. Caspian's jaw dropped, and Xan eyed him with a questioning gaze.

"Wait... so... you bonded with him too?" Caspian stuttered, his hand waving back-and-forth between Drayce and me. I nodded, unable to drum up much care, feeling like I was about to explode from greasy burgery goodness.

"That's right, Sprinkles, you're stuck with me," Drayce flirted with Caspian, a smug smile curling his lips.

"Can I get you anything else?" our waitress asked as she started to collect the empty plates. "Any dessert?" She chuckled at the collective groan at the mention of dessert. Xan reached for his wallet and handed her a card before any of us could protest.

"One check, please!" he said with a polite smile. She gave him a wink at our protests and walked off.

"Thank you," I said softly, giving him a big smile. It was a sweet gesture, and I didn't want to make him feel weird about it. When she brought the card back to him, we filed out, ready to keep moving before we fell asleep right here in our booth. Drayce led us through town to the mini-golf course, paying and ushering us through to pick our clubs and golf balls. I grabbed the pink ones right away, excited to start now that I got the best ones.

"Pink? I'm so shocked at your choice," Kye teased, rolling his eyes at my predictability.

"Oh, did you want it? Sorry," I shot back, holding it out to him.

"Nah, I'm more of a black kind of guy," he snorted, holding up the dark black equipment. We stopped at the first course, the others ushering me to go first. Stepping up, I placed the pink golf ball in its slot before lining up my shot and hitting it, hoping for the best. It bounced off the back before falling easily into the hole.

"Yes!" I celebrated, doing a victory dance in my spot before moving to let someone else go.

"Impressive, Sweets," Kye grinned, taking his turn next. He managed to make his in after it bounced off the back wall like mine. Each of the guys took their turn, but Drayce was the only one who managed to sink it in the hole without the aid of the wall.

"Oh! That means I get to go first," he cheered, impressively mimicking my victory dance. "*Everyone* has to answer, don't forget," he started, getting groans all around. "When did you lose your virginity?"

Before I could even process, I pointed at Caspian, singling him out in front of everyone. "Uh, my first day here," I mumbled, my cheeks flaming at being called out.

"Easy, never. Being a councilor's son means going on arranged dates that are torturously close to business meetings," Xan said, a slight bitterness to his tone.

"When I was seventeen, some girl I was talking to at the time," Kye answered, looking uncomfortable at the invasive question.

"Uh," Caspian coughed, his face flaring as he avoided everyone's eyes. My brows dipped down as I waited for him to answer.

"Come on, Sprinkles, everyone has to," Drayce pushed with a cocky smile. Caspian glared before snapping back.

"Well, when did you then?"

"When I was nineteen with the girl I had been dating, but we broke up last year. Now, your turn."

"Aris'firstdayhere," he mumbled under his breath.

"I'm sorry, what was that?" I asked, my eyes wide. He flashed me an apologetic smile.

"Uh, surprise?" he hedged with a shrug.

"You little shit! You freaking asked about me and made me admit to it!" I balked and tossed my other ball at him, and he curled into himself, and the pink projectile hitting him in the side.

"Aww, that's adorable. I love when you two go at it,"

Drayce teased, curling us under his arms. "Come on, onto the next course!"

The next course was a bit more complicated. This one had actual magic infused into it, a swirling vortex sitting in front of the hole. We stuck to the same order, which meant I was first to make a fool of myself. My ball got caught in the vortex, shooting out at me, so I had to dodge out of the way, letting Kye catch it for me. He snorted at my smooth move, handing my ball to me as he sauntered up to the course. He bounced it off the back wall, launching it straight in for a hole in one. The sexy smirk he sent me after was *definitely* worth it. A small tingle of need fluttered in my belly, and I looked away to hide the blush on my cheeks.

Everyone else sent their balls flying into the vortex, one way or another, shooting back at us at varying speeds. *I bet the humans don't have this.* As we walked to the next course, Kye remained quiet, apparently thinking hard about his question.

"Who has a tattoo, and you have to let us see it if you do," he asked finally, chuckling to himself, probably assuming he'd be the only one.

"I'm a Summoner, we all have one to keep ourselves grounded," Drayce revealed, lifting up his shirt to show us the runes that glowed on his chest. Well, I'm sure the others saw the tattoo, but I saw his abs first, and holy black cat in a box did I want to run my tongue over them! *Down, girl!*

"I don't have one," Xan answered quickly.

"Nope, me either," Caspian said with a shrug, turning to me.

"Well," I hedged, remembering that one rebellious streak I had back home. I turned and lifted my shirt to expose my back, showing them the pretty pair of pink wings on my shoulder blades. Even though I'd had sex with two of them, we hadn't been in any position for them to see it.

"See, nickname was perfect," Drayce chuckled, tracing the outline of the wings, making me shiver at the soft touch.

"Fuck, I didn't expect that one," Kye groaned as I dropped my shirt back down.

"Show us yours," Caspian said to Kye, seemingly desperate to change the attention off me as he not-so-discreetly repositioned his legs.

"I have a rune spiral on my arm," he answered with a shrug. "It's easier to activate them," he added, lifting his sleeve to show off a band of different colored runes swirling around his toned bicep and ending on his wrist. I'd seen it before, but now that I had my full attention on it, I stepped forward and ran my finger along it, taking in the intricately designed runes. He smiled down at me as I studied him, leaning down to press his lips against mine as I looked up to say something. Once his lips were on mine, I forgot about everything until Drayce cleared his throat to try to hide his laughter.

"Alright, moving on," Caspian said, turning to take his turn. This time the victor was Xan, who looked like he was actually having fun for once.

"What's your favorite thing about going to Aether?" Xan asked, his question seemingly simple, but a hint of something deeper in his tone.

"All of you? My freedom? Not being judged constantly? The fact there are actually seasons here? I have a list," I countered as I took my turn at the next course.

"I can agree with the freedom thing. I feel like I can actually breathe here. Even though I'm still being watched by the staff and other students, it's nothing compared to the scrutiny back home," Xan revealed with a deep sigh.

Yup, we need to give him more opportunities to loosen up.

"Not being judged, other than by my asshole brother," Caspian answered, taking his turn on the course.

"He's not that much of an asshole normally," I challenged. Caspian threw me a look over his shoulder, his eyes narrowed, lips thinned.

"Maybe not to you, Cupcake, but he certainly is to the rest of us. He just likes your ass." He stuck his tongue out playfully, Drayce swatting at it. I gasped and stomped several steps away so they couldn't get me.

"Not fair!" I huffed, "Kye and Drayce, your turn!" I sing-songed, having more fun than I'd had in years.

"The free food in the pantry," Kye deadpanned, refusing to give another answer, but really, I knew he was serious. *I've caught him in there enough.*

"Teasing Caspian is my new favorite hobby. Other than that, it would be flying," Drayce said, blowing Cas a kiss. Caspian blushed and looked away from us, but a definite hint of heat flared in those ocean eyes of his.

"Xan wins again," Caspian whined after Xan kicked our cauldrons at the next course. He took longer to ask this time, his question a bit more thought out than the others.

"If you could choose another affinity, what would it be?" he asked, watching me intently as I took my turn. Somehow, I managed to get a hole in one without any trouble, even though the course was more difficult than the others we'd done so far.

"I wouldn't change. I hate how every other magical ability is shunned; it's ridiculous. I don't like the judgment, but I'm proud of what I can do," I huffed, getting fired up as I thought it over.

"I'd wish to be a Mixta. Then I would be forced out of the spotlight," Xan revealed, giving us another peek at the intensity of his life. A small flare of magic built within me as I looked at Xan, but it fizzled out quickly as Kye answered.

"I'm pretty happy with where I'm at, and if I can control the shadows again, that'd be cool," he said as he lined up his shot and missed, his ball disappearing before dropping in front of him with a thud.

"It'd be cool to see how life would be as a spell caster like my family, but I do love making potions," Caspian added, giving me a soft smile. We'd both been there.

"I'm happy too," Drayce said with a shrug. "Oh, look! Aris won one!"

"I've got my question already too. What is your favorite thing about the person to your left?!" I asked, looking pointedly at Kye standing on my left. "My favorite thing about you is you share your sweets with me," I answered, giving him a happy smile. With Kye, I felt like that was a rare thing, and it made me feel special.

"My favorite thing about Caspian is he didn't hesitate to be there for Aris when she was having a bad day," Kye said quickly, avoiding everyone's eyes. All attention on him was not his thing.

"I like that Drayce isn't afraid to be himself, unapologetically so," Caspian said, giving Drayce a grin. This time it was Drayce's turn to lightly blush at the compliment.

Aww, that's so cute! Can you hope for a relationship between two of your own boyfriends?

"Xan, I love that you stepped up to take some heat off of Aris when her dad was here and bringing us together to make sure she was alright," Drayce said, giving him a pat on the back. When Xan turned to me, his expression softened a bit, a small smile on his lips.

"I love that you show me it's okay not to be professional all the time, not to be perfect, to be myself. I feel like this is the first time I've truly taken a deep breath in a long time," he said, taking a breath as if to punctuate his point. At this point, Xan won again, earning him the next question.

"What's your dream familiar?" he asked with a grin, this question a bit more fun than deep. I could visibly see him loosening up, and it made me so happy.

"I want something cute and fuzzy! Like a bat," I cooed, picturing an adorable, fuzzy, black bat.

"You're so weird," Kye said, shaking his head at me and laughing. "I want something fierce like a wolf."

"Oh! I always wanted a fun familiar like a fox," Caspian said, his eyes lighting up excitedly.

"A sloth, those guys are so calm and still adorable, kind of like me," Drayce teased, giving us a toothy grin.

"I want something ridiculous to add a little excitement to life. Something big and bold like a tiger," Xan said with a chuckle. "Can you imagine one of those in a council meeting?"

"That'd definitely be exciting," I chuckled, imagining the councilors all freaking out as he walked in, companion by his side.

"Yes!" Caspian cheered, making us all jump. We looked over to see his victory dance as he sunk his ball in one try. "I finally get a turn!"

"Well, hit us with it," Drayce said, holding out his hands like we've been waiting forever already. Caspian rolled his eyes but started walking toward the next course without answering right away. After Kye's second exaggerated sigh, he finally asked his question.

"What's your biggest turn on?" he finally asked, his smile laced with a hint of devious.

"Pink hair, apparently," Kye said in a tone I couldn't quite read. He might have been joking, but I gave a sexy smirk and a flip of my bubblegum hair, anyway.

"I'm a sucker for smiles. I've been around too many grumpy people in my life, so I live for bright smiles," Xan said, smiling at me. My blush deepened, still unused to compliments so freely being sent my way.

"It's a toss-up sometimes, but I'm an ass man, and I've got my eye on two perfectly sculpted ones right now," Drayce said, winking at me before checking out Caspian's ass as he bent over to place his golf ball on the course.

"I can't argue there," I agreed, reaching over and smacking Caspian lightly on his ass.

"Thanks," he grinned, shaking it toward us before taking his turn. When he missed, he turned around with a pout. "That leaves you, Cupcake. Piggybacking on someone else isn't good enough."

"Well," I started, looking at each of them slowly before finally giving up with a pout. "That's not fair. I like something different about each of you guys. Let's just say, my biggest turn on is confidence."

"We'll take that," Kye said, giving me a wink and a half-grin before taking his turn. "That makes me the winner of this course," he announced, landing his golf ball in the cauldron after somehow bouncing it off the sidewalk. *I swear these boys are using magic!*

"Why am I more nervous about your question than anyone else's?" I asked, starting the final course. This, of course, was the hardest. With more than one magical barrier in our way, it would take some serious skill to even make it in, let alone on the first try.

"Don't be," he said with a shrug, chuckling at my easy miss. "Do you have any siblings?"

"I have two brothers and a sister... and yes, they're clones of my parents," I said with a crinkle of my nose.

"I'm an only child," Kye said, "but I always wanted more. My parents were busy, so it was fucking boring growing up."

"I'm surprised! I thought for sure the way you hide in pantries with your snacks, you must have come from a huge family," I teased.

"Nah, I just hate sharing. It's an only child thing," he said, laughing at being called out.

"I have Torryn," Caspian deadpanned, not sounding happy about it.

"Well, I have a feeling you won't be against that much longer," I said happily... *not if I have anything to do with it.*

"I have five siblings... all girls," Drayce said with a happy smile. "My house is chaotic, loud, and perfect."

"It's just me," Xan said, looking a bit jealous at Drayce's answer. "I always wanted a big family."

"Oh, look, Xan made it... again," Kye grumbled as Xan grinned happily. Magic swirled in the air above the course, showcasing Xan's color as the winner.

"Come on, Xan, this is how you victory dance!" I cheered, coming over and dancing in a circle around him, shimmying my hips and doing ridiculous dance moves until the others were cracking up too.

"You've got the last question, let's hear it," Caspian said as he wiped tears from his eyes.

"What do you want to do after Aether? What do you want out of life, not just what anyone else wants for you?" Xan asked, the mood turning serious while we thought about the loaded question.

"I'd like to open a potion shop or something like that. Be my own boss," Caspian said quickly, his cheeks tinting a bit at admitting his dream.

"I want not to be around people for a while," Kye half-joked, though knowing Kye he was probably serious. "I think I'll figure it out when the time comes, but for right now, I don't have much of an idea."

"I just want to be my own man. I love to paint, and I want to do that freely, and I want a future not in the council's shadow, though I know that's unlikely," Xan added with a sigh.

"Why is it unlikely? Just because dear old dad is a councilor doesn't mean you are," Drayce asked, clearly confused about Xan's conclusion.

"No, but he does expect it. His father was a councilor as well, and since it's the High Council, I don't have much of a choice." His voice was pained but resigned to what he thought was fact. He wasn't his own man, and he never would be. It broke my heart. I knew all too well the disappointment of not living up to parental expectations.

"Sure, you do. We all have choices. Your choices could be staying with the council and being miserable or doing your own thing and living your life how you want. It's that simple. They can't force you. If they're disappointed, then they're selfish, and you'll be fine without them," Drayce countered, conviction clear in his eyes.

Needing to ease the tension now that he stated his point, I jumped in. "I can agree with that sentiment... I just want to be myself. Travel. I want to do something that goes down in history that doesn't include my powers, to show them it's not all about affinities or family names. I want to make a difference."

"You're just too pure," Drayce joked.

Glancing over at him, I warmed from the inside out at his proud smile that told me how much he liked my answer. Seeing the brightness of his smile and the happiness shining at me through his eyes, I wanted it all that much more. To show my guys, who all had people look down on them or saw us looked down on in some way, it was okay to be yourself.

"I'm not as bold as my Angel. I want to teach. I want to inspire students to be themselves," Drayce said. I thought over all their answers, my heart growing at their answers, loving that we all seemed to be on the same page. I loved that we are all trying to be unapologetically genuine.

"Okay, enough of this deep shit," Caspian joked, coming over and leading us out. "Let's grab some ice cream!"

I couldn't stop the bright smile that had been permanently affixed to my face as we made our way to the small, brightly colored shop.

This was the perfect date, minus one thing.

Ah, here we go, the one thing I missed during our night out. Standing outside Torryn's classroom door, I don't exactly know when it became our meeting spot, but ever since we decided to blur the line of student and teacher, we met in his office. Feeling giddy and nervous about seeing him, I took a deep breath and headed into his classroom. Soft music was playing, and the flickering light from his fireplace lit up under the bottom of his office door as I neared it, not even bothering to knock as I pushed it open.

My breath caught. Torryn sat on his couch, a glass of wine clutched in the hand that rested against the arm of the leather furniture. One leg was crossed, his ankle resting across his knee as he looked at me. The blue in the fire intensified the turquoise tint in his seafoam irises as they centered on me. As much as his eyes held my attention, I couldn't help as my gaze drifted down to his dress shirt, the top couple buttons opened, showing his smooth skin underneath.

"Hey there, Gorgeous," he murmured, getting up from the couch and coming over to me. Placing a hand on my lower back, he pulled me fully into his room and shut the door behind my frozen body.

Apparently, seeing Torryn ooze sex appeal breaks my brain. Who would have guessed?

"You thirsty?"

I nodded, not trusting myself to speak in case something rambly or weird came out and ruined the moment. Flashing me a tiny grin, he turned, pouring me a quick glass of wine before handing it over to me, but when I tried to take it, he pulled it back.

"Have to pay the toll first, miss." Cocking a brow, I started to grow more sure of myself, his confidence fueling my own.

"Oh, yeah? What would that be?" The sinful smile that appeared made my toes curl and my blood pump, eager to do whatever the hellsticks he wanted at that moment.

"Need to give me a kiss first. I've had to wait all damn day to touch you, and I'm not going to wait any longer," he murmured.

Seeing the fire burning in his gaze had me closing the distance between us in an instant, popping up on my toes and grabbing the open lapels of his shirt. His lips were smooth, but his kiss was demanding. Moving surely against me, he took control of our kiss but pulled away too soon, leaving me pouting.

"Don't give me that lip, Gorgeous, the night's just getting started."

Handing me my glass, he led me to the couch, situating

me next to him. I angled slightly so I could face him, nerves growing as I realized I had no idea how to act. I mean, this was Torryn, my professor, who was both cool and sexy at the same time while I was... *me.*

"How was the town?" he asked quietly, his hand coming to rest on my knee. I took a sip of wine for encouragement, the red liquid decadent with hints of fruit, chocolate, and something slightly earthy.

"It was fun. We went to get dinner and did a round of mini-golf," I explained, feeling good about the fact I hadn't embarrassed myself yet. "I wish you could have been there." His smile was breathtaking as he squeezed my thigh.

"Me too, Aris. Maybe one of these days, I'll get to take you out and show you off to all the other witches. Let them know I have the sweetest and prettiest one around," he teased, but a hint of honesty shone in his gaze reminded me he was telling the truth about how he felt.

My chest warmed as I nibbled on my lip in a futile attempt to keep a giggle contained, but it ended up bubbling out of me, anyway.

"I would like that. Maybe we could find some time for the Samhain festival in the capital, I mean, if we go," I stumbled over my words, but Tor didn't seem bothered as he beamed.

"Absolutely."

I perked up, taking another few sips to finish off my glass as we sat in comfortable silence, the blue light from the fire casting a romantic glow around the room. Feeling confident from the wine and Tor's hand on my leg, I reached around him to place my empty glass on the table, my chest brushing against his. Instead of pulling back to settle on the couch next to him, I latched on to that bravado and pressed my lips to his.

Torryn's hand tightened against my leg as I cupped his face, his upper body leaning into me. He nipped my bottom lip, brushing his tongue to help ease the sting as he set his glass down and grabbed me around the waist. Our kisses deepened, growing with intensity as he pulled me onto his lap, my legs straddling his trim hips. Sinking down onto his legs, I felt just how turned-on Tor was as his cock pressed into the seam of my jeans.

He groaned as I decided to push him further, rocking my hips at a leisurely pace. Hands gripped my hips tightly as if he was struggling to control himself from laying me on the couch and taking me like I knew he wanted. Not wanting to push him too far, I slowed, focusing more on kissing him.

"You're absolutely perfect, Gorgeous," he whispered against my lips, his half-lidded gaze looking at me. "But when we have sex, it'll be in an actual bed where I can shower you in the attention you deserve, not on my office couch where we have to be quick, in case a student comes in." I smiled, my chest squeezing at the sweet sentiment.

"Deal, Sir," I agreed, kissing him once more briefly before pulling back.

"But I'm not missing the opportunity to hold you, so come here," he murmured with a lazy, yet happy smile. Shifting, he angled himself until he was half lying on the couch and maneuvered me until I was curled into his side, my head and hand resting on his chest. We cuddled and watched the flames of his fires dance into the early hours of the morning, neither wanting the moment to end.

Is it Samhain yet?

CHAPTER 15

September 19th
Thursday Midday
Xanthius

After the trip to Crystal Borough, I hadn't been able to keep my mind off Aris. Something about her made me want to enjoy life, throw away everything I'd been forced to work for and find out what I really wanted. Ever since the questions, I'd been asking myself that, but I kept coming up blank.

I started mixing the two colors in front of me, adding a bit more red until it was the perfect shade of pink. My paintbrush danced across the canvas, adding soft waves to the long pink hair. Aris' smile beamed up at me as I added the finer details. I hadn't painted in a long time, but when I couldn't get her image out of my head, I decided to put it on canvas.

I checked the time again and realized an entire hour had

passed, meaning I'd have to rush to get to mentoring on time. After last week's mentoring session getting interrupted by her terrible family, I hoped this one would go more smoothly. She was already waiting for me by the time I got there, her smile still in place.

"Hey, Xan!" she said, giving me her signature quick wave.

"I'm sorry I'm a bit late, I had a project I wanted to finish," I said quickly, closing the door and taking the chair opposite of hers. "So, I thought we could delve a bit into your family's magical history to try to see where we should start figuring out this bonding situation. So, what affinities are in your direct household?"

"Mother is an Earth elemental, Dad is a fire elemental, my brothers both ended up with fire, and my sister is air," she said, looking down at the table, a bit of shame marring her gorgeous features.

"There is *nothing* wrong with being a Mixta," I reminded her firmly. "You have amazing powers and apparently, more emerging every time you bond, so you're stronger than all of them." She grinned at that, a spark of excitement in her eyes.

"Can you imagine what they'd say if they knew?" She snorted and threw her voice into a fake deep tone, mimicking her father as she continued, *"We knew a Calisto would never be a Mixta."*

"I feel like they look at your powers the same as mine look at art. That was my only escape as a kid, but my father would literally set fire spells to them in front of me," I revealed. When I caught the quick grimace she tried to hide, I realized I was saying more than I intended, yet again.

"That's terrible," she said, fire dancing in her eyes as she clenched her fists. "I would practice the only skill I had, telekinesis, and my parents or siblings would snatch things out of the air and tell me to stop playing around and practice 'real' magic. That's what I hate about Akasha. People want to fit us into these five pretty boxes some asshole set up and fuck everything else. Let's not care that witches use herbology to make our fucking lifesaving medicines and tinctures, that some people can work with animals and form a magical connection to them all, that some people maybe aren't Mixtas, that they have a power we can't find because fuck everything that doesn't follow their standards," she finished her rant, meeting my eyes. I couldn't look away from hers, her anger and resentment at the injustices mirroring my own sentiments.

My fingers tingled as I clutched the table, a burning smell reaching my nose and forcing me to look away. Smoke billowed out from both ends of the table as our palms flared a molten red, fire shooting out of our palms. Magic tethered us together at that moment, something in the flames connecting us and bringing us in for more. The fire burned brighter still, dancing along the table until it started to crumble under the heat. A loud squeal echoed through the halls as I grabbed Aris' hand and our stuff before darting out of the room.

"Somehow, the table in our room just caught on fire. We weren't even doing magic, just discussing family history. Something weird is going on here!" I yelled over to the gathered faculty before pulling her outside with the crowd of escaping students. As soon as we were out of earshot, Aris' eyes met mine, and we lost it, knowing damn well it was our fault, but they couldn't prove it. As silly as it sounded, I felt a bit like a rebel at that moment and loved every second of it.

September 20th
Friday Afternoon

Aris

"So," I heard a familiar murmur behind me, "what is this I heard about a fire in one of the mentoring rooms? One specifically involving a councilor's son and a tiny pink witch."

Turning, I came face-to-face with Torryn looking down at me with a raised eyebrow. I plastered a smile on my face but didn't respond. *If he's asking about this, I'm thinking he already knows enough to have figured it out.* "Is this that situation we have... discussed previously?"

"Uh, yes," I mumbled, "but it was the last one I know of." He shook his head but didn't say anything more as more students filtered into the area.

"Try to behave yourself for now, at least," he ordered, his hand starting to reach forward before dropping down to his side and clenching into a fist.

"No promises, Sir," I said, putting a bit of heat in the name. His eyes darkened, and he let out a small groan as he walked away. I wasn't even a little sorry for riling him up.

"Hurry up, someone said new animals were incoming!" a girl yelled, almost knocking me over.

"Whoa there, Sweets," Kye said, his strong arms wrapping around my waist as he placed a soft kiss on my neck. "We really need to get some alone time soon. I miss you."

"That can be arranged," I said, turning in his arms and using the other students' distractions as a chance to kiss him without judgment, pulling his head down, so I could claim his lips with mine.

"Holy Hellsticks!" a guy nearby yelled, "Do you guys see this?" His friends erupted into chatter, ruining our moment.

"To be continued," he rumbled, nipping my lip before pulling me along with the crowd. The ring of students was so thick, we couldn't see at all. Using my size to my advantage, I squeezed between the students and made my way to the front, spotting a grouping of animals standing in the middle of a huge ring of students. Kye and I spotted Caspian on the edge, and I left them behind as I snuck forward to try to catch a peek.

"What is it?" Caspian's called out as he grasped my hand and pulled me back toward him and Kye.

"New familiars, it seems," I explained excitedly, wanting to go back and look. News must spread quickly at Aether because it looked like the entirety of the faculty and student body were coming to check it out like it was some kind of animal lottery. "Does this happen often?" I asked, waving at Drayce who had no hope of getting near us with the mass of witches between us.

"Not that I know of," Kye shrugged, grabbing my hand and pulling me forward, having enough of standing back. I latched onto Cas' hand and pulled him behind me until we were standing at the front of the crowd. A few students mumbled angrily, but nobody bothered to speak up to Kye's glowering.

"What are they doing?" I whispered, stepping up beside Kye, confused why the group of familiars were standing in a group, not moving. When Caspian stepped out from behind me and joined us in the front, it was like the catalyst for the moment. The animals immediately started moving, and before I could stop myself, a different sort of magical pull was moving me forward. Looking to my sides, Caspian and Kye were doing the same, along with Torryn, Xan, and Drayce from different parts of the crowd. *What the hell is happening?!*

I could hear someone's feeble attempt at moving us back to the crowd, but we couldn't have obeyed if we tried. Before

I could even process it, I was standing with the others around this random group of animals. *What the hex made them think this group would go well together?* A chicken, otter, lemur, hedgehog, piglet, and red panda.

Before I could ask any of the others, the animals all moved in unison, claiming each one of us as their own. The cute little lemur jumped, wrapping his little hands and feet around my arm. The moment we touched, a quick shock zapped at the point of contact, and I could feel the first sparks of a bond as his little beady eyes stared up at me. My heart swelled as I felt him take his place as my companion, something in me knowing he was happy at that moment. *Me too, little guy!*

"A... chicken..." Kye grumbled, eyeing the little golden feathered farm animal that was looking up at him from the ground. "I... bonded with a chicken..."

"Aww! Look how much she likes you," I laughed, loving the way the chicken seemed to be sassing him back, turning her tail to Kye and ruffling her feathers.

"But she's a chicken! Chickens aren't vicious," he complained, gesturing wildly at the cute little familiar at his feet.

"Don't listen to him! You're a fierce, vicious warrior, just like a little raptor!" The chicken puffed out her chest at my praise, screeching what seemed to be a chicken battle cry and running at Kye's ankles. He huffed and tried to stand his ground, but she was quick and kept pecking at him until he ran.

"Okay, okay! You're fierce! Stop it!" he complained while I laughed so hard, I was crying. I turned my attention to the others, smiling at Caspian who was snuggling his otter and showing him off to anyone who would look. Torryn was in shock while he crouched down in front of his red panda, the cute little guy cocking his head to the side as Torryn spoke to him as he stood on his back two feet. Drayce was petting his piglet and feeding it treats Thane brought over as he excitedly talked about how lucky we were. Xan walked over, his little hedgehog curled into his palm as he tickled its belly, the look of pure joy on his face making butterflies dance in my stomach. It was nice to see him so happy and relaxed for a change.

Thane called us all back to attention, dismissing everyone back to their classes. I absently petted my new friend as the professor went on to talk about basic familiar care, his excitement palpable for the rest of class. He eventually cut his explanations short to take questions.

"What kind of area does he need in my room?" I asked as I raised my hand, not bothering to wait to be called on.

"He'll need something to climb on, but he'll just want to be near you at first. Hopefully, he's not a bed hog," Thane joked. "Ring-tailed lemurs also spend a lot of time on the ground, unlike their counterparts." He stood with a small smile, waiting for my next question.

"What does he eat?" I asked next, knowing I wouldn't be able to just share my pizza and Hex Mix with him. *That's what Kye is for.*

"Fruits, leaves, flowers, tree bark, and sap, but mainly fruit," he listed off easily and without judgment.

"This may be a dumb question, but Lulu tends to take up a lot of my attention, so I apologize in advance. What do familiars do, exactly? Like, do they have magic of their own?" I gave him a pained smiled which just made him shake his head and laugh, but much to my surprise, he didn't lecture or belittle me for not previously paying attention during his long, boring speeches.

"The connection a familiar has with a witch is unique

and can manifest in many ways, which is why it's seen as an honor within Akasha to have one choose you. Downside to that is, it may take a while for the connection to form and may be difficult to identify right away, so for the next month or so, I would focus on getting to know one another and adjust to your new furry partner."

"Is there anything else I need to know? I mean, like right at this minute before I can go cram read a 'How to Care for your Familiar' textbook?" My awkward smile only got wider, making me look crazy I was sure, but I felt bad I hadn't paid attention before.

Note to self—pay more attention in class.

"Two small things. First, try to remember they were actual wild animals before this, and while the magic has adjusted their mindset, they still need to adjust, meaning they'll possibly be standoffish for the next few days or a week. Second, as cool as it would be to have your furry animal with you all the time, you both—especially your familiar—need time alone. Same with the first point, give it a week before you expect them to come with you more consistently."

"Okay, I think that's all I have. Thanks, Professor!" I squeaked, hugging my familiar who was hanging on my torso.

I can't wait to get to know Mr. Stripes.

———

Ever since the animals bonded with us, my magic felt like it was trying to burst from my skin. I tried to keep it contained, but even walking down the hall, I had to use all my focus not to be noticed, the sensation growing until it was severely uncomfortable. *What the heck is happening?* The hallway was thankfully empty, most students either in the town at the pub or hanging out in their rooms, so I had taken the opportunity to shower when the bathroom was empty, and Mr. Stripes was happily napping.

"Aris," Xan's powerful voice filled the stone hall, slightly echoing off the barren walls. "Wait up."

"Hey, Xan," I greeted, smiling at him. His eyes darted up to the wet mass I had balled up and secured atop my head before meeting my gaze.

"We were supposed to have a mentoring session," he explained.

My eyes narrowed in suspicion because, while I had been very out of sorts the last few days, I knew we weren't *actually* supposed to be meeting. So, something was obviously going on.

"Torryn asked me to have you take me to your off-grounds meeting spot."

My eyes narrowed for a second, trying to figure out where this was all going. *Everything about this is so odd.*

"Okay..." I trailed off, "let me drop my stuff in my room first." He followed me quietly, something about his demeanor more closed off and restrained than he had been lately. I thought we'd made some progress with his social skills. *Maybe he's overwhelmed.*

Once I dropped my bag off in my room, I led Xan outside, hating the tension between us. Mr. Stripes climbed up my arm and rested on my shoulder, giving my neck a small squeeze. *I need to learn more about this familiar bond. Poor guy must be picking up on all the tension.* I could feel his worry through our bond, and finally, I couldn't take it any longer.

"What's up with you? You're quiet and acting weird, and

it's worrying me," I rambled, all of my thoughts tumbling out.

"Sorry," he answered quietly, his voice still sounding off to me. "It's just been a bit overwhelming. The familiars, the bond, then this magic that seemed to come out of nowhere is all a bit much. I'm just used to being analyzed all the time, so I tend to clam up when I'm stressed."

"I know the feeling," I said, bumping my shoulder against his. He smiled over at me, a look of understanding on his face. I reached for his hand, locking my fingers with his as I led him, offering what comfort I could.

I froze as we entered the forest, the sound of cracking sticks coming from a few feet in front of us. My tension ramped up as we both froze, looking around. I didn't fight my magic this time, holding it close in case I needed to protect us. A laugh cut through the quiet of the forest, everything in me relaxing when I recognized it as Caspian's, followed by Kye's low chuckle. *Why are they here?*

"He said it was near here," Kye said in frustration. "We've circled this spot four times. It's not funny, you ass." I could hear Raptor clucking his agreement.

"It's a little funny. My brother's a dick, so he probably did this on purpose," Caspian shot back, though he picked right back up, laughing at Kye's continued grumbling.

"He's a dick to you, not to me, and I'm not surprised why. It's around here somewhere," Kye countered, their little quarrel letting us catch up to them on the path. "Sweets?"

"Hey, guys, it's just up here," I said, giving a wave as I got closer. Kye and Caspian both smiled, their familiars standing close by as I let fire dance in my palms, illuminating our way. "Look for a patch of hanging vines. Once you know what it looks like, you can't miss it."

"Oh, is that all?" Caspian joked, nudging Kye who glared

over at him. "Torryn told us to go straight north until the path curved, then we'd find it."

"He probably figured I'd be by. Oh! There it is," I exclaimed as quietly as I could, pointing them toward the hidden entrance.

"So obvious," Kye joked, following me into the tunnel. Nobody else said anything as we walked further in, but the moment they saw the illuminated crystal room, they gasped, jaws dropping as they took in the beauty of the space.

"Glad you guys could make it," Drayce teased, his piglet off to the side, rooting in the dirt. He stood next to Torryn, who had his red panda snuggled in his arms. Torryn glared at the others, more than likely for taking forever, but his seafoam-green eyes lit up when he saw me.

"So, Tor, want to explain why we had to sneak out in the middle of the night?" I questioned, glancing around the cave. "I mean, you're a teacher, shouldn't you be the one keeping us in line?" I teased, but my question had his eyes flaring and his lip curling in a sexy smirk.

"Please don't fucking flirt," Caspian fake gagged. "I don't know if I can handle it."

His dramatics made me laugh, and just because, I skipped over to Torryn, grabbed the collar of his shirt, and pulled his lips to mine.

"Ew," Caspian whined.

"Aww, Sprinkles, feeling left out? Come over here, and I'll give you a kiss." Drayce winked, licking and biting his lower lip seductively. *Oh, my broomsticks, hot as a cauldron on a fire.* I melted in Torryn's arms as I watched Drayce. Kye coughed, cutting through the moment. Moving to stand beside Torryn, I clutched his hand, treasuring one of the brief times I was actually able to show he was mine.

"Alright, for real though, why are we here?" Kye questioned.

"I think it's safe to assume we're all bonded to Aris?" Torryn asked, easily slipping into his role of mentor.

"Yes," I blurted before anyone could come up with a smartass response. *Of course, I had to get bonded to the sassiest witches possible.*

"Yeah, and this magic is insane," Kye said, holding up his hands, showing us the black smoke that seemed to languidly weave in and out of his fingers.

"Same," Xan said quickly, showing the fire sparking in his palm.

"I think, now that the bonds are in place and we have familiars, it's hit its peak," I said, hating they were all dealing with side-effects from our bond. I didn't do it intentionally, but it was hard not to feel guilty. Mr. Stripes made a little chirping noise, ambling away from the group of familiars that had formed when we were entering the cave and jumping up to my side, clinging to the collar of my jacket in a small hug as his little furry face nuzzled into the crook of my neck. Hooking my arms under his bottom legs, I clutched him to my chest and snuggled him.

"With these new magics so close to the surface, we'll have to be careful about them being seen, so we're not drawing too much attention," Torryn took over again, addressing the group. "Since I'm still a teacher, I'll have to keep my distance for the most part, so any issues with our powers will have to be played off as a mentoring session or a teacher-student meeting."

"That was the entire reason you made me crawl out of bed? To say we need to be careful?" Caspian huffed, glaring at his brother.

"I called you here to tell you to not be stupid and flirt up a storm with Aris in front of everyone. With the way our magics are connected to our emotions and *her*, that could cause a flare up, so yes, that's exactly why! Last time I told you to keep under the radar, you ended up practically blowing up the house with some crazy potion you were trying to brew!"

"Dude, it was one time!" Caspian countered in exasperation. "And I was seven! Can I claim I was a child?"

"Alright, you two," I cut in, shaking my head, unable to stop the laugh that bubbled out of me at their antics. "It's late. Let's go get some sleep before one of you ends up blowing up the pretty crystal cave."

Caspian grumbled but didn't argue as we started out of the cave, leaving in pairs to keep any eyes off us. Before leaving with Caspian, I turned and gave each of the guys a quick kiss, lingering a bit longer when I reached Torryn. *If I only get small moments with him like this, where we don't have to worry, I might as well make the best of them.*

"Come on, Cupcake, let's head back. I heard there's a new episode of Boos and Brews we haven't watched yet," Caspian smiled, tucking me under his arm as we left.

Boos and Brews? Count me in.

CHAPTER 16

September 21st
Saturday Midday
Aris

My eyebrows furrowed as I grew a cluster of vines down one section of my wall. Tiny blades of grass sprouted from the floor, creating a soft, light-green carpet while a small tree spiraled up to the ceiling, giving Mr. Stripes plenty of room to adventure. Heading for my wardrobe, I grabbed an old scarf and tied it into the lowest branches, forming the perfect hammock for my excited familiar. He let out a loud chirp before scurrying across the floor and scaling the tree, depositing himself in the hammock, leaving only his beady eyes and a tuft of fur poking out.

"I take it you like your new home?" I asked, laughing at his happy coos and the feeling of contentment that filled my mind. It felt weird being away from my guys, but life had been a whirlwind since arriving here, and I needed some alone time to process all the craziness. First, I had made real friends, then accidentally bonded, made some enemies, found my place in the world, and now, I had all this crazy extra magic to figure out. *My life is definitely not boring anymore.*

I took out my basket of nail polish and plopped down on my bed, painting my toes, then moving on to my fingernails. Sure, most witches would use magic for a task like this, but I preferred the human way. *Not everything is better with magic.* Just as I started waving my hands back-and-forth to dry them, a paper airplane flew through the air and beaned me in the forehead. Grumbling, I opened the note delicately, not wanting to ruin my nails.

Hey, Sweets,
We had a discussion, and I won. So, you want to go to the Aether Annual Mabon Feast with me tonight? It would be nice to hang out, just the two of us. Let me know.
-Kye

A smile spread across my face at the invitation, and I hopped up to write him back, using some air magic to dry my nails quickly. Once I sent it off, I hurried for my wardrobe to pick out something to wear. The thought of Kye dressed up in a black button-up that showed every ridge of his muscles had heat pooling between my thighs as I rifled through the closet.

An hour later, I was ready and waiting, wearing a cute flowing, black dress with pink accessories that matched my hair and nails. Mabon was one of my favorite holidays. It was about being outside, celebrating the harvest, and giving thanks. I kept my shoes off, knowing bare feet was the best way I could connect to nature directly. I'd never been to a Mabon celebration outside of the stuck-up one my parents threw each year, and I'd hardly call those the proper way to celebrate. Their "festivals" had nothing to do with the purpose of the feast and everything to do with their appearances.

A soft knock on my door had me running to answer, throwing it open with a huge grin. "Ready?" I asked excitedly, not even bothering to hold back my happy dance. Kye's welcoming grin grew even more at my dancing, his entire demeanor more carefree now that it was just us two. *Hopefully, in time, he'll get used to the others.*

"How did I know you would be this excited?" he joked, pulling me in for a searing kiss. "You look gorgeous."

My cheeks flamed at the compliment, taking that moment to run my eyes over his outfit. My daydreaming was clearly on point—his dark button-up was as glorious as I expected. Fitted, it hugged his toned torso, making me want to yank open the dress shirt to revel in the tanned planes of his chest and abs. Trailing my eyes down, I admired his dress pants and the black belt that cinched them to his trim waist, lingering on the quickly growing bulge even the dark material couldn't hide.

"Ready, Sweets?" he asked, pulling my eyes away from his body and up to his heated, half-lidded gaze. If we hadn't been running late, I would have pulled him in my room to have some *real* alone time. Nodding, I hooked my arm through his before looking over my shoulder at Mr. Stripes.

"You coming, buddy?" I cooed in a soft voice, hoping to coax him out. One beady little eye opened before he let out a little chirp and snuggled deeper into the hammock. *Like witch, like familiar. I'm not always the easiest person to drag out of bed either.*

They had really gone all out for Mabon. The halls were strung with spiraling ribbons in deep reds, burnt orange, and the startling yellow that can only be found in the heart of autumn. As we wandered, wide-eyed, the sweet scent of baked apples floated through the air, the hint of cinnamon making me aware of just how hungry I was as my stomach growled. Kye led me through the halls and outside to the courtyard, his eyes darting to me every few moments to see my reaction, his smile still in place.

I let out an audible gasp as my eyes landed on the courtyard. Floating candles illuminated the area, helping us see the flowers, streamers, and stacks of pumpkins and gourds decorating nearly every surface, giving that Fall feel. The scents were even stronger out here, mixing with the savory smells of stews and roasted vegetables lining the buffet tables on the pathways. Tables and chairs were set up banquet style, faculty and students already filling them.

The gentle tunes of a string quartet filled the air, drawing my attention toward the clock tower. Instead of finding a group of musicians, the instruments were each standing on their own, the strings plucked and bows waving completely on their own, transitioning from one song to the next seamlessly. Whoever enchanted them did well. A group of barefoot witches danced and swayed to the jazzy tune under a cluster of sparkling lights.

"It's so perfect!" I exclaimed, tugging on Kye's hand and dragging him to the closest table.

"You hungry yet? Thirsty?" he asked, suddenly looking a bit awkward as he tucked his hands into his pockets. *Of course, his first thought was food.*

"Not yet, we can go get something in a bit when the lines slow down. You want to dance or sit?" I asked, hoping he would say dancing but knowing better.

He studied my face for a moment before letting out a sigh, smiling just a little as he tilted his head toward the dance floor.

"Come on, Sweets."

Beaming, I followed him, my fingers intertwining with his as he spun me into his waiting arms. His free hand curved around my lower back, holding me close enough, I could see every tiny speck of gold in his eyes that were only amplified by the romantic overhead lights. With my arm resting on his shoulder, my fingers lightly brushing over the back of his neck, we started to slowly sway to the beat. I knew it was more of an upbeat tune, but right now? I was too engrossed in the romantic and soft way Kye was holding me, my chest warming as he leaned down to give me a kiss.

It was light at first, just the briefest touch of his lips against mine before he pulled away, his eyes lighting up as I pouted slightly before moving in to kiss me deeply. My eyes fell shut, and when he moved our clutched hands to his chest, I felt the rhythmic beat of his heart thudding. When his tongue darted out against my bottom lip, I barely held back the tiny moan that wanted to escape. I had just started to open my lips when a large crash sounded to our immediate left, startling me enough to jump and shriek.

"Hells bells and tarot tells," Kye breathed, his heart rate racing against my hand. The lights above us had fallen to the ground in a wave of broken glass and cords. If I hadn't of jumped toward Kye, a collection of broken shards would have shot out toward my legs and bare feet. Glancing around, now that my breathing had evened out and my heart rate had slowed, I noticed everyone else had moved toward the outskirts of the dance floor or toward the food and drinks.

"That was really close," I mumbled, a niggle of anxiety worming its way into my stomach before I pushed it away.

"You alright, Sweets?" Kye asked, his eyes scanning my legs and feet before looking back at me, his brows furrowed as if he could read my worry. "What's wrong?"

"Nothing, Honey, it just startled me," I assured with a smile, pushing the last of my concerns away as I saw my other guys making their way out of the crowd to join us. There was no reason to worry him or the others who I saw slowly moving out onto the dance floor.

"Are you guys alright?"

"What happened?"

A thousand questions were fielded our way from our group until I finally got them calmed down. When that was accomplished, I moved us out of earshot as discreetly as possible.

"I'm fine, I promise," I reassured again as the questions started back up. "If you guys get worked up, the magic will too. Go have fun, I'll be fine. Kye and I are going to hit the buffet now," I said confidently, so I could put an end to their fussing. They didn't look happy with my answer, especially Torryn who hung back from our group, trying to keep some semblance of professionalism.

Knowing I was fine and not wanting to argue, I grabbed Kye's hand and started toward the food. All my annoyance washed away as I took in the array of deliciousness spread in front of me, piling my plate high before finally heading for the table. I powered through half of my plate before looking up. It took one look at him licking a bit of chocolate frosting from his lip for me to want to drag him back to my room.

"Uh, I'm ready to go. You?" I asked awkwardly, his eyes drawing down in confusion.

"What? You love this kind of stuff," he pointed out, taking another bite of his oversized cupcake, leaving more frosting and crumbs on his lip. Not wanting to explain, I darted forward and licked the frosting off, his eyes widening in realization.

"Yup, yup, I'm ready to go." He snatched my hand and practically ran for the door, gaining an annoyed look from Torryn we passed by where he loitered near the clock tower. *I hate that he has to keep his distance like this.*

We had just gotten into the staircase when he pushed me up against the wall, kissing me with such intensity, my breath left my lungs. I reached up, grabbing the lapels of his shirt to hold him tightly against me as I kissed back, our tongues brushing together as I felt just how turned-on he was as he pressed against my hip.

We were panting when we finally pulled apart, my body buzzing as we practically sprinted up the stone steps and into my room. Before the door even closed, we were back at it, battling for dominance in a fierce kiss. Wanting to feel his tanned skin against my fingertips, I smiled and yanked his shirt open. The buttons popped off, splaying around the room as I palmed the hot, cut planes of his chest.

"I liked that shirt, Sweets," he murmured huskily, his rough kisses traveling across my jaw and to my neck as he whispered against my skin. I tried to chuckle, but it turned into a moan as his hands cupped my breasts in a light squeeze. Running my hand over his hardened bulge confined by his dress pants, I stroked him at a leisurely pace, content to enjoy feeling his hands on me as he massaged my breasts and rolled my peaked nipples over the fabric of my dress. Shifting as our hands continued to rove over each other, I pulled Kye over to the closest piece of furniture and hopped onto the top. Kye flowed easily into the new position, stepping between my parted thighs, one hand shifting from my chest to my thigh.

Stars flared in front of my eyes as soon as Kye's fingers ran over my sensitive clit, the barely-there touch enough to send me spiraling into a wave of need and desire. His nipping bites along my neck and collarbone had me wanting more, so when he pulled my dress up my hips and torso, I yanked it over my head and unhooked my bra. As soon as my chest was on full display to his nearly molten golden-brown eyes, he dove in, sucking a pebbled peak into his mouth, picking up a rhythm with his fingers as they stroked me over my underwear.

My hips bucking against his hand, I grasped onto his muscled back and shoulders to keep from completely melting at his ministrations on my breasts and pussy. The signature building fire within my core flared, pushing me that much closer to release when his fingers slipped under the thin material of my underwear to slick up his fingers.

"Kye," I breathed, nails digging into his back as he pushed into my wet entrance. I could barely breathe as the fiery tension built to a higher level with his thrusting fingers, until finally, my body convulsed, falling into a pit of release. Shuddering in his arms, I waited until my body settled before turning my attention to him. I quickly unbuttoned his pants and wrapped my hand around his shaft as he shucked his bottoms and boxers. When he was bare except for his shirt, I palmed his balls, circling them in my palm as I stroked. Leaning forward, I flicked his lower lip with my tongue, a tiny smirk curling my lips as he growled deeply within his chest.

"Enough teasing, Sweets. I want you," he murmured softly, cupping my cheeks and kissing me hard. Before I could even kiss back, he was sliding my underwear down my legs until he had them off, letting them drop haphazardly on the floor. Moving back in, he spread my thighs, eyes flaring in appreciation as he lined up. I held my breath as he slid in, inching ever so slowly until I was a moaning, shivering mess with the need to feel him thrust in earnest. "Teasing isn't so fun, now is it?" he whispered with a cocky smirk and half-lidded gaze. Narrowing my eyes at him, I wrapped my hands around his jaw roughly and yanked his lips to mine, wanting him to know exactly what I needed at that moment.

Taking the hint, he wrapped his arms around my waist and hips, moving in rhythmic thrusts until I was shaking with my impending release. When I thought I couldn't handle the building tingles, Kye sucked on my neck, and I exploded in his arms, my pussy clamping around his cock. My moans turned to cries as he picked up his pace through my orgasm, pounding into me until he shuddered, reaching his own climax in our intense but quick moment together.

"Holy hellsticks, I think I need some sugar to replenish after that," I huffed in his arms, my body coated in a thin layer of sweat from our exertion. He chuckled, pulling out of me before lifting me off the desk.

"I want a nap and to feel my sexy girlfriend in my arms," he stated simply as he carried me over to the bed. Laying me down, Kye curled around me and reached into my nightstand. "Besides, I know you always have a stash in here." I chuckled as he pulled out a bag of Hex Mix, our favorite treat. We spent the rest of the night tangled up in the sheets, playfully fighting over the bag of honeyed goodness before finally falling asleep in each other's arms.

September 24th
Tuesday Afternoon

Aris

Potions seemed to be one of the classes I didn't feel as out of place. Our last class, we were learning about making a simple healing tincture. Everything on the list was familiar to me, simple things we grew in our garden back home. Well, our gardener grew, and I tried to help when I needed to escape my family. It was nice to feel like I was actually grasping a topic. Even with the added magic, I still felt like such an outsider here. To everyone else but our group, I was still just a Mixta.

"You'll need to get your cauldrons hot before starting the mixture, and when it is completely dissolved, it needs to be cooled immediately," Professor Brogan started his lecture, his loud voice booming through the room. "Use care when dealing with this while it's hot because it will be thick and can cause serious burns." I didn't miss the look he gave me, clearly remembering the few clumsy moments I'd had since starting here.

I got to work adding water to my cauldron and boiling it, putting Mr. Stripes safely on the chair behind me. As the water boiled, I ground the herbs I would need. Once that was ready, I slowly added the ingredients, following the instructions meticulously so I could nail this one on the first try. I stirred slowly, my mind so focused, I was startled by the commotion behind me. Looking back, I saw Mr. Stripes lunging for Delilah's bag, knocking it on the floor, her books and papers spilling out.

"I'm so sorry!" I said, crouching down to help her clean it up. "No, no, Mr. Stripes, not cool!" I scolded gently, turning toward him and scooting out of the way as she reached for the pens under my chair. He was munching happily on something I had no chance of getting back now. "I'm so sorry, I think he ate something too." I winced, hoping it wasn't bad for him or something she needed.

The smell of something burning caught my attention, and I gasped, suddenly remembering how close my potion was to being finished before the commotion. When I glanced in my smelly cauldron, the thick liquid was no longer a liquid, but a black, burned goo. *Hellsticks*, I mentally groaned.

"Miss Calisto, I see you didn't get it cooled off quickly enough. Start again," he encouraged, not looking annoyed as most would be. I gave him an apologetic smile, taking my ruined potion to the cleaning counter, scraping the blackened gunk from my cauldron. Mr. Stripes scurried over, climbing his way up my pastel-purple skinny jeans until he was seated on my shoulder, his tiny hands clutching my hair and forehead as he held on. A flood of happiness filled me, telling me my tiny lemur had enjoyed his unexpected treat —*little troublemaker.*

"Well, baby, at least I didn't blow anything up this time," I perked up as I continued to scrub.

Baby steps.

CHAPTER 17

October 1st
Tuesday Midday
Aris

The past week had been a whirlwind, flying by before I even realized. Between learning how to take care of Mr. Stripes, keeping up with classes, and trying to keep all this extra magic under control, there was little time left for relaxing.

My absentmindedness had been worse lately, but even I couldn't explain away the random objects moved in my room and that more of my stuff had gone missing. I had no clue what this person was looking for, but they wouldn't find much of value in there. I hadn't had a chance to mention it to the guys or the incident with the cloaked figure, but now that I had power, I could defend myself.

I don't want to make them feel like I they have to babysit me all the time. It seems like some new situation pops up every time we're together.

Grabbing my bag off the floor as soon as the clock tower chimed the end of class, I started toward the cafeteria for lunch. Lunch had quickly become my favorite time of day; all the animals got along so well, and we got to see them really interacting. On the first day of having them all together, we moved to one of the tables near the door that wasn't as cluttered with people, giving our familiars a chance to interact without people practically stepping on them.

Mr. Stripes was in his usual spot, using my bag as a seat as he held onto the strap and my arm, chattering happily as we walked through the halls. He loved the attention he got as we wove through the crowds, puffing out his chest as the other witches cooed and petted him. It was odd to feel the emotions of another creature so deeply, but I welcomed it wholeheartedly after spending years alone.

The moment we stepped through the doorway to the dining hall, he leaped from my shoulder and took off for our table, the familiars holding our spot as we all headed for the food lines. Seeing how long the lines were today, I headed for the restroom instead, figuring it was going to be a long afternoon, so I may as well go now.

Thankfully, the restroom was empty when I went in, and it wasn't until I was washing my hands the door opened, revealing the Curse Crew. Esmerelda's smile curled up the corners of her mouth the moment they spotted me. *Keep your magic under control. They won't hurt you, and you don't want to reveal your magic yet.*

"Excuse me, ladies. All yours," I said quickly, tightening my ponytail and walking for the door. Before I could step around them, Amber was pushing me back, so my denim-clad ass hit the floor. *Ew!*

"Look, the Mixta is finally alone. Tell me, how does a lowly Mixta manage to get a familiar? Did you fuck Thane?" Tasha asked, cackling at her own taunt. "That's the only explanation that makes sense."

"Some of us don't have to fuck our way to good grades, and last time I checked, familiars choose who they want. Maybe they thought your personality was too hateful for theirs. Maybe you should wait for a snake or something," I shot back, done with being treated like this.

"Why a snake?" Amber asked, clearly not getting it.

She's obviously not the shiniest cauldron in the cupboard.

"She's calling us sneaky and vicious," Tasha clarified, giving me a hard look.

"We aren't vicious. We haven't hurt you once... at least, not yet. But I'll admit we're a bit sneaky... maybe. I mean, how else do you expect us to find out how a girl like you keeps men you don't deserve? Especially men as strong as them," she snarked.

"Step one, don't be an asshole," I deadpanned, pushing through them and walking toward the door again. I kept my head high, not wanting to stay here and fight or show them how much they had gotten to me. As my hand wound around the knob to pull the door open, I was yanked back by my ponytail, hitting the nasty bathroom floor for a second time. My magic sparked to the surface, dancing under my skin and fueling my emotions higher. It took everything in me to pull them back, my breathing slow and steady as I fought to keep from exposing myself and my guys by extension.

"Don't you dare think you can be rude to us and walk away," Esmerelda seethed, a few strands of bubblegum pink hair hanging from her fingers. Her nostrils flared as an ugly sneer contorted her features.

"Do you even have a reason for hating me, or is it just petty jealousy? Because I don't see any other Mixtas at the brunt of your hatred," I asked, standing up and brushing off my jeans before staring them down. *I just want to wash my hands and leave. What the hell?*

"We just don't like when peasants try to move above their league. Caspian, Kye, Drayce, and Xanthius are all above you. They deserve better. Can you imagine what Councilman Eideann would say if he heard his son was hanging out with a no magic witch like you?" Esmerelda shot back, both of her minions nodding like bobbleheads behind her.

"The Councilman has nothing to do with me hanging out with Xanthius, and neither do you. You've known them for this long, and yet not a single one of you were dating, so I'd say they're not your territory," I said, finally turning to the side and washing my hands again before pushing past, this time forcefully enough to knock them back and giving me a chance to properly escape.

My anger bubbled the entire way through the lunch line until I slammed my tray down on our table. The guys all looked up at me in shock though nobody said anything right away. I slid Mr. Stripes his plate of fruit before glaring down at my own food, not even seeing what was on my plate.

"Uh, Cupcake, you doing alright?" Caspian asked slowly, leaning away from me like I was going to explode any second.

"Yeah, why?" I asked, my voice harsh. *Fuck, rein it in, Aris.*

"You picked a salad for lunch, have no dessert, and

you're glaring at your plate like it personally offended you," Kye said, giving my tray a pointed look.

I grabbed what?

"Oh, gross," I finally realized what I was seeing—a green leafy bowl of blandness. "Someone want this?" I pointed to it, but Mr. Stripes darted over, taking an armful of the salad, and running it back to his fruit. "Never mind then, guess my baby wanted it." I slid the rest of the salad over to him where he gave me a happy chirp, shoving the leaf in his hand into his mouth.

"So, going to tell us what's wrong, Angel?" Drayce questioned with a raised brow.

I hesitated, nibbling on my lip before finally responding. *I guess they should know... I mean, it kind of has to do with them.*

"The Curse Crew struck again. I thought they were finally getting over this shit, but they just cornered me in the bathroom and started in on me again. I handled it," I added when they all opened their mouths to interject something. "Someone just talk about something else for a bit," I pleaded, not wanting to dwell on it anymore, not to mention the magic was still too close to the surface for comfort.

"Coral and I are getting along well, and she has the coolest set up in my room now," Caspian said, giving his otter an adoring look.

Could he get any cuter?

"This chicken and I are tolerating each other," Kye grumbled, shooting his sweet chicken an unpleasant look. "I'll never say she's not fierce again, though."

"Chickens aren't gentle creatures most of the time," I pointed out, laughing at his annoyed expression. "She's a fierce little raptor; her name fits."

The conversation lulled for a second as we all looked over at our odd assortment of familiars. They were kind of like us, a group that didn't seem to fit together but somehow did.

Having them with us now makes me feel like we can actually make this bond work.

October 3rd
Thursday Evening
Aris

After sitting alone in my room for a while, I decided to visit Xan. I'd been feeling bad we hadn't gotten as close as I had with some of the others, so I figured a visit might help. Maybe I could even convince him to go out with me this weekend.

The moment I turned down his wing, I noticed there were more students in the halls than normal, all of them facing one door and whispering. My confusion only grew as yelling and clattering came from the door in question... which happened to be Xan's room. I knocked on his door, waiting for a few minutes before knocking again, louder this time.

The guy who opened the door looked nothing like the Xan I knew. His hair was disheveled, as were his clothes, and a streak of bubblegum pink paint that matched my hair perfectly was on his cheek. Part of me loved that it matched me, but the other part was worried he was mid-breakdown.

"You okay?" I asked as he stood there, breathing heavy and looking confused.

"Yes," he said quickly, pulling me in and pushing the door closed behind me before running back for the mess in the middle of the room. I let out a giggle when I saw his little hedgehog run over his paint, leaving the most adorable paw prints all over his stone floors. "He just won't stop messing with my paint!" He looked ready to pull his hair out, and I just lost all self-control. One tiny hedgehog making my tall, adept boyfriend lose his mind—it was far too comical not to laugh.

"Come here, Hedgie," I said, dropping to the floor and holding out my hand for him. He scurried over to me, taking a detour in the orange paint and leaving another trail of footprints behind. "You didn't mean to drive him crazy, did you?"

"Oh, he meant to. He runs right for it!" Xan yelled, his arms gesturing wildly to the mess on the floor.

"You aren't used to anything in your life being messy, are you?" I asked, imagining the same scenario but with multiple crazy toddlers running around. *Though let's be real, Caspian, and maybe Drayce, would be running with them.*

"No, I'm not," he said with a sigh, dropping down onto the stool behind his easel. He gently turned it away from me, but I didn't mind. Art could be private, and I would never demand he show me what he was working on.

Spotting a roll of paper towels by his desk, I gave Hedgie one last rub, then tore a few off and went to work cleaning up his floor. Most of it was easy. The tubes were already closed, so it was just his palette that was ransacked by a spikey little trickster. When I had it cleaned up, I tossed the papers in the trash can and led Xan over to his bed to sit.

"Take a deep breath, Picasso," I said, giving him an amused look. It was kind of nice seeing him not so 'perfect.'

"Wait... who's Picasso?" he asked, his head tilting to the side. I could practically see him searching his brain for the unfamiliar name.

"He's a famous human painter," I answered, laughing at his exasperated expression. "I like to learn about the humans and collect things from their realm sometimes."

"You know, that's something I love about you. How did you manage that with those parents of yours?" he asked, his eyes soft as he studied me.

"Well, I live by the 'what they don't know won't hurt them' code. They were always training my siblings or too busy showing off to really care what I did. You should have seen the relief in my mom's eyes I was going here. Dad managed to get me a spot in a school closer, by sheer status alone, but Mom was worried about how much people would talk. And dammit, I'm rambling again," I said, wincing. I hated when I got nervous and started talking, and the feeling of his leg pressed against mine definitely wasn't helping that problem. Inappropriate thoughts flew through my head, increasing my nervousness among other sudden... feelings. *How am I going to keep getting closer to my guys when the magic is so meddlesome?*

"I wish I could be like that. Say, 'fuck it,' and do what I want. To paint and travel. To not have to keep up appearances," he said emphatically, standing up and waving his arms as he listed everywhere he wanted to go.

"Well, you can, and we will go to all kinds of places," I said, my smile bright as I watched him.

"That sounds nice," he said quietly, a wistfulness to his voice that made my heart ache for him.

"You don't have to give up living just to follow a career you choose. Emphasis on you... not your father. It's your future," I said firmly, willing him to believe it.

"It *is* my future," he agreed, turning to me and closing the distance. He pressed his lips against mine, no hint of sweetness as he showed me how much he wanted this, us, our future... all of it. "All because of you, my muse. Come look." He took my hand and pulled me behind the easel, his smile proud as I let out a gasp. He had painted a picture of me, the work so realistic, it looked like I was coming to life on the canvas. My heart clenched at how sweet it was, how beautiful he had made me look.

"It's so pretty," I said, admiring the way the colors blended perfectly.

"Yes, you are," he said, pulling me into his lap. Feeling bold, I turned to straddle his legs, his hands moving under my ass to support me as he fused his lips to mine. He was forceful and demanding in his kiss, no tension in his movements, just pure passion and fire as he gripped my ass tightly and nipped my bottom lip. Wasting no time, he pushed my shirt up and over my head, hands reaching behind me to unclip my bra. It took him a few tries, but with him peppering the tops of my breasts, I barely noticed, nearly drowning in his kisses. As soon as it was off, he swirled his tongue over one of my nipples, sucking it into his mouth.

His hair was silky against my fingers as I ran my nails up the back of his neck, making him shiver. Xan made me feel sexy with his strong and demanding movements as he picked me up, laying me on the bed under him, but instead of nestling between my thighs as I thought he would, he immediately slipped my skirt off. Grabbing my ankle, he pressed a row of kisses down my calf before trailing down my thigh, his deep brown eyes centered on my face as he finally reached the edge of my underwear. Knowing he was a virgin, this bold and confident Xan was completely unexpected, but I absolutely loved it.

My eyes fluttered shut as he kissed over the wet spot, nipping slightly at my clit, making me jump at the jolt of lightning that shot through me. I couldn't stop the breathy moan that left my lips. Slipping his fingers under the hem of the one barrier left between us, he shifted back far enough to pull them off. My eyes refocused on him when he didn't move back in right away, worried there was something wrong. My chest squeezed, and I nibbled on my lip and watched the way his eyes filled with such heat and adoration as he took in my naked body laid out on his bed.

"You are a work of art, Muse," he murmured, running his hands gently over my thighs and stomach to cup my chest, thumbs gently running over my peaked nipples. The warmth flooding my body had me nearly tearing up. Feeling worshiped—like the goddesses—was something I had never expected, but with Xan, I did.

He pulled off his shirt to reveal his lean chest and abs, leading to trim hips—all of which had my mouth watering. When he folded over me and captured my lips, it was softer, slower, drinking me up completely, instead of a flurry of movement like most of my times before. I wrapped my arms around his bare shoulders, neither of us hurried to break our embrace as we leisurely nipped, licked, and made out.

"I want you to lie down," I murmured against his lips, my eyes opening to see him watching me with a curious expression. Doing as I asked, he traded places with me on the mattress. Taking the same reverence he did with me, I pulled his pants off and ran my hands over his thighs until I reached his cock. Wrapping my hand around him, I stroked him slowly as I bent down to wrap my lips around him.

"Aris…" he breathed, his eyes falling shut as I bobbed my head.

I wanted him to feel just as good, just as wanted and worshiped as I did, so I poured all my attention into what I was doing. His sharp gasps as I swirled my tongue around the head of his cock had me moving faster, empowered knowing I was turning him on so much.

"Aris… I'm going to come if you keep that up," he ground

out, his hands coming to pull my mouth off him. Looking up at him, I smiled before crawling up on top of him.

"Maybe next time, I can finish you like that," I whispered, my body flaring as I talked, my cheeks burning at my first attempt at trying to speak aloud those kinds of things. His cheeks flushed, but he smiled at me.

"I would like that, but right now, I want you. I... uh, I've never..." he stuttered, the pink flush on his cheeks darkening to red as he struggled to explain he was a virgin. Pressing my finger against his lips, I silenced him.

"I remember, babe. Just let me start, then if you want, you can take over. How does that sound?" I proposed, wanting him to fully enjoy his first time. Reaching between my dripping core and his cock, I repositioned him against me. He nodded, jaw clenching as he pressed against my slick entrance. Groaning, his head pressed back against the bed as I sank down onto his cock, going slow enough for both of us to adjust.

Sitting up, I braced myself against his chest, rocking my hips gently at first before bouncing up and down. His hands moved from my hips to my chest, rolling my sensitive peaks between his fingers. Our moans mixed together, both of us getting lost in the intoxicating feelings and sensations of being together. The longer I rode him, the more confident he became until he grabbed my hips to thrust into me.

"Xan..." I breathed, barely able to speak as my body tensed. Nearly painful waves of tingles shot through me as I clamped around him, falling blissfully into release. I felt myself go slack as aftershocks ran through me, but instead of folding over into his chest, Xan shifted us until he was sitting and clutching my torso in a warm embrace.

"You're absolutely the most beautiful work of art I have ever seen, Aris," he murmured, continuing to pound into me. Peppering my chest in loving kisses, his rhythm faulted, and his breathing hitched. I rocked slightly, and that was all he needed until I felt him pulse inside me in orgasm. He continued to hold me, his sweaty forehead resting against my chest, his fingers lightly trailing over my back until our breathing evened out.

"I couldn't ask for someone more perfect, my muse," he whispered. His deep brown eyes had my chest squeezing. In that one look, I felt a lifetime of love and caring, and in his arms, and I nearly melted into a puddle of girly giggles and butterflies. "Can I paint you?"

"You already painted me," I reminded with a soft smile. His lips curled, a small chuckle rumbling his chest.

"But I didn't get to paint you like this," he stated simply, his hands moving to lift me off his lap and onto his sheets. "Will you let me?"

I beamed, nodding as I let him position me the way he wanted. I had to nibble my lip to keep from moving as he sat in his stool, naked, behind a fresh canvas.

"You know," I started, the silence was nice, but we hadn't gotten a lot of time alone, and I didn't want to waste it. "You never asked me out on that date."

"I suppose I didn't," he chuckled again, the warm and deep sound radiating to my very bones. "Aris Calisto, my beautiful muse, will you go on a date with me?" His eyes lit up as he looked at me over the top of the canvas. This time, I couldn't stop the girly giggle that bubbled out or the flush I felt heat my pale skin.

"Of course, but when?"

"Can we go after Samhain? I don't want us to be worried about midterms or focused on the festival," he explained.

I agreed, letting my body relax into the position he wanted, allowing him to focus. Before long, I saw his little hedgie peek his prickly head out from the top drawer of Xan's dresser.

So, that's where he ran off to, little troublemaker.

October 4th
Friday Evening
Aris

With the prospect of a night of fun since it was Friday night, I rushed out of mentoring with Torryn. I was still bummed he wouldn't be able to go with us, but I didn't mention anything because I knew it would make him feel bad, and I didn't want that. Besides, we had more fun in this session than actual work. We'd watched and laughed as Mr. Stripes and Ruby played. We even snuck in a few kisses.

The guys said we'd go do something after dinner, so I wanted to stop in my room first. I hurried through the hallways, getting quite a few strange looks from my peers. After last night with Xan, some of my magic seemed to settle. *At least we didn't set the bed on fire.*

As I turned my key in the lock, an unusual magic seemed to emanate from the door, and even Mr. Stripes jumped back in alarm. *That's strange, there shouldn't be any magic here.* I considered going to find one of the guys, but the thought of lugging my textbooks across campus sounded like a form of torture I wasn't interested in.

Taking a deep breath, I pulled my key out and pushed the door open. Peering into the room, nothing looked weird, so I took a step forward. As soon as I moved over the threshold, it was like I moved through a pit of fire, agony blistering across my skin until it felt like it was melting from my body. I fell to the ground as a scream tore from my throat, a scream I knew would go unheard, thanks to dinner being across campus at that moment.

My eyes slowly closed, and a sense of hopelessness flooded me, knowing it could be too late. Mr. Stripes howled sadly as he watched on, helpless to fix this. I knew nothing of poisons. I couldn't move a muscle in my body, not even to alleviate the burning. Darkness slowly overtook me, my last thoughts before I passed out were of my sweet boyfriends.

CHAPTER 18

October 4th
Friday Night
Drayce

"Dude, will you stop?" Kye hissed under his breath as his chicken yanked another piece of food off his plate. Raptor clucked but proceeded eating her catch.

I chuckled, unable to stop myself as Kye glared at me. Caspian sank into the seat next to me, his cheeks tinting pink as I rested my knee against his thigh. *Flirting with him is just too much fun.*

"Has anyone seen Aris?" Xan asked, his deep voice startling me from my teasing. Now that he pointed it out, I realized he was right; Angel was always here by now. The lunch lines were practically empty.

"Mentoring?" Kye asked, leaning around to try to get a view of the faculty section.

"Nope, Torryn is eating. I saw him in line grabbing his

nasty healthy food earlier while I was grabbing a piece of cake."

"That's not good," Xan said, standing up and using his height to peer over everyone's head. His frown deepened as he came up empty.

"Should someone go check on her?" Caspian questioned, looking worried. Xan had just opened his mouth when Raptor shot straight up, her head whipping back-and-forth until she was yelling out an odd clicking screech. A sense of worry wormed into my stomach when I noticed all the familiars had stopped eating and clustered together.

"I think they're trying to tell us something," I murmured, moving to stand. Kye scoffed and mumbled under his breath, but I wasn't paying any attention to him as the group of animals shot to the ground and barreled toward the door. "Come on," I directed, following quickly, our trays forgotten on the table.

"What's going on?" Torryn's commanding voice echoed down the hall, running to catch up to us. His red panda, Ruby, was sprinting as fast as her little legs could carry her to join the rest of the familiars. His gaze darted around the group, his face paling when he didn't find who he was looking for. "Where's Aris?"

"She wasn't at dinner, then this happened," I explained, waving a hand at the animals as they started up the stone steps. As we neared, a loud ear-splitting screech filtered down the space, but no one who was around seemed bothered to go check despite their creased brows and frowns—*what assholes.*

Dread filled my stomach as we neared Aris' room, and the screaming became even louder. A mix of shadows, fire, water, and air formed a miniature tornado as her room came into view. *Please let her be alright*, I pleaded, but my stomach sank as I saw a wave of pink curls fanned out on the stone floor, Mr. Stripes frantically hopping around screaming, darting around Aris' prone body until he crawled onto her chest and started frantically patting her cheeks.

"Holy hellsticks," Caspian raged, Torryn and Xan immediately falling to their knees next to her as we crowded around. Bending down, I scooped up the distraught lemur and rocked him softly, attempting to calm him. "What the hex happened here? Is she okay?"

"We need to take her to the infirmary as soon as possible," Torryn commanded, whispering an incantation until Aris was floating between him and Xan. "Let's go. Caspian, go tell the nurse we're coming. Kye, are you able to do a rune scan?"

Caspian bolted down the hall and stairs, not even bothering to apologize as he ran into several of the people who stood with nosy expressions. Mr. Stripes must have realized none of them had come to help and gave a weird hiss, slashing out at them with his little claws. Holding tight, I cooed to him until we were out of the dormitory and in the courtyard.

"There are no runes or anything on her person, so I don't have any idea what could have caused this," Kye explained, slowly growing more and more unhinged as he ran his hands through his hair. I hung back, gripping his shoulder with my free hand.

"She'll be alright, she's tough. She's too happy to be down for long," I exclaimed, even though I felt acid burning my stomach in fear. Kye's chuckle was slightly hysterical, but he calmed, nonetheless.

Everyone moved out of our way, Torryn's glaring and Aris' floating form enough to deter anyone from getting in the way. I moved ahead of them and pulled open the door, allowing Torryn to guide her down the hall to the infirmary. Caspian was already there, pacing with wide, worried eyes near the door. As soon as he saw us, he yelled for the staff. A moment later, four witches in white doctor's coats converged on us, taking her easily from Torryn and rushing to the back, leaving us in stunned silence.

"She never messes with anyone, and I feel even her bullies wouldn't go this far. Who would do this to her?" I asked, unable to hide the frustration in my voice, feeling helpless there was nothing we could do but wait.

"I thought the same thing," Xan agreed, his voice deeper than usual as he joined the pacing.

"What bullies?" Torryn asked, his voice hard as his eyes flared in anger. Caspian opened his mouth to say something, but I shot him a look to calm the negativity before it started.

"A few girls have been giving her a hard time, but she handled it. This seems worse than your average student," I explained, keeping my voice soothing to try to alleviate some of the tension, though it proved useless. They started in on each other, despite the warnings, the others joining in the argument.

"Why am I just now hearing of this?" Torryn grumbled, squeezing his hands into tight fists to try to contain his anger, but it still radiated off him in waves. It clearly ran deeper than just finding out she was bullied a bit.

"We didn't realize we answered to you, big brother," Cas bit out, taking some of his anxiety out on Torryn.

"I still need to know things, even if I have to stay further back than you. She means as much to me as she does to you, as much as you don't believe it," he bit back, his voice low to keep our conversation from the wrong ears.

"This isn't helping," Kye bit out. "We need to figure out who the fuck is targeting her."

"This fighting isn't going to help. When we hear she's stable, we need to check her room. Something got her right in the doorway, so maybe a hex bag?" Xan rambled, pausing his pacing to hash out the details. "Torryn and I are probably most equipped for that."

Our heads snapped to the door as it creaked open, revealing Headmaster Tallis and a man I recognized from Aether's security team, a severe, scowling, bald man. His eyes were sharp, making the green seem volatile. The nurse hurried from the desk to greet them, wringing her hands as she clearly gave them more information than we had gotten so far. After a few moments of thick tension, they followed her as she held open the door to the room. As if we all were on the same thought process, we moved together, swarming the space without invitation.

"You all found her?" the headmaster inquired, a look of annoyance on his face that boiled my blood. The two men distracted us from checking on Aris as she laid in the bed unconscious. The witches who were working flittered around, weaving between us as they ran their scans but didn't ask us to leave, no doubt detecting the tension running rampant through the room.

"Yes, she was lying on the ground, unmoving, and clearly hexed." Kye's voice was cold and angry as he answered, and I couldn't help but brace myself for an argument.

"Now, let's not jump to conclusions, you don't know she was hexed," the headmaster blustered, looking stricken at Kye's boldness. "Mr. Windle is here to determine the details, so please give him honest answers."

Without hesitation, Mr. Windle grabbed a notepad out

of his pocket, turning his fierce gaze on us. "Now tell me, were there any visible signs of magic, runes, or hexes? Any distinct smells or sounds?"

"No, I did a rune scan, but it must have dissipated before we found her," Kye answered, sounding a bit less angry now that they seemed to be doing something.

"So, nothing to show it was a hex as you previously thought?" he challenged, causing Kye's nostrils to flare.

Not wanting to cause more trouble, I rested a hand on Kye's shoulder to calm him, trying to silently remind him what was at stake.

"Has she had any recent issues at school?"

"Just some bullies. She's a Mixta, so they were teasing her," Caspian said slowly, unsure if he should share it with these assholes or not.

"There you go. It was likely just a prank, she'll be fine," the headmaster cut in, his smile forced and fake.

"So, you're writing it off as a prank before even doing a search of her room or making sure she's alright?" Xan asked formally, his eyes dancing with an angry fire behind them. A small flame started in his hand, but he extinguished it before I could even process what I was seeing.

"I don't like what you're insinuating, young man. You may be the son of a high councilor, but that doesn't mean you get the choice to be disrespectful," Tallis barked out, his eyes darting side-to-side as if Xan's dad would step into the room at any moment.

"He's asking why a headmaster and head of security are not investigating an attack on a student. I also would like to know who will be heading the investigation," Torryn asked, his voice holding a bit more of that commanding quality.

"I want what's best for Miss Calisto, though I'm curious

why you are so invested in her wellbeing, Professor Callahan?" Tallis asked, his eyes narrowing in on Torryn.

Oh shit, he looks suspicious. My heart pounded, and the moment seemed to stretch on forever as they stared each other down. A breeze formed at my panic, and I stuck my free hand into my pocket to stop it before anyone noticed, though all eyes were on the two men arguing in front of them.

"I care about the wellbeing of *all* of my students, Headmaster Tallis," Torryn bit out, his face turning red at the creepy vibe emanating from the man.

"Then perhaps you should head the investigation of her room since you seem so determined to find evidence. We will be monitoring the investigation and speaking with teachers to find if there is any gossip floating around pertaining to this. As for right now, let the medical professionals handle her recovery, and we'll see what they say," he explained before patting Aris on the leg.

The sight of his hand on her knee made me irrationally angry, and despite my laid-back nature, all I wanted to do at that moment was punch him.

"I want what's best for Aris as much as you do." With that, the headmaster stormed out, his sidekick at his heels. We stood in stunned silence, the familiars standing vigil with us. I couldn't wrap my head around the fact they brushed it off so easily.

"Fuck this, I'm going to check her room as soon as she wakes up," Torryn bit out to no one in particular. Mr. Stripes abruptly let out a chirp and lunged from my arms, scurrying on top of the bed and up Aris' chest. All of us surrounded the bed, determined to see our girl.

"Well, I guess we don't need to give you a report since she's awake now," the head nurse said with a hint of disapproval as she walked over from her spot by the medical cart. "There were no signs of any magic in her blood or on her skin. Clearly, something knocked her out, but there are no signs of it left behind. Either someone was very smart with their magic, or she had a reaction to something." She looked every bit as baffled as we were.

How could the magic leave no trace?

"We'll find the evidence," Torryn promised, shifting his attention from the witch to Aris. My heart clenched at the sight of her looking so shaken and weak in the hospital bed.

"Cupcake? Are you alright?" Caspian choked out, his voice wavering a bit with relief. Our magic had been fighting to break free from our holds this entire time, but now that she was awake, everything seemed to have calmed.

"I feel alright, just weak," she rasped, hugging Mr. Stripes to her chest. "I just opened my door, felt a bit of magic, and *bam,* all I knew was burning pain before I passed out." She shivered at the memory, her eyes haunted as they looked up at us. "How did you know to come find me?"

"Because of him," Kye said, nodding to Mr. Stripes, "and the other familiars. We were sitting in the dining hall, wondering where you were when Raptor went crazy. Then the others followed suit. They all rushed out of the dining hall, and we ran to keep up 'til we got to your room. If it wasn't for them... we might not have found you in time. He was inconsolable when we got there."

"Thank you, friend." Aris hugged Mr. Stripes and kissed his head. Mr. Stripes purred and sank into the embrace.

"I'll inform the headmaster you're awake," the head nurse announced, leaving us to speak with Aris. Nobody acknowledged her, none of us even caring she was still around, so she slipped out without another word.

"I'm going to check your room. They say your blood is

clean, but something must be there," Torryn said angrily, giving her a kiss on the forehead after glancing around to make sure we were truly alone.

"I'll go too," Xan offered, giving Aris a tight hug before rushing after an already retreating Torryn.

"They'll probably keep you here awhile. Kye and I can go get your snacks and clothes. I'd hate for you to be uncomfortable," Caspian said quickly, bouncing anxiously on his feet. I could see his relief, but he also seemed unsure how to process or handle seeing her like this. She gave him a soft smile, seeing through his intentions.

"I'm okay, Sprinkles," she promised. "But I wouldn't say no to some comfier clothes if I'm stuck here for a bit."

"You got it," Kye said, leaning in and kissing her softly before pulling Caspian away. Now that it was just me and my Angel, I settled onto the bed next to her, stroking her hair softly.

"So, how are you really?" I asked, giving her a soft smile.

"I feel like a witch who fell off her broom," she said, flopping back down on the bed with a small sigh.

"You scared me," I admitted, thankful to see those gorgeous gray eyes looking back at me. Seeing her on the floor like that was going to haunt me for a very long time.

"I'm sorry," she sighed, her bottom lip poking out in a cute pout. "I didn't mean to."

"Angel, it's not your fault. All I care about is you're okay," I explained, brushing her hair off her face lightly. Her forehead was hot against my fingers, her cheeks flushed slightly with a minor fever, but other than that, she didn't seem to have any outward signs of whatever happened. "Even laid out in the infirmary, you're still the most beautiful witch I have ever seen."

"I doubt that," she challenged, but try as she might, she

couldn't hide the tiny smile or happy glint that lit in her gray eyes. I smiled at her and leaned forward to press a soft kiss to her cheek.

"You are, I just haven't gotten much of you to myself to be able to tell you, and I want my girlfriend to know how special she is to me." Needing to show her how I felt, I leaned in and captured her lips with mine, the magic tingling along my skin as I poured my emotion into it. She met my kiss with the same amount of intensity, both of us panting as we pulled away.

Before I could say anything else, a frantic Caspian and Kye came running in with their arms loaded, their familiars not far behind, holding lettuce and fruit in their mouths for Mr. Stripes who hopped off the bed to accept their gifts. I had to hold back my laughter at the ridiculous number of treats Kye had grabbed for her—enough to feed *all* of us for days, let alone our petite witch.

"I just grabbed a t-shirt and shorts for you. I hope they fit," Caspian explained, holding out the clothes to her.

"They're perfect," she said sleepily, taking the clothes and raising her eyebrow at Kye's haul.

"Don't judge me, I didn't know what you'd want," he half whined at her, dropping the snacks on her blanket.

"I'm not," she laughed, grabbing a bag of roasted pumpkin seeds and munching on them. "Open up," she commanded, holding a seed in her hand, ready to throw. Kye looked at her like she was crazy, but Caspian opened his mouth right up. Seeing her giggle as she tried and failed to land a pumpkin seed in his mouth helped calm my frazzled nerves.

I'd been at this school for four years and not once had I met a person who I would have found capable of attacking Aris like this. She was cheerful to everyone, maybe a bit sassy at times but never without reason. What reason could this attacker possibly have for doing this? The fact they knew exactly the best time to strike was even more unsettling. The thing they hadn't anticipated was she had five men and five familiars bonded to her who were willing to fight back. I hoped Xan and Torryn would find something upstairs so we could prove to the headmaster it was no prank.

And if they won't protect her, we will.

Torryn

Anger pulsed through me as we stomped up to her room, white-hot and blinding as I shoved away the image of my gorgeous girl on the floor. I was determined to find something up here, then go punch Tallis in his face. This was no prank. Pranks didn't put you in the fucking hospital.

Xan was just as mad, his mouth forming a tight line as he breathed angrily through his nose. Students dove out of our way as we hurried through the dormitory and up to her room. It was sort of satisfying to have such an effect on people.

We slowed as we reached her doorway, both of us holding out our hands as we scanned for magic. A white tendril of magic moved from my hand and enveloped the area below it like a fog, but nothing seemed to jump out at me. Xan's sigh told me he found the same... nothing—either that or the magic already dissipated after it did its job.

Feeling like it was safe enough after our double scan, I stepped forward, only letting out the breath I was holding when I safely stood on the other side of the threshold. Crouching down, I scanned the stones surrounding her door, trying to find any trace of runes or magic before moving around the door frame. My eyes stopped on a small bag resting above the door, tucked so close to the wall, I almost missed it. Grabbing a nearby towel, I used it to pull the bag down.

"I found something, and this is definitely not Aris'," I said, calling Xan over. His eyebrows furrowed as he studied the mesh bag, the assortment of herbs inside seemingly unfamiliar, but we needed a better look. Xan mumbled under his breath until the bag untied and flipped, dumping the contents into my linen covered hands.

"Blood magic?" Xan hissed out in alarm, pointing out the small red droplets covering the herbs. *No wonder our scans didn't work. Blood magic isn't something you can detect with a normal magical scan.*

"It's less likely to be a student then, right?" I asked, more to myself than Xan. He looked up in alarm as he processed what I said, starting to shake his head.

"Someone on the faculty? But why?" he asked, the disbelief clear in his strained voice.

"That doesn't feel right either, but I guess you never truly know people. Even the seemingly normal witches can surprise you," I mumbled, folding the towel around the contents and storming out of the room. Xan closed the door behind us and hurried to catch up, mumbling under his breath as I made a beeline for Tallis' office.

He let out a startled yelp as I threw the door open, not bothering to knock or play nice before slamming the towel down on his desk. Tallis started to screech out at us that we were being disrespectful, only stopping when I unfolded the towel, exposing the evidence.

"What is the meaning of this?" Tallis finally thundered, looking apprehensive now. He knew exactly what it was, even if he was afraid to admit it.

"We found it above Aris Calisto's doorway. We took precautions when opening it, but that is blood magic, sir," Xan explained calmly, yet looked two seconds away from choking the headmaster.

"Blood magic isn't practiced in *my* school. How *dare* you imply such a thing!?" he seethed as he pressed a hand to his chest in a display of overexaggerated shock, still avoiding looking at the materials in front of him.

"I'm not implying anything, I'm pretty sure the evidence speaks for itself, sir. And as someone who doesn't want dark magic around, I would think you'd want to check it out and find the culprit quickly. You have obvious dark magic and a girl in the hospital; I'd say that warrants a full investigation," Xan said, taking the lead when I couldn't form a full sentence through my anger, building with each word out of the headmaster's mouth—*fucking idiot.*

"I'll have Windle look at this, rest assured it will be dealt with," Tallis said, puffing out his chest in an attempt at keeping his pompous airs intact.

"See that you do," I said, the comment an obvious threat as I glared down at him. He gulped audibly, adjusting his tie as he tried not to look intimidated. I didn't miss the slight narrowing of his eyes as he was likely once again questioning why I cared so much. *Let him be suspicious! He can't fire me without looking like he dropped the ball on this investigation.* Having a teacher who cared more about his students than he did would not be the image he strived to portray. Striding out of the room, Xan and I made our way into the hall and turned toward the infirmary, intent to get back to Aris as soon as possible.

God, I can't wait to be able to kiss her senselessly like I want. Damn this fucking school.

CHAPTER 19

October 9th
Wednesday Morning
Aris

After a few days of the guys being overly protective and smothering, I was ready to get back to class. The nurses insisted I take off until today, and I obliged, but I was ready to lose my mind. Professor Bellario, however, was not the right way to start the day. As soon as I walked in, she started to make a scene, fawning over me and asking if I was alright. *Like I didn't stick out enough already... thanks, crazy woman.*

"Are you better now?" she asked, the fake sympathy dripping from her voice, making my skin crawl.

"I'm fine," I promised, giving a cheerful smile as I slipped away to my desk. Mr. Stripes let out a grumble of annoyance, clearly as unimpressed with her as I was. The little guy walked over and snuggled into my lap as I started to pull out the notebook I needed for class. He'd been just as bad as the guys—*but he gets away with it because he's so cute.*

By the time basics finally ended, I was ready for the change. Even though she didn't approach me again, the stares were starting to be overwhelming. Word traveled fast at this school, and clearly, I was once again the topic of conversation.

Magic 101 wasn't much better though at least it wasn't smothering and fake like it was with Bellario. That woman was just a bit too much for me. Once the clock tower chimed at the end of class, I grabbed my stuff and practically sprinted to the cafeteria, even leaving Caspian behind.

Thanks to my hurrying, I was the first of our group inside the dining hall, leaving my favorite lemur at our table before going to get my lunch. As I moved through the line, piling my tray high with food, rumors were whispered around me—everything from me surviving a duel to a self-induced magical mishap—solidifying my spot as the number one gossip topic for the week. *Ugh, why can't I just stay out of the spotlight?*

Magic sparked along my fingers at the next accusation of a stupid Mixta blowing up her own dorm room. Of course, they had to assume it was me and my lack of affinity fucking things up. Needing to get away, I grabbed one last cookie and hurried off to our table. I tried to calm my breathing as I watched Mr. Stripes take his lunch from the tray and dig in.

The others slowly trickled into the dining hall, none of them looking any happier than I felt, though Cas' displeasure could have been from me running away. I gave him an apologetic smile as he dropped Coral, his sweet little otter, off at the table. He just shrugged and smiled, understanding the reason behind it. The whispers seemed to get louder as everyone sat down to eat. The gossip was getting to some of us more than others, Caspian and Kye looking downright murderous as they stabbed their pasta with way more vigor than necessary.

"Caspian!" I hissed as his water swirled around in his cup. The sound of his name startled him, and he grimaced as I pointed out what he was doing.

"I have a theory," Xan said slowly, bracing for our reactions. "I think us being together all at once makes it worse. Just sitting here, we are all having to strain to keep it under control."

Not one of us could argue with that. Kye kept having to rein in the shadows, and I felt like magic was fighting to burst from my fingertips.

"He has a point, but she shouldn't be alone," Kye protested, giving the others a hard look that was more of a challenge. I doubted any of us would have really protested.

"No one disagrees with you, but Xan might have a point. I have a few classes with her, so that covers part of the day," Cas started.

"I'll have to be alone sometimes, guys. I have my own room," I pointed out, not letting them have the conversation around me.

"Not if someone stays the night with you," Xan pointed out, the others quickly agreeing. It's not that I minded having a sleeping buddy, it was more I was starting to feel like a burden.

"I can't just avoid all of you," I protested again, hating the idea of having to sit with only one of them at meals or having to walk away, so we didn't get too close to someone else.

"It's not avoiding, we know you want to be with us," Drayce finally chimed in. Until now, it seemed like he was just silently thinking over everything. "We could alternate nights; that way, she never goes into her room alone. Then we all have a few classes with her, so no need to change anything but meals."

Hello, I'm sitting right here!

"Fine, but if nothing changes after this, I'm done. Things go back to normal," I huffed as I sank further into my seat and pushed my tray away, no longer hungry.

"Chin up, Cupcake, we don't like it any more than you do," Caspian said softly, reaching over Kye to squeeze my hand.

"I'll take tonight," Drayce said quickly, the others calling out their spots to form a schedule. I didn't bother to say anything more, letting them figure out the plan they'd cooked up. I hated everything about it, hating even more everything we did had to be kept hidden.

True to his word, Drayce was waiting for me outside Torryn's classroom door at the end of mentoring, his lazy smile still in place, making it impossible to be frustrated. *Maybe it will be nice to spend some quality time with each of them.* I needed to focus on the positives and not let all the chaos in my life keep me down.

"I thought we'd do dinner in your room tonight to make the transition a bit easier. I even downloaded a human game for us to play," he said cheerfully, wrapping his free hand around mine as he walked with me upstairs. My mood perked up at the prospect of something fun, forgetting all about my protesting.

"You did?! What's it called?" I asked, trying to peek into the bag he was carrying. He tucked it further up his arm, refusing to let me look.

"You'll have to wait and see," he teased, shaking his head at my obvious pouting.

I paused outside of my room, the memories of the attack

flooding me every time I went inside. It made me angry someone had made me feel unsafe in my personal space. Drayce paused with me, giving me a second before he pulled me into the room, giving me the push I needed to move past it and enjoy my night.

Since we were staying in for the night, I grabbed pajamas from the wardrobe and stepped behind the partition to change while Drayce did the same. Now that we were both ready for bed, he finally spread a blanket on the floor and let me see what he had brought. An array of sandwiches, snacks, and treats sprinkled across the blanket. He even laid out a little spread for Mr. Stripes and Petunia, who wasted no time in partaking of their meal.

"Alright, the game is called Life. You get to choose the path you take, pick jobs, kids, and all that," he explained as he said the incantation to open his witch's glass. A bright and colorful animation sounded before the game board appeared in front of us, a cheerful melody playing in the background.

"It sounds kind of boring," I admitted, wondering why they made a game of the mundane things they go through in life.

"We might just be surprised. What's wrong, Angel? You aren't usually so negative," he pointed out quietly, a hint of concern colored his words.

"True, I'm sorry. All of this separation and the weird attacks," I mumbled, shaking out my limbs dramatically. "Okay, okay. You're right. I'm ready!" I grabbed the plate with chocolate cake and dove in while he started the game.

"Aw, look. The game piece is pink like you," he teased as an odd-looking person-shaped game piece jumped in a car. We read the directions before starting the game, both of us choosing a career path. I laughed when he picked the artist card, knowing Drayce wasn't exactly the artsy type. I picked rock star, getting the highest salary of the two.

We played for a while, making our way around the board, though I protested when he said I had to pick a husband.

"What do you mean I have to choose? I don't want only one, I have five guys," I protested and pouted when the game automatically gave me one. *Humans just don't know what they're missing.* The rest of it went smoothly, both of us retiring. Drayce won by only a hundred dollars, but by the end, I was smiling without reservation.

I guess I was wrong, a game building a different kind of life was actually fun.

I started to clean up, but Drayce waved me away, choosing to do it himself. I sat on my bed and watched, waiting for him to join me. When he finished, he slipped his tank top off, revealing his bare chest. The soft caramel color of his smooth skin called to me, practically begging me to touch it. Drayce wasn't a big guy, but his muscle definition was delicious, the hard planes of his chest making me drool. All thoughts of playing games were gone as he approached me, his eyes darkening as he took in my hungry gaze.

When he was within reach, I pulled him down to me, a breeze already blowing through the room as I crushed my lips to his. Drayce lost all pretenses of being laid-back as he kissed me, his kiss demanding as he maneuvered us on the bed, so he was underneath me.

Wanting fewer barriers between us, I slipped my shirt off and unhooked my bra before throwing them onto the floor beside the bed. His hands moved over my bare skin, fingertips gliding lightly over me, leaving a trail of goosebumps that had my body perking up. I moaned and threw my head back as he leaned up, swirling his tongue over the sensitive peaks of my breasts.

"I knew you'd be perfect," he murmured against my skin, torqueing us again, so he was on top, slowly licking his way down my body until he grabbed the waistband of my pajama shorts in his teeth and tugged them down playfully. I giggled, but it was pretty hot. He just grinned up at me before kissing his way back up my legs, need causing the ache between my legs to grow as I watched the predatory way he moved over me, discovering and claiming every inch of my bare skin.

Hiking one of my legs over his shoulder, he held my hips steady and brought his tongue to my pussy, licking along the seam before flicking his tongue over my clit. My body bucked at the sensation, but he just chuckled and dived back in, licking and sucking until I felt my orgasm crashing over me, barely having time to build. A heated cry flew from my mouth as the waves of pleasure washed through me, fire burning my veins as my legs shook around him. My hands released the death grip I had on the sheets, reaching for him.

The only thing the orgasm did was drive my need higher, making me desperate for more. As he pulled away, I moved with him, kissing him and forcing him to turn so I could be on top again. I could taste myself on his tongue, only turning me on more. Moving down his body, I took his gym shorts and boxers with me, freeing his thick length. I moaned at the sight of him before wrapping my hand around the cock that slightly intimidated me, moving over his silky skin and watching as his eyes filled with heat. The breeze turned to full-on wind as I worked him up, the cool air making me shiver slightly. Something about the elements being involved in our times together made me feel even more powerful and sexy.

Wanting to taste him, I leaned forward and wrapped my lips around the head of his cock. Using my hand as a guide, I took him further into my mouth before pulling away, my tongue swirling around him as I moved. He moaned and tightened his hands in my hair, guiding me in a pace he needed. I worked over him, bobbing my head, loving how he was losing control and the deep moans he let loose, not bothering to be quiet up here in my tower.

"Enough," he growled, shifting me off him and up across his defined body until I was over his slick length. I slid over him, taking him easily with how wet I was. We moaned as my body adjusted to him, not pausing for long before he was bucking into me, holding me steady with a strong grip on my hips. He was gorgeous, my bronze Adonis lying beneath me, claiming me as his own. My hand slid over my body, the feeling of him inside of me too much to just take. He groaned as I slid my hands over my nipples, teasing them when I saw how turned-on he was. I worked myself up, a new orgasm building slowly this time as his eyes stayed trained on me with rapt attention.

His hand slid between our bodies until he could tease my clit, the touch speeding up the impending orgasm even more until the tingles burned through my body, and my core flooded around him. The sensations of him filling me, my hands teasing my breasts, and his hand between us brought me to my climax, waves of pleasure pulsing through me as my body tightened around him. He moaned and thrust into me faster, working me over him until he lost control. We panted as our bodies calmed, and I moved off him, snuggling into his side. He pulled a blanket over us before kissing my cheek and settling into the pillows.

It was funny to me how different life was now. I came here wanting more out of life, hoping to make a friend or two, for the first time. Instead, I managed to find five guys who I cared about more than anyone else in my entire life. They first became my friends, then swiftly wormed their way into my heart. Each of them was so different and unique in personality, tastes, even down to the way they were intimate with me. I never had a dull moment when they were around. Despite all our differences, we somehow fit into this group perfectly, making us all stronger. I was happier than I had ever been.

Let's just hope this happiness lasts.

October 11th
Friday Afternoon
Aris

I sank into my seat, my familiar running over to Ruby, where she sat on Torryn's desk. The little red panda perked up, fluffy tail swaying back-and-forth as Mr. Stripes jumped onto the desk, both making funny noises as they talked to each other. Too engrossed in watching Ruby and Mr. Stripes, I hadn't realized Caspian wasn't there yet until I felt a sweaty hand resting on my arm. Glancing to the side, I saw Delilah leaning over Caspian's desk with a sympathetic expression.

"Hey, Aris. Are you alright? You seem kind of down, and I haven't seen you with your friends lately. I just wanted to make sure you were doing okay," she stated, giving me a soft smile. Grinning at her, I tried to fake being peppy, but it was difficult.

"Yeah, I'm great! We've all been really busy," I explained, happy to know someone besides my guys seemed genuinely concerned about my wellbeing. Though her concern was a nice change from the bitchy treatment I was used to from the Curse Crew, I still felt hollow and weirdly empty with the guys' presence being so reduced from my life.

"Yeah, I understand that with midterms coming up. I was just checking," she added, patting my arm one more time before sitting back up in her seat and pulling out her book. I kept the smile plastered on my face even though all I wanted to do was wipe my arm on my sweater. *I mean... I know witches can get sweaty palms, but they freaking make potions and salves for that.* Pushing away the snarky thought, I turned back toward the front of the class. Torryn came out of his office at the same time, his seafoam-green eyes centering on me before his shoulders relaxed.

"Hey, Cupcake," Caspian greeted breathlessly, flashing me a smile. "Sorry it took so long, the men's restroom was out of order, so I had to run over to the one at the other end of the floor."

"It's alright, you made it just in time," I exclaimed. As Torryn started teaching, my stomach turned slightly, making me frown. *On top of everything lately, I have to feel nauseous.* Maybe lunch wasn't sitting well... or honestly, I had one too many soul cakes. Caspian gave me a concerned look as I fought the nausea, rubbing my stomach and waving him off as I focused on the lecture.

I hope I'm not getting sick.

CHAPTER 20

October 13th
Sunday Night
Aris

I was hot, cold, grouchy, nauseous, and all I wanted to do at that moment was throw something and watch it break. I had been sick before, plenty of times, but this was a hundred times worse than Broom Cough. Kye was lying next to me, fingers tapping away at his chest, and the longer he tapped, the more irritable I got.

Thud.

Thud.

Thud.

Right when I had had enough and opened my mouth to snap at him, a familiar red plane came zooming into the room. I huffed angrily as I rolled out of the dive-bombing plane's path. Reaching out, I snatched it from the air, the paper crumpling in my fist. *What the hellsticks does Torryn want now?*

> *Gorgeous,*
> *Meet us at the crystal cave as soon as possible. I found something.*
> *xoxo*
> *-Tor*

"We've been summoned," I bit out, already feeling weak and achy from getting up so fast, but I focused on throwing on my shoes and jacket. Mr. Stripes took his usual spot on my shoulder, nudging my head as though he knew I needed the extra comfort.

"Ready, Sweets?" Kye asked, his lips curling up a bit as he looked down at me. Plastering what seemed to be the hundredth fake smile on my face, I took his hand and headed out. It was quiet around the dormitory in the late Sunday evening, the cold outside air keeping students tucked in their rooms where it was warm.

And yet, here we were, fucking walking in the wet, soppy forest.

By the time we reached the cave, I was a dripping, shivering mess and angrier than I had been in a long time. The rest of my guys were waiting in a circle for us, all looking as cold and irritable as me.

"Alright," Torryn started as soon as Kye and I stepped up into the circle. "I found out what Aris is." Even feeling down and angry, I stood up straighter, excited to finally know what the hell was happening to me. "In some *very* old archives, I found written records that made me think you are what they call a Conduit."

"A what's-it?" I mumbled, my sick witch brain unable to process what he was saying.

"A Conduit. Basically, you're a powerful witch who can unlock and amplify any dormant elemental powers within your Tethers, a.k.a. the witches who form a bond with you.

"Tether? That's what we are?" Drayce questioned, and Petunia, his piglet familiar's head tilted as if she was trying to understand. *Well, that's just cute as hellsticks.*

"Yes, we all had latent elemental powers, but they weren't brought out until we emotionally aligned or 'vibed' with Aris."

"So, why did you call all of us out here to tell us that?" Caspian asked with a frown, his messy hair clearly showing he had been asleep before being summoned.

"Well, I figured the fact every Conduit in the history of Akasha had been used by the Council or killed because of the power they held was a pretty good reason to meet out here. Excuse me for thinking of Aris' safety, little brother," he snapped before looking at the rest of us.

"I also brought you out here because we have one final step, one more bond to complete the connection to Aris. This bonding is called a Circuit Bond, and essentially, it'll solidify the overall connection between the Tethers and the Conduit. It should, hopefully, make the powers less unstable, so they'll be less active when we're together or emotionally charged. Right now, it's as if Aris is the center of a spoked wheel. Each of us is one of the spokes connected to Aris, but we're missing the most important connection—the outer wheel that's a secondary connection between all of us, giving our bond a stronger structure. This ceremony should, in simple terms, bond all of us together."

I nodded, glancing around the circle. Everyone wore pensive expressions, thinking over what he just told us, and much to my surprise, no one argued. *First time for everything, I guess.*

"Alright, let's do it," Xan commanded after everyone had nodded their agreement. Torryn instructed us, having all of them hold hands with me in the center as we stood under the glass top of the clock tower. Looking up, I saw the full moon was close to completely filling the clear, circular crystal.

"When the moon fills the circle, everyone needs to think of why they care about Aris. Let it be the only thought in your mind. There's no activation word or incantation, just another emotional alignment with Aris like the previous bonds," Torryn stated, looking up. "Ready? Now."

As if I was dreaming, the crystals started to pulse and glow in the moonlight as it filtered down the inside of the clock tower into the cavern. All five elements swirled around the space, mixing together until I couldn't make out where one element started and another ended. Spinning in wonder, my eyes wide as I watched, feeling wave after wave of magic flow over me, filling me until I felt like I was going to burst, until finally, I collapsed to my hands and knees, vomiting. When the power subsided, I still wretched, pain radiating through me as a black goop sprayed out on the ground in front of me.

"Holy shit, Aris!" Caspian called in distress, but I was too lost in the intense pain and pulses of nausea that were slowly lessening.

"No! She needs to purge," I heard Drayce explain. No one approached me until I finally stopped. Sitting back on my heels, I felt like I had run a marathon and been run over by a witches' competitive broom race, but emotionally, I was back to my old self, not realizing until now how irritable and agitated I had been.

"Gorgeous," Torryn murmured, kneeling in front of me, taking care not to touch the goo. "You okay?"

"Yeah," I whispered, my voice raspy from all the bouts of sickness. "What the hellsticks just happened?"

"You were poisoned," Caspian bit out, looking into the puddle of black mass. "The bonding cleansed your system and pushed out the potion that was wreaking havoc on your body."

"Okay, this has gone way too fucking far. First the hex and now poison," Kye nearly screamed, pacing frantically until Drayce laid a hand on his shoulder, stopping his back-and-forth motions.

"Those aren't all," I whispered, finally realizing that all those previous instances that tripped my gut instinct were correct. "Things had been randomly missing from my bag and my room, my stuff ending up in different places than where I left them. I thought it was just witches being well... witches, but that's clearly not the case."

"Anything else?" Xan questioned, his deep voice bouncing off the crystals that no longer glowed in the moonlight. I nodded, taking a deep breath and hoping they wouldn't be mad at me, but Torryn spoke first.

"That night when there was that cloaked figure in the classroom," he breathed, his face dumbstruck as he processed. Knowing Tor, he was questioning how he could have missed such a detail. I reached out, stretching over the puddle to grab his hand.

"It's okay, I didn't think of it until now. But Torryn's right, there was a cloaked figure following me when I went to check on him and get him snacks after he had been hexed. I figured it was just someone trying to scare other witches because I never saw them again."

"Hells bells and tarot tells," Kye muttered. "So, it's definitely someone targeting Aris since there's not another witch being laid out in the infirmary. What do we do?"

"Tell the headmaster and that bald motherfucker," Caspian ground out in agitation, his hand coming out to rub my back, showing me he wasn't mad at me but at the situation in general.

"And how do we explain the fact we were out here in the cave in the middle of the night?" Torryn muttered, his hand coming to rub his eyes. "Fucking hellsticks, we can't tell that useless bastard anything. That's opening a lot of questions we don't want to answer."

"The best we can do is stick together and hope they'll get their shit under control," Drayce added, Xan nodding his agreement before taking over.

"We can try to look into it more, but we lack the resources required to conduct such an investigation. We keep an eye out for Aris. Our top priority is keeping her safe while not arousing suspicion about our connection or powers."

"Does that mean we can go back to doing group stuff?" I perked up, hope filling me. I had missed them terribly, and the only thing I wanted was to be able to spend time with them without shame or worry about being discovered.

Hopefully, this bond worked, and it mellowed out the powers.

"Yes," Drayce smiled at me, knowing where I was going. I did a little dance from my spot on the ground, a wide smile spreading over my face. "I've missed that smile, Angel. Let's get back and get some rest."

I nodded, each of us leaving in pairs, as we usually did, back to the campus.

At least there was one good thing that came from this—I got my guys back.

October 21st
Monday Night

Aris

"I literally can't read anything else about potions," Drayce groaned, closing his level four potions book and sliding it across the table. The past week had been a blur, every professor throwing every last ounce of teaching they could muster in before we had our exams. It felt like everything was due at once, so most of it had been nonstop homework and studying. *Only a few more days until freedom!*

"I take offense to that," Caspian chimed in from his spot a few chairs down.

"Yours is the only potion I want to brew," Drayce flirted, throwing him a wink. Cas' face burned a brilliant red as he groaned and adjusted in his seat, flipping his book to the next page as he actively ignored us.

My eyes grew fuzzy as I read over my notes, closing slightly despite my best attempts. We'd already been studying for a few hours, preparing for our midterms on Wednesday, and I was about to lose my mind, along with my energy. It didn't help that Xan had snagged us a mentoring classroom to use, so it was secluded and quiet as well. *If it gets any deader around here, I'm going to fall asleep for sure.*

"You with us, Muse?" Xan asked, laughing lightly as I blinked up at him with bleary eyes. "Your snores are distracting me."

I glared at him, the second guy to call me out for snoring.

"I don't snore, they're cute little breaths of air," I protested with a huff. "I'm just struggling to stay awake, and I still have History and Magic 101 notes to cover," I groaned, lightly hitting my head on the table at my to-do list.

"We just learned how to make Brainiac Brew. You want one?" Caspian asked excitedly.

"Bring it on." I should probably be afraid to be his guinea pig, but I was desperate at this point.

"Hell, yes."

"Give me one."

"Good thing I made a double batch," he mumbled as he took a pack of vials out of his bag and passed one to each of us. I popped the cork, the liquid inside a brilliant shade of gold, smelling like fresh, crisp apples. I was expecting something along the lines of rotting apples, but I was pleasantly surprised.

"Cheers! Here's hoping Sprinkles doesn't kill us all," Drayce teased, clinking our glasses together and downing them all at once. The concoction tasted as good as it smelled, a slight warmth working its way from my belly and moving through my body, waking it as it moved. Moments later, I was wide awake and alert, feeling like I could take on the world.

"Damn, babe, that was some good shit. It's not my first energy aid, but it's probably the best," Drayce complimented, handing the empty vials back down to Caspian, who gave us a proud grin, his whole face lighting up as he tucked them away.

"Now to focus. Let's study until this alarm goes off," Xan said, fidgeting with his witch's glass and setting it on the table in front of us. "Then we can reward ourselves with a pantry run."

He knows me too well.

"First one to hit their goal gets the Hex Mix. You know they only keep one bag in that pantry," I sang out to Kye, who narrowed his eyes at the challenge.

"You're on. And just for that, I'm not sharing," he said before focusing back on his project.

With the help of Cas' energy mix, I was able to power

through my notes. The concoction also helped me not be so bored studying, so things actually soaked into my brain as I read them, all of it seeming interesting now. Hopefully, he had another round for tomorrow and maybe, even for Wednesday.

The sound of The Hex Girls' 'I Put a Spell on You' playing shocked us out of our studying. I gave Xan a sly smile at his song choice before Kye and I glanced at each other, a challenging grin on both of our faces. I shoved my books away and hurried out the door, sprinting down the hall to the pantry. By the time he got in there, I was happily munching on a bag of Hex Mix.

Maybe I'll be nice and share... probably not though.

October 23rd
Wednesday afternoon
Aris

Our study night started with the Brainiac Brew from the night before, meaning we were all a bit more cheerful. Not to mention Xan, always the responsible one, brought the snacks with him. *Clearly, he's already learned how to keep me from getting cranky.*

Two successful nights of studying made me feel like the exams wouldn't be so bad. Though all of that flew out the window as soon as Professor Bellario slid an exam across my desk. I opened it and started reading, realizing she was quizzing us on the handbook instead of our individual study plans. Thankfully, we would be having a one-on-one individual exam with her after.

Thanks to Xan, I was humming The Hex Girls as I took the exam, the catchy tune actually helping me breeze through the monotonous questions. As soon as I turned it in, she pulled me aside to show her what I could do. She decided we all should be capable of simple spells, so I had to light a lantern and put it out again before using a simple communication spell to send an airplane. The latter was something I didn't realize not all Mixtas could do.

"Let's see what you've learned," Professor Bellario said in her fake voice. The more time I spent with her, the more I hated her. Focusing on holding back what I could do, I let the lantern fizzle a few times before finally lighting it, using everything in me to keep the light small and controlled. Thanks to our completed circuit, the magic was far easier to control. Before this, I probably would have exploded the poor lantern, giving us away.

"How's that?" I asked in a fake hopeful voice. She tsked for a moment as she jotted some notes.

"It's impressive for a Mixta; you could barely start a small flame before. I'd say the mentoring has done you good," she answered, something else in her voice I couldn't place.

"I've been studying hard," I promised, walking over to the papers she had laid out for the next part. I wrote a quick note, thanking her for helping me find my magic and sent it off. The paper flew around the room for a moment before dive-bombing her hair and getting stuck in the frizzy mess on top of her head. "Whoops," I said, wincing at her angry expression.

"Impressive, Miss Calisto," she said, narrowing her eyes at me suspiciously. "You're dismissed." My heart pounded in my chest as I gathered my stuff and hurried from the room. I wasn't sure if she suspected me of cheating, or if she knew I had more magic than I was showing, but either way, she was someone I needed to look out for.

October 25th
Friday afternoon
Kyelerian

The Divination technical exam was mind-numbing. Thanks to the boost of magic we all got the other night, mixed with Caspian's knack for making powerful Brainiac Brew, I was killing this round of midterms. This was the last exam I had before Familiar Studies, which I wasn't worried about in the least. Thanks to an angry little chicken, I had learned to pay better attention in class. That particular chicken was pecking away at seed I had put on the ground, occasionally hitting at my shoes, which I was sure was not an accident—*little feathered brat.*

As I filled in the last answer, I glanced at the clock on the wall, groaning inwardly when I realized I still had a thirty-minute wait. This professor was a stickler for time, making us all wait until the end of class to turn our tests in and leave.

My thoughts drifted back to the night in the cave, bonding as a group. The fact I had bonded with four other guys *for life* should probably weird me out—especially because I hate people—but it didn't. Somehow, our little ragtag band of witches seemed to work. Aris drew us all in, her cheerful personality and bubblegum pink hair so hard to get out of your head. The mere thought of her cute smile had me grinning down at my test.

What Torryn had told us about Aris being a Conduit and us being her Tethers made sense. She made us stronger, pulling out magic we hadn't known we'd had in us. After we completed the circuit, my magic settled, and it was the most balanced I had ever felt.

As class droned on, I thought over my other exams,

wondering how well I did on them. The only one I was really questioning was my history class; boring classes really aren't my strong suit.

The moment the clock tower chimed, I hurried to grab my bag, slapped my test on her desk, and booked it out of the room with Raptor at my heels. Thoughts of Samhain and spending extra time with Aris had me grinning the entire way.

October 25th
Friday early evening
Aris

My brain felt like Witches Brew gone wrong after two days of studying, followed by three days of exams, though I thought I did a lot better than I expected. Now that we were all free, I sent airplanes to the guys, hoping to round them up for a night out in Crystal Borough. I got ready as the airplanes came back, one-by-one, everyone quickly agreeing. Of course, Torryn sent back his usual response.

Man, I can't wait until we don't have to hide this anymore.

I grabbed a sweater to keep me warm and hurried out, locking the door behind me as Mr. Stripes took his usual spot on my shoulder. The guys were waiting by the front door, all of them looking more settled and happier than I'd seen them in what felt like weeks. Guilt bubbled up for a moment like an overheated cauldron, but I pushed it down, knowing it was out of my control.

"Come on, the vendors will be closing in an hour, and I'm starving," Kye complained, giving me a wink as he took my hand and led me down the main pathway. This time, our walk to town was accompanied by other students apparently having the same idea.

The Friday night vibe in Crystal Borough was energetic and fun. Musicians sat in the middle of the bazaar, playing a lively tune for the dancers surrounding them. Shoppers milled around the stores, and the smells of food and sweets permeated the air, making my stomach growl as my excitement grew.

"Where to first?" Xan asked, looking a bit overwhelmed at the activity. I took his hand in my free one, giving it a reassuring squeeze.

"Food first," Kye mumbled, already scanning the closest stalls. I laughed but didn't argue—food should always come first.

"I want to stop by this cute little shop in town before we go," I said, remembering she had a stall but preferring to see what she had in her store.

In preparation for Samhain, decorations were everywhere. Corn stalks and Fall flowers lined the streetlamps, the usual blue glow enchanted to a beautiful burgundy to fit the theme. A huge altar to the God and Goddess was near the square entrance, lined with offerings, the pristine statuettes on top adorned with silks and flowers that matched the Fall theme. A new addition to the open-air market was a vendor selling cider and Cauldron Corn, the cast iron cauldron fired up, the sugary and spicy scents completing the perfect atmosphere.

"Here," Caspian said, pulling me over to one of the fresh flower vendors, picking out an adorable floral circlet adorned with flowers and ribbon. The burnt orange, burgundy, and purple hues were gorgeous and even matched my cream-colored sweater perfectly. Once he paid for it, he adjusted it on my head, smiling down proudly. "You're as pretty as the Goddess," he whispered, sweetly kissing me once before pulling me along after Kye who was already moving toward the food.

We split up at the food vendors, everyone insisting on grabbing their own favorites. I couldn't choose, so I just followed Kye around and let him help me decide. I smiled as my eye caught Drayce and Caspian leaning close and whispering to each other, Drayce's hand casually on Cas' hip. I was sure some girls would be jealous of their closeness, but honestly, I loved it. They might like each other, but that didn't mean they felt less for me. Drayce was unapologetically himself, not afraid to show affection to both me and Caspian. I admired that. Not to mention, seeing Caspian's blush under his flirty attention was one of my favorite pastimes.

Grabbing the tray of goodies, Kye led me to the first empty table we could find. Cas and Drayce joined not long after, each with a cauldron float and a shared plate of homemade Hex Mix, which Kye immediately eyed. Xan was the last to join us, his tray full of Witch fingers, meat, and veggie kebabs that smelled amazing. We dove into our dinner, not wanting to wait for it to cool down before we were shoveling it in.

"I need to walk this off," Xan groaned, pushing his tray away as he stood. Everyone else had already finished, so we all followed him to throw our trash away before I wandered the stalls. We walked the square, browsing the stalls and joking around for close to an hour. I managed to keep my purchases contained, though I didn't want to. When I spotted the dreamcatcher that caught my eye last time still hanging in the stall, I headed straight for it and snatched it, handing my coins over, a huge grin plastered on my face as I showed it off to my guys. Before I could step away, I spotted the perfect dress for the upcoming holiday hanging on a nearby display. I hurried over, slipping expertly through the crowd until I reached the stall.

"What sizes do you have this in?" I asked excitedly, pointing to *my* dress. The witch eyed me up and down before a measuring tape flew toward me and started measuring me for her.

"Your size. You want this one?" she clarified with a smile. I nodded enthusiastically, and she chuckled, whispering something under her breath as she held the dress up. A pastel, yellow glow flared around it before slowly dissipating. "All yours," she said, taking the coins from my hand and laughing harder as I squealed excitedly and danced around as I appreciated my purchase.

I can't wait to wear this on Samhain!

"Man, it's nice seeing everyone smiling," Drayce said happily, laughing at my ridiculous dance.

"Well, I'm bonded to five sexy guys, I've got the best lemur around, and I'm finished with exams. I'd say those are all things to smile about," I teased in a low voice before heading out of the main hub toward the little shop I'd found last time.

"That's a valid point," Caspian laughed, wrapping his arm around my shoulder as we walked the less crowded side street. When I opened the door to the tiny shop, the bells tinkled overhead as the owner hurried to greet me.

"There you are! I wondered when you'd come back. Oh! You got your dreamcatcher too and a new companion! My, you have been busy," she chattered excitedly, taking my arm and leading me back to the section where she kept the human items. "I got a few new baubles in,"

"Awesome!" I said, breaking away from the guys to follow the excitable witch to the back. She held up a few items I didn't recognize, but a small square screen with buttons on the bottom caught my eye. "What's this?"

"It's a game system, kind of like those you find on a witch's glass, but it plays on that small screen. You'll have to use magic to make it work, but it's all the rage with the human kids."

"I'll take it!" I said excitedly, barely able to stop myself from checking it out in the middle of the store. I followed her to the cash register, happy with my choice. After paying and promising to come back, we headed back toward campus, everyone full, happy, and ready to wind down for the night.

"I claim Angel's room tonight. You coming, Cas?" Drayce asked, a hint of promise in his eyes. Caspian was quiet for a moment, eventually giving a determined nod.

"I'm down, plus I want to see what that game is all about," Caspian teased, looking down at the weird device in my hand.

"I'm out, you three have fun," Kye teased, not needing spelled out what Drayce had planned.

"I'm with Kye. I think I'll just head to bed early," Xan agreed with a chuckle.

When we reached campus, we split up, Xan and Kye heading for the dorms while we hurried for the pantry, wanting to grab drinks and snacks for our night of fun. I'd like to say I was excited to check out my new gadget, but I was more excited about whatever Drayce had planned.

"I'm changing first," I said as I unlocked my door, tossing my sweater on the back of the desk chair.

"Can I watch?" Caspian asked, giving me a wink. Feeling feisty and not able to step away from a challenge, I lifted my shirt over my head, depositing it on the floor before dropping my pants along with it. Their mouths dropped open in shock as I stood there in front of them in only a matching lacy bra and panties... pink, of course.

"Well, tonight took a sexy turn," Drayce mumbled, moving toward me as his eyes roved over my exposed skin. "You're fucking gorgeous, Angel."

"I couldn't agree more," Caspian mumbled, moving around my back and sweeping my hair out of the way so he could place a kiss behind my ear. "I think you've still got too much on."

"I think you two do," I mocked, folding my arms across my chest, Drayce's eyes zeroing in on me as the action pushed up my breasts even more.

"That's an easy fix," Drayce said playfully, moving around me to take Caspian's hand, pulling him forward. My mouth went dry as I watched him take the hem of Cas' Henley, pulling it slowly over his head. Caspian's cheeks tinted pink again, but he didn't protest, his eyes locking on mine, full of heat, excitement, and a hint of trepidation. His lips quirked up in a smirk as he watched me clench my thighs together before turning and facing Drayce. Drayce paused for a moment, looking a little taken aback at his boldness, but it didn't last long before he pulled Caspian closer. Heat flooded my body as I watched Caspian take a deep breath and lean in for a kiss. Drayce was reserved, letting Caspian lead at his own pace. My heart warmed at how thoughtful Drayce was, never pushing, always a gentleman under all his flirting.

Cas seemed to grow bolder as the kiss went on, his hand coming up to cup Drayce's jaw as the other rested on his hip. Heat flooded my core as I watched them—seeing the two of them together like this was even hotter than the fantasies I'd cooked up.

When they broke the kiss, Caspian rested his forehead

against Drayce, his shoulders no longer tense, a lighthearted chuckle bubbling out of him. I loved that he was letting himself get comfortable with us and more importantly, himself.

"What about you, Cupcake, what do you want?" Caspian asked, looking at me.

"I already told you, I want you both naked," I declared, quirking an eyebrow at them in challenge. Drayce pulled his shirt off quickly before unbuttoning Caspian's pants and letting them drop to the floor, then quickly moving on to his own. Cas shrugged out of his own underwear, kicking them aside and moving toward me. Drayce took a long look at Caspian's ass as he moved away, a sexy smirk adorning his lips.

Caspian unhooked my bra as Drayce slowly moved my panties down, their hands roving over my skin. Feeling both of their hands on me had me so turned-on, I felt my legs go weak.

"Angel, on the bed," Drayce ordered, ushering me to my bed. I settled on my back, following his orders, my eyes glued to his.

"Caspian, can I touch you?"

"Yes," Caspian agreed quickly, no hesitation in his response, only heat.

"Then come over here with me," he said, trailing his fingertips over Caspian's hard cock. Caspian let out a shiver of pleasure as Drayce moved away, quickly following behind. Drayce grabbed my legs and pulled me toward the edge of the bed before hitching one leg over his shoulder and placing a kiss on my inner thigh. Caspian was within his reach, so his fingers wrapped easily around Cas' cock, pumping his hand over him as his tongue licked along my folds. My eyes fluttered closed at the sensation, but I forced them open, needing to see what was unfolding between my two boyfriends. Cas' eyes locked on mine as Drayce worked him over, his moans mixing with mine. Drayce was a fantastic multitasker, his tongue never stopping its assault, thrusting into my core at the same pace he moved his hand, bringing us both to the edge.

"Drayce, you need to stop," Cas warned, his voice husky with need.

Drayce gave one last thrust before he turned his attention fully to me. *Holy hellsticks*, watching him move his mouth up and graze his teeth over my throbbing clit as he pushed two fingers inside of me, pumping them while he sucked me into his mouth was hot as sin and made me melt into a puddle of pure need. It didn't take long for my orgasm to crash through me, my legs shaking around him as pleasure swirled through me, and I cried out with my release.

"Caspian, sit against the headboard," Drayce ordered again, his eyes darkening when Cas answered with a 'Yes, sir.' "I think our boyfriend over here needs some attention, don't you agree, Angel?"

I nodded, moving out of Caspian's way before shifting toward him, my mouth wrapping around his cock. Caspian's hands moved to my hair, winding it around his hand, holding me tight as I moved my tongue along his cock, bobbing my head slowly, wanting this to last. I felt the bed dip as Drayce moved behind us, my pussy aching with need as he settled in, his cock pressing against my entrance. He thrust in slowly, giving my body time to adjust before he started to move faster, setting the pace for me and Caspian, as well. Being with both of them was one of the most exciting things I'd done, their moans mixing with mine as we pleasured each other.

"I'm coming," Cas warned, his fist tightening in my hair,

the slight sting turning me on even more as I continued to move my mouth over him. As he came, Drayce reached around, moving his hand between us, teasing my clit. The simple touch was enough to throw me into orgasm with Caspian, my body tightening around Drayce as Caspian filled my mouth. I swallowed him down as Drayce found his own release, pumping into me as he relaxed against my back.

I pulled away from Caspian, my breath coming out in pants as I came down from the high of my orgasm. Drayce pulled out of me before grabbing a nearby towel and cleaning me. Caspian repositioned himself, so he was lying on the bed properly before I snuggled into his side. Drayce came back to bed, curling around my back as we all soaked in the moment.

My first time with them both couldn't have been more perfect. Drayce was gentle with us, guiding us into it slowly, making sure we all enjoyed the experience. I loved the way they looked at each other, realizing it was the same kind of look they gave me. Honestly, everything about them and this was just perfect.

Holy hellsticks, how did I get so lucky?

CHAPTER 21

October 29th
Tuesday Midday
Aris

I could barely contain my excitement as the cart rattled down the cobblestones, the wheels crunching over fallen leaves as cool air entered the space. It was crazy to think, just two months ago I was leaving Ignis, and here I was, happy and falling for five amazing guys on my way to enjoy my first Samhain festival—really enjoying it. All the previous festivals had been clouded by my parents' constant need to push me aside. *It's hard to enjoy something when you feel like an outcast.* I rolled my eyes at my family's insanity and turned back to my guys, loving the wide smiles on each of their faces as they watched the passing scenery, the familiars looking just as happy as their witches.

This is what true happiness is, I realized, curling into Xan's side, his arm coming to settle on my shoulder. He had lightened up, smiling almost all the time now as he had grown more into himself these last couple months and out of the 'councilman's son' mold he had been forced to live in.

As the cart entered the main gates of Divus, I couldn't peel my eyes away from it. It was like an entirely new world, nothing like Crystal Borough. The streets were bricked, unlike the shaky cobblestone of the other towns I'd seen. The buildings and homes were close together, the small stone structures adorned with colorful shutters and thatched rooftops. The buildings started to look more uniform and sleeker as we rode further in and were spaced out reasonably here, instead of being built stacked one on top of the other. One loomed above the others, a large building with shiny brass encasing the dome on top of the stone structure. It was eye-catching and imposing but beautiful.

At the center of the city stood a large fountain—a detailed carving of the Goddess with water flowing from her hands into the basin below. The fountain was carved from a beautiful stone with rivets of inlaid amethyst. The sun caught the jeweled veins perfectly, giving the flowers and trees around it a beautiful purple glow.

Everywhere I turned there were Fall-colored flowers and ribbons adorning every surface, window, and pole, giving the whole town the perfect Samhain feel. They wouldn't be setting up the booths and festival fully until tomorrow, so travelers could move through the streets. Everything here seemed so colorful and lively, and I couldn't wait to graduate so I could move somewhere exciting like this.

"Sweets? You might want to close your mouth, you're drooling," Kye teased. I gave him a playful glare, but that was all the time I'd give him, more interested in soaking in everything I possibly could.

"Just wait until tomorrow when we look around, it's going to seem like a whole new world!" Xan said, letting out a relaxed laugh as he smiled over at me. He seemed content just to watch me as I experienced it all, the smile on his face spreading wider.

The carriage finally came to a stop outside a tall, gray brick building. The doorman ran forward as soon as the cart stopped moving, trying to reach us before we could open it ourselves. Two more doormen stepped out, levitating our luggage and leading us inside. Xan stepped up to the counter, insisting we wait for him in the main lobby.

The inn itself was gorgeous, a huge candlelit chandelier hanging above a plush woven rug. The tile gleamed under the glow from floating lanterns, and the walls were adorned with murals and paintings that seemed to come alive the longer you stared at them.

The staff fawned over Xan for a while before he finally escaped their attention. His shoulders were tense as he walked back to us, his entire demeanor screaming he was back to being the councilman's son. My smile dimmed for a moment before I caught myself, fixing it before he could approach.

"I got us a suite, so there are three bedrooms and a common room. The restaurant down here is included in the room price, so we can have dinner here and relax tonight if you want," Xan said and even his voice was stiff.

"Who body-snatched you?" Drayce mumbled as we all dutifully followed him upstairs. I gave a shrug, knowing he was back in his former element and appearances had to be upheld—that didn't mean I had to like it.

The doormen opened the door and stepped aside,

letting me walk in first. As much as I'd seen today, my mouth still hung open in awe as I looked around. Our room was fancy, having a common room with huge fluffy couches, a food and drink bar, and a balcony with what seemed like an incredible view. The lanterns in here were glowing a bright blue, giving the room a cozy glow.

I claimed the first room I opened since it had only one bed. *The guys can fight over what's left.* Plus, I would have an entire bathroom to myself, and I wanted to dress up for tomorrow's festivities. By the time I stepped back out, everyone had already claimed their beds and the doormen had left, leaving us in peace. At least Xan seemed a bit more relaxed again, my happy boyfriend back. Our familiars all settled in along the fluffy rug, nestling together in a pile of fluff, feathers, and sass.

"We still have an hour or so until dinner. If you guys want a snack, they're complementary," Xan said, pointing out the snack bar. "I have to call my father, or he'll come find me. Nobody wants to hang out with a high councilman all evening."

"Do you want some company?" I asked quietly, feeling awful he was in such a rough place.

"Nah, I'm just going to go onto the balcony," he said with a smile, stepping out and closing the door behind him.

"Don't worry, Angel," Drayce said quietly as I stared at Xan's turned back. "He'll be fine, and we'll learn to adjust when his family is around. Until then, you better hurry if you want to snag that honeyed Hex Mix," he whispered conspiratorially. I lunged for the bag, snatching it as Kye approached, his answering scowl worth the extra effort.

"That's just plain rude," Kye grumbled, reaching for a box of moon cookies instead. Feeling generous, I grabbed a drink cup and poured some in before handing the bag over.

"Don't be so dramatic, I can share… sometimes," I joked, taking a bite and flopping down on the couch.

"This place is so nice. It's hard to find a room for Samhain. I'm glad Xan has connections. Everyone from school is across town at the big hotels. I like this place way more," Caspian added, flopping down next to me on the couch, resting his head in my lap. I absently played with his russet locks as I munched on my snack. My eyes flickered back to Xan every few moments, watching as he paced back-and-forth and ran his hands through his hair, sure signs he was struggling with the conversation.

Xan stayed on the phone for close to an hour, the rest of us getting restless in the meantime. It felt wrong not having Torryn here with us, but at least he was staying with some of the faculty in the same building, instead of across town.

"I'm going to get ready for dinner," I said, finally standing up and stretching. "Once he's done, we can head down. We only have thirty minutes before they open."

Since the place was so fancy, I wanted to dress up a bit. I grabbed a pretty, deep purple lace dress before starting on simple makeup. Sure, I could probably use a charm to do it, but I loved to do mine by hand, just like my hair. Once my smoky eyeshadow and deep purple lipstick were in place, I slipped on my black heels and went off in search of the others.

A catcall rang out from the open balcony door where Drayce was leaning against the railing as he chatted with Kye, both dressed in black pants and button-downs, looking classy and sexy as hell. Kye even styled his dark hair a bit, giving me a better view of his gold speckled eyes.

"You like it?" I asked with a grin, spinning slowly, so the skirt flared out a bit. It was one of those outfits that made me feel beautiful.

"You look sexy," Kye said in a low voice as his eyes slowly moved down my form. I grinned back at him, feeling even more confident thanks to their attention. Cas and Xan walked out a few minutes later, both looking equally delicious as the others.

"Look at us, all looking perfectly respectable," I joked, taking Xan's extended elbow as he led me out of the suite and down to the dining room like a true gentleman. Waving a quick goodbye, I left Mr. Stripes lounging with the other familiars.

Walking in with Xan made me feel like a celebrity with the way everyone whispered and talked when we entered; even a picture or two was taken as we stopped at the hostess stand. As soon as the staff recognized him, we were whisked off to the back of the restaurant, getting a private room for our group. It actually gave me a glimpse of what kind of life he lived before us, his stuffy, boring demeanor making a whole lot more sense now.

"Welcome, Mr. Eideann, your other party is already here," the hostess said as she opened the door to the private room. My heart sank as I realized what she'd done, and Xan's arm tensed under mine.

"We would like a normal table, please," he said, stopping her from opening it the rest of the way.

"Oh... but your father insisted," she said in a wavering voice, her hands starting to wring together as she looked up at him.

"This will be fine, we can handle it, right, guys?" I said quickly, looking to the others for confirmation. They all put on their serious faces, giving me a determined nod, knowing this would probably be the first of many we'd have to go through. With a sad sigh, I let go of Xan's arm and stepped back to stand in line with the others, knowing his father wouldn't approve of his son being with a Mixta.

We can address that in the future.

Xan started to protest, but I gave him a firm nod, and he gave up with a sigh. Gesturing for her to open, he squared his shoulders and led our group in. A woman who looked like Xan stood, rushing around the table and air-kissing his cheeks. I almost expected her to embrace him, but she simply patted his cheek and gave him a soft smile before returning to her seat. His father was easy to spot, a stoic expression on his face, looking like a sterner version of Xan. The others at the table stood and bowed to Xan before taking their seats. His father simply gave the rest of us a calculated stare.

"Xanthius, care to do an introduction?" he asked, his deep voice holding such a bold command, I almost saluted.

"Of course, Father. My apologies. This is Kyelerian, a Rune Drawer, Caspian, a Potions affinity, Drayce, a Summoner, and Aris Calisto," he said, wincing as he added my last name, but honestly, it was his best option to deal with this.

"Ah, Calisto. You must be Councilman Calisto's daughter?" Xan's dad asked, eyeing me before nodding slightly.

"Yes, sir," I said quickly, internally praying he didn't ask *why* I was here and not at school in Ignis, so I gave him the most diplomatic answer I could think of off the top of my head. "They thought me going to school here would be a better fit and broaden my options for the future."

"Being this close to the capital didn't hurt, did it?" he asked, this time a hint of a smile on his face, shocking the hellsticks out of me. "There's a reason we sent Xanthius to Aether Academy."

"This is Councilman Altermin and his wife, Sircey," Xan introduced, trying to drag the conversation away from us.

"It's a pleasure to meet you. Thank you for offering us to join you in your private room. It was a kind and appreciated gesture," I gushed, giving my best smile and taking the seat Kye pulled out for me. We all sat, looking over the menu, not bothering to hold a conversation. The other table started discussing something about a new law they were planning to introduce.

Dinner was excruciatingly slow, but thankfully, the conversation was much less intense when we were all finished. It didn't hurt that the food was delicious, down to the chocolate tart I was convinced was infused with some kind of charm to make it even tastier.

The only rough part was the dinner took so much longer than normal, leaving us no time for any other plans. We all decided our best option was to go to sleep early and spend tomorrow exploring the town.

I hope Xan can handle being here with his dad and doesn't lose the Xan I'm falling in love with.

October 30th
Wednesday Morning
Aris

The next morning at breakfast, Xan was still tense, which threw the others off as well. I nibbled on my toast and considered what to do about it, but after the fifth one-word answer, I'd had enough.

"Nope... nope, this isn't happening. We played the game last night, but this weekend is about fun and relaxation. You need to push aside that unemotional side of yourself and give us Xan back. We are going to go to the pumpkin festival today, carve pumpkins, and enjoy Samhain," I said firmly, his eyes flying open in surprise at my outburst.

"I have to agree. I don't care much for Xanthius... but Xan, I like," Caspian said, giving him a nudge with his elbow. Xan nodded, letting out a breath as some of the tension left his shoulders.

"Sorry, old habits die hard, I guess. I'm definitely fine with having fun. Thank you for last night though. You won over my father, and that's not easy to do."

"What can I say? I'm a charmer," I teased, grinning like a fool at the prospect of actually carving a pumpkin. My family wasn't much for *messier* activities.

"Come on, it's only a block away," Caspian said excitedly as he showed us the map they'd handed out at the front desk with all the major locations and activities listed. We followed his lead as he left the dining hall, stopping only long enough for Xan to tell the front desk we'd be out for the day. As soon as I stepped into the crisp autumn air, my stress melted away.

We left early enough the crowds were thin, mainly families with young children making their way to the pumpkin patch with us. All the kids were pointing to our familiars, the odd assortment catching a lot of eyes. I couldn't help but grin as they cooed over at our little companions. Even broody Kye looked like he was having fun, grinning down at me as I intertwined my fingers with his and led him ahead.

"Pumpkins first," I declared, already leading Kye over to the rows of pumpkins in the field. We veered off to the side, not wanting to pick the first rows of pumpkins or right alongside the families. They continued to dart around the different sizes and shapes of pumpkins in chase, squeaking and chirping to each other as they played tag.

"Look," Drayce called, lifting a perfectly round pumpkin, after magically separating the vine. "I've got mine! Now I've got nothing to do but wait for you slowpokes," he teased. After a moment, his eyes lit up with a wicked gleam, and he continued, "That's okay though, I'll just wait here and check out Caspian's ass as he bends over to find his pumpkin."

"It's a pretty fantastic ass," I agreed, giving it a smack as I passed him. His cheeks tinged pink again as he turned his back to Drayce and did a shimmy before smacking his own ass and cracking up. I was glad Cas was starting to retaliate to the flirting, especially as I watched Drayce's eyes light up at the returned teasing. A memory of our night together popped into my mind, making my own cheeks heat up. *Easy girl!*

"I like this one," Xan said, picking up a pumpkin that was a bit odd. It had swirls of green and orange as if it was confused on what to grow into and stayed that way. It was artsy and perfect for him.

Caspian was being picky, choosing one before setting it back down and moving on. Which only gave Drayce more chances to quietly catcall and tease him. Kye let go of my hand so he could choose a bit easier. I took the opportunity to wander down the rows of pumpkins, waiting for one to catch my eye.

The others were finished by the time I found mine. Cas chose an oblong pumpkin he was oddly proud of while Kye picked one almost too big to carry. The one I found was completely white with a twisted stem. It reminded me of something out of a fairytale story.

"Isn't the hotel a bit fancy to be scooping out pumpkin guts?" Caspian asked with a chuckle.

"Um, YES!" Xan exclaimed, looking half startled at the very thought of it. "They have a section for that here." He pointed out a row of tables to the side of the patch, just for prepping and carving. They even had a witch separating out the pumpkin seeds next to a huge kettle so she could roast them. The smell of roasting seeds wafted over as we approached. By the time we'd found our spot, it was starting to get a lot more crowded. I picked up one of the spelled daggers from the table and started to carve the pumpkin, using my magic to lift out the guts and deposit them into the pail they provided. Once the inside was cleaned, the witch came by to collect them to clean and roast. I agreed happily, my stomach rumbling at the idea while I watched the knife carve out a perfect depiction of my favorite fuzzy lemur. He squeaked proudly when it finished, clearly recognizing himself.

With handfuls of carved pumpkins and roasted seeds, we made our way back to the inn an hour later to drop them off. Drayce was insisting we check out the magical circus that was in town. It was the one thing I'd seen enough of as a kid, but I refused to say that to him, he was too happy. Plus, it wasn't my guys' fault my parents had made us go each year, then forced me to sit a bit away from them. I would swear most of their friends probably thought they only had three kids, not four.

Pushing the wave of negative thoughts away, I followed them up to our room, setting our loot on the table before heading back out. Picking up on my mood, Caspian hung back and tugged on my hand, forcing me to stop.

"What's the matter, Cupcake?" he asked, his brows furrowing as he studied my face.

"No worries. It's just the circus doesn't hold the best memories for me. It'll be fine, please don't say anything. We can make new memories," I said in a pseudo-cheerful voice, pulling him out the door with the others.

"There you are, Gorgeous," Torryn's voice said from behind me, his hand trailing down my back as he joined us. "Where are we headed?"

"To the circus," Drayce answered excitedly. "You finally joining us?"

"Hell yes, I am," he said, his hand still moving over me until it rested on my lower back, teasing the band of my jeans.

"Actually, I forgot something upstairs," I said, giving Torryn a pointed look. Cas snorted, clearly catching on.

"I can run back up with you," Torryn offered, picking up on my meaning as well.

Caspian surprised me, giving a smile and a wave.

"We'll meet you there," he said quickly, giving me a wink before putting his arm around Drayce's shoulder and leading him away, leaning close to whisper something in his ear, probably explaining what was happening.

I owe him some serious snuggle time later.

As soon as we hit the hallway upstairs, Torryn stepped forward and nipped at my lip, excitement and anticipation dancing in his eyes. When he slowly moved his kisses down my neck, I let out a small moan, fumbling for the room key as I tried to coax him to our room.

Laughter echoed down the hall as a group of witches turned the corner. We pulled apart as if we were on fire, trying to look innocent as Tor tried to hide the obvious bulge in his pants. I noticed a few people in the group, including Delilah, who gave me a small wave, looking from me to Torryn. *Shit, she definitely noticed.* I returned the wave, and they continued walking, not letting myself relax until they were out of sight.

"You think they noticed anything suspicious?" I asked, worried I just got him in major trouble.

"I don't give a fuck. This isn't high school, we're adults. I kept it out of the school, but I've decided I want you, and I shouldn't have to treat you like a dirty little secret. I should be able to spend time with you outside of class how I want," he said firmly, capturing my lips once more.

I pulled away long enough to unlock the door and close it behind us. Torryn took the click of the door closing as invitation not to waste time, pulling his shirt over his head and pulling me close. Our lips crashed together in a flurry of long-awaited kisses, my skin practically buzzing with the anticipation of what was about to happen.

My hands roamed down Torryn's chiseled body as our tongues danced together. I broke the kiss long enough to rip my shirt over my head, Torryn's hands snaking behind me and unhooking my bra before I even had the chance. His eyes moved slowly over my body, the desperation giving way to reverence. He moved closer, tucking a piece of pink hair behind my ear as he stared into my eyes, his seafoam depths showing me how much he wanted and cared about me. Heat burned my cheeks at his attention, but I was too turned-on to care about the flush of pink. My fingers moved to the button on his pants, quickly undoing and sliding them down, taking his boxers with them.

I looked up at him from under my lashes, giving a sexy grin before falling to my knees and wrapping my lips around his cock. My hand moved over the silky skin as I bobbed my head over him, taking him further into my mouth with each pass. His deep groan had my own arousal practically dripping down my thighs as I swirled my tongue over him, teasing him to the point of losing control.

My eyes drifted up to his, the heat flaring in them as he watched me made the moment even sexier than it was a moment ago. Every flowerpot in the room exploded with life, distracting me for a moment before I moved my tongue away from him, swirling it over his abs as I stood. *I've always wanted to do that, and it was hard to resist the dips and cuts in his muscled torso.*

Torryn was done playing games, bringing his lips back to mine as I stood, backing me toward the bed. In one swift movement, he picked me up and threw me onto the soft mattress, giggles bubbling out of me as I landed. Heat flooded me at the predatory look on his face as he crawled onto the bed, slowly moving his body over mine.

"I feel like this is a bit unfair here," he teased, pulling the rest of my clothes off, every movement deliberately slow and calculated as he took his time with me. I wanted more, and I wanted it now, but I fought with myself to find patience, knowing Torryn had to wait this long, and now, it was my turn to wait. *Wouldn't want to spoil his fun.*

Tossing my clothes haphazardly to the side, he peppered kisses over me, starting at my feet and moving up my body, pausing only to take one peaked nipple into his mouth, grazing his teeth over it and sending a shiver of pleasure down my spine. His other hand moved up to tease the other, pulling a moan from my lips. I was lost in sensations, needing more but loving the attention he gave me, my pleasure building as he continued his torturous teasing.

His hand slid down my body until he reached my slick core, my legs falling open for him as I tangled my hands in his hair, bringing him in for another kiss. He pumped his fingers inside of me, capturing my moans with a kiss.

"I could listen to that sound all day," he groaned, moving his thumb over my clit, making me moan even louder. I rocked my hips into his hand as he moved his fingers faster, my building orgasm making me lightheaded with its intensity. He moved away from my lips, nibbling on my ear as he whispered, "Come for me, Gorgeous."

His encouragement was the final push, my body following his heated command as pleasure rolled through me like a tidal wave. He continued pumping his fingers while my body pulsed around him, shaking with the intensity of my release. *Holy hellsticks, that was amazing.*

Wrapping his hands around my waist, he pulled me with him as he rolled. Knowing what he needed, I sat up, positioning myself over him before slowly sinking down. We both moaned as he filled me, my body already sensitive from his previous ministrations. Moving over him, I loved how powerful and sexy this position made me feel. His fingers moved over my body, teasing my nipples as he watched me fuck him. Leaning forward slightly, I braced my hands on his chest as I moved faster, hitting the perfect spot.

He took over as my movements faltered, gripping my hips as he guided me, throwing me into a second orgasm. Torryn thrust up into me in a frenzy before he tensed underneath me, his muscles rippling as he came. Neither of us spoke for a moment, reveling in the sensation of coming down from the high before I moved off him. I'd barely started to catch my breath before he sat up and pulled me with him to the adjoining bathroom, fiddling with the knobs quickly.

"Let's clean you up, so I can make you dirty all over again," he teased, pulling me into the hot shower he'd prepared for us.

How could I refuse an offer like that?

CHAPTER 22

October 31st
Thursday Afternoon
Aris

I hummed as I put on my black lipstick, using a glittery gloss over the top to complete my Samhain look. The dress I bought at the market the other night fit perfectly, the skirt flaring out with a layer of pale pink tulle lining the bottom. It matched the pale pink dreamcatcher design that adorned the top. I loved the cheesy, traditional design of the dress.

With one last look in the mirror, I was finally happy with the look. The others were once again waiting on me, but they didn't seem to mind. *I'm a lucky girl.* After a perfect evening with Torryn, I couldn't keep the happy grin off my face.

"The council hall courtyard is where they hold the harvest dance and main celebration. We need to get there early if we want any chance of getting close enough to enjoy it," Kye reminded us, already heading for the door, holding it open.

"True, and the vendors are still out, so we'll have something to do to pass the time," Drayce agreed as he picked up the map from the counter.

"I just want to show off that we have the hottest witch in the entire city," Caspian said proudly, checking me out, ending his perusal with a smirk.

"I can't argue with that," Xan said, pulling me close as he walked by, kissing me with enough passion to leave me weak in the knees. Seeing him let loose more since that dinner was even more satisfying. Knowing the positivity we brought into his life was a stronger force than his parents' negative one was gratifying.

"Before we go, we got you something," Kye said, the others grinning stupidly, which only had me bouncing on my toes in excitement. Extending his open hand, a small pink box with a white bow on top rested in his palm. I snatched it from him with a squeal, untying the bow and ripping it open. Resting on a small bed of satin fabric was a rose gold necklace with a small pumpkin charm dangling from the dainty chain.

"Guys! I love this so much!" The small necklace was perfect, a symbol to remind me of my first Samhain with the guys. I pulled it out of the box and put it on, my eyes getting blurry with tears before I blinked them away again.

"We couldn't resist," Xan said with a smile, looking down proudly at the jewelry they'd chosen.

The fact they were able to choose it together and get along perfectly meant more to me than anything.

"Alright, alright, let's go!" Kye grumbled, though I could see how happy he was under his broody mask. We hurried through town, the crowds already thick, holding our familiars, so they didn't get lost in the crush of people. Just as we reached the entrance to the courtyard, I reached up to touch my charm, only to find the necklace empty.

"My charm!" I cried out, letting go of Caspian's hand and slipping into the crowd, my eyes trained on the ground as I retraced my steps. I heard the guys calling my name, but they'd have to wait, my mind solely focused on finding my gift as tears threatened to fall. The little golden pumpkin sparkled in the sun, the crowd parting just enough for it to catch on my fallen trinket. With a relieved gasp, I dove forward and snatched it up, reattaching it quickly, making sure it was secure this time.

When I finally looked up at the crowd passing me, I realized I was on the edge of an alley, not one of my guys in sight. Just as I stepped forward to find them in the courtyard, rough hands yanked me backward, my head smacking sharply against the stone wall behind me. As I groaned and turned, a painful blast hit me in the back of the head, my vision fading as I was plunged into darkness.

Not again...

October 31st
Thursday Night
Aris

Everything hurt, my limbs alternating between painful tingles and numbness. When I tried to move them, I found I couldn't, and the pain only grew as I pulled. Groaning slightly, I peeked my eyes open. *What the hellsticks happened?*

"What the..." I murmured, the two whispered words rough and accompanied by pain. A wall of tears filled my vision from the sharp pain, but I pushed it away until I could see around me. It was dark, save for the small flickers of candlelight that danced across the ceiling, illuminating the cobwebs and dust that coated the corners and walls. Turning my head slowly, in an attempt not to aggravate the thudding in my head, I looked left to right, finding myself secured to a large black stone. When my eyes focused on what was holding me to the cold surface, I realized they were chains which had a spike on each chain. Every time I moved, the spike dug a little more into the inside of my wrists and ankles. Adrenaline flooded my body along with the quickly increasing thudding that echoed through my head. The pain was only overshadowed by the adrenaline starting to surge, triggering my fight-or-flight instincts.

"Aris Calisto," a soft girly voice called out in the darkened room, but no matter how much I looked around, I couldn't see who was speaking. "Daughter of a well-off elemental family and yet, *somehow,* just a Mixta. A disappointment."

"Who are you? Show yourself!" I whispered as loud as my voice would allow. *Something* definitely *burned my throat, but I'll be damned if I let whoever this is see me cry. I need to try to figure out what the hellsticks is happening.*

"I wasn't finished talking!" The voice hardened, whipping sharp and fast through the room. "As I was saying, a Mixta with no successful affinity and yet, somehow, manages to land the attention of several male witches, including Torryn Callahan Kersey."

Tilting my head back, I finally spotted who was talking.
Delilah.

"What?" I mumbled, my brain short-circuiting from all the questions floating around my mind, and instead of asking one of the ones that might prolong whatever plans she had or give me answers, I went with 'What?' *Why am I like this?*

"Goddess, you are so stupid sometimes. I don't know how you ever caught Torry's attention," she hissed, looking at me with disgust.

Torry? Is she serious right now?

"Is that what this is about? Torryn?" I asked, finally relaxing slightly against the stone as she sauntered around the stone slab. Despite being scared, my limbs trembled slightly with the dump of adrenaline. I kept my face flat, unwilling to show her any emotion.

"Don't say his name!" she screamed, her eyes widening as she snarled at me. In her anger, her normal light blue eyes tinted red. "You don't get to say his name, you little useless Mixta!" she ranted. Fear overpowered the adrenaline, and it took everything in my power to keep myself from trying to yank my arms and legs from the makeshift bear traps they were locked in.

"Alright," I soothed, "I won't. But are you going to tell me what this is about?"

After a few tense moments, she seemed to get a grip of herself, her demeanor changing like a flip of a switch, and suddenly, I was looking at the Delilah I knew from my classes.

"I suppose I should. It's not going to matter much longer, anyway." She gave a disinterested shrug, continuing circling down to my feet.

Her words iced my veins, and my eyes darted around, trying to find any possible way out of this.

"Well, why should a useless witch like yourself catch the attention of a man such as Torry? He deserves someone who is on the same level of intelligence and power, someone who can not only warm his bed but also hold more of a conversation with him than a dimwit like you."

She opened her mouth to continue when I heard a familiar little screech sound from the corner of the room. My head snapped up, my vision dimming slightly at the jarring movement before I saw my familiar crammed into a dingy metal cage, hunched into a little ball to fit. Mr. Stripes' screeching only got louder as our connection flared. I saw red when I realized he must have been knocked out as well.

If she hurt my baby, I'm going to give her a taste of her own medicine.

With that thought, I tried to pull forward my elemental magic, but the clasps around my wrists and ankles flared bright red, the heated metal searing my skin. I couldn't hold back my scream as I involuntarily tried to flail away from the contraptions and accidentally dug the spikes further into my sensitive, burned skin.

"Tsk, tsk," she cooed, shaking her head as a concerned mother would. "Trying to use your powers on me is a big no-no, Aris. I suggest you don't do that again... Damn it all to hex with you, you infuriating fleabag," she snapped at Mr. Stripes who had started to scream again. Kicking out, she smacked the cage into the wall, the metal rattling as it collided with the broken plaster and back onto the ground.

"No!" I called out, my voice barely audible against my lemur's whimpers. "I'll get him to be quiet," I pleaded. She glanced over at me with a pensive expression and pursed lips before finally nodding with a wave of her hand toward the cage.

"By all means, please do, I can't stand to listen to that infernal screaming."

I almost cried with relief. Looking over at Mr. Stripes, I tried as hard as I could to mentally convey he needed to stay quiet. As if he understood, he dipped his furry head and stopped making noise. I breathed a sigh of relief as I relaxed against the stone. *Now that was handled, time to figure out how to get the bat out of hell.*

"Now, that better be the last interruption," she huffed haughtily, tossing her hair over her shoulder. "You, *Aris*, stole Torry from me."

I wasn't sure if it was slowly impending unconsciousness, hysteria, or straight up stupidity like she said, but I laughed—so hard and loud, my laughing was no longer audible, and tears streamed freely from my eyes. *Torry. Oh, my broomsticks, to see Tor's face if she called him that...*

"Shut up!" she raged, and finally, unable to handle my chortling, she strode over to my left side and smashed the spike into my wrist.

My chuckles turned to silent screams as I felt the metal pierce my skin and embed in bone. Warm, deep red rivulets poured freely from my wrist onto the stone, the dark surface illuminating in glowing red runes as soon as my blood touched the material.

"Ah, there we go, the whole reason we're here."

"What... are you... doing to... me?" I barely breathed out, my mind suddenly growing foggy, my eyelids slowly closing as if I wanted to sleep for a million years. I forced myself to stay awake, envisioning my guys' faces, chanting their names in my mind, trying to stay grounded.

"Well, if my love wants to toss around with you instead of me, then I'll just become you," she exclaimed simply with a cocky smile. "I might look like a Mixta, but I'll still have my powers. Moving things with my mind certainly wouldn't hurt either," she hummed, proud of herself as she pulled an athame from under her ugly, pink argyle sweater and eyed my restrained form with a blood-red gleam and unrestrained delight.

Oh, fuck.

Torryn

The festival was in full swing, witches singing, dancing, and overall, extremely cheery. While I'd finally had a taste of Aris, all I wanted was more. *Fuck that she's my student or I'm a teacher, she means more to me than a magical bond or the tenuous situation of me maintaining a professional image.* She was my girl, and all I wanted at that moment was her soft skin under me, her lips locked with mine, and my cock buried in her perfect pussy. *Ugh*, I groaned, discreetly adjusting myself as blood rushed between my legs, hardening in less than a second thinking about Aris spread out in front of me.

Ruby perked up, her little head swiveling back-and-forth, which immediately put me on edge. There had only been one other time this had happened, and it had turned out Aris had been hexed. She bounced up and down on my shoulder, nudging my head to the left where I saw the rest of the group collecting at the edge of the crowded city square.

"What's going on?" I questioned when I reached them, my voice low to not draw attention. They all looked as panicked as I felt, our familiars nudging us in a specific direction until suddenly they stopped.

"I think it's safe to assume something is happening to Aris. Wasn't she with you guys? Who was the last to see her?" I questioned in anger. *I can't believe they lost Aris. How hard is it to keep track of a witch with pink hair!*

"She pulled back from me just a few minutes ago, something about her charm necklace. We've been trying to find her in this crowd," Caspian explained, his eyes wide with fear. Biting back the urge to snap at him, I looked toward our familiars.

"Well, clearly, something is wrong, so we split up and find an official guardsman," I commanded. "Xan, you take Caspian and Drayce. Kye, you're with me. Meet back here in ten minutes if the animals don't pick up another trail."

Splitting up, we scoured the crowds, but no matter how hard Kye and I looked, we couldn't find a guardsman in the crush of people. Glancing at the clock, a wave of panic filled me as we neared the ten-minute mark, but before we started back to the meeting spot, Ruby and Raptor started up again. *Please let the others have found some sort of help.* I pushed through the crowd in the direction the familiars led us. It only took a few minutes for all of us reach it, Xan leading a set of four guardsmen, but the relief was short-lived because as soon as we entered the house, a manic laughter reached our ears.

I darted down the hall, my only focus on getting Aris, and when I burst into the room, my instincts took over. Shouting a binding spell, I threw my hand out toward the figure standing next to a large slab in the center of the room. Time slowed as my brain processed what I was seeing—Aris unconscious and bleeding out onto a rune-carved altar and a disfigured Delilah Thana bound and lying on the floor screaming. I had to swallow the bile I felt rising in my throat when I realized the reason she looked so disfigured was half of her face had started to look like Aris', and half of her messy brown hair turned into a cotton candy pink.

The guardsmen darted forward, two going to Delilah, securing a pair of power-dampening handcuffs on her while the other two safely maneuvered Aris off the stone slab. Mr. Stripes' screeching filled the space, and Caspian ran around the room to where Aris' lemur was caged. Grating metal sounds filled the space until I saw the fluffy black-and-white striped tail puff up into the air. Before going to Aris as I expected, he scurried over to Delilah and pounced on her, clawing at her face with a blood-curdling scream.

My lips curled into a smug smirk, leisurely walking over to the crazed lemur before pulling him off her, not caring in the slightest her face was now back to normal, albeit cut up. *I noticed the guards didn't move to stop him, either.*

"Come on, let's go see Aris," I cooed softly, my nerves rattled and frayed, but I stayed grounded as I stepped up to our girl. "Here you go, Mr. Stripes." He gingerly crawled up onto her chest, his little hands patting her cheeks, but she remained unconscious as the healers I hadn't seen arrive loaded her up onto a wheeled cot.

"What in the hells bells and tarot tells was going on here?" Kye asked quietly, eyeing the table and the discarded potion bottle on the floor. "These are some very dark runes, and I only recognize one or two."

"She was trying to morph herself into Aris," Drayce explained, his upper lip curling back in disgust as he pointed to the glass bottle. "Even used a Flame's Ignition potion, for what, I'm not sure, but that's a nasty piece of work to use on someone."

"It looks like she used it to burn her throat," one of the healers explained as she looked in Aris' mouth in a brief assessment. One of the other healers was checking her arms and legs, bandaging and healing the visible injuries as well as they could.

"Why?" Caspian huffed, running his hand through his hair as he actively avoided looking at her injuries. Couldn't say I blamed him; I could barely look at them without fear of destroying the house in a rocky earthquake.

"Can't call out for help if you can't talk," the healer whispered, her eyes filled with haunted shadows as she closed Aris' jaw. "Don't worry," she reassured when she saw our shocked and angry expressions. "She'll be alright. There was no major internal damage picked up by our scans. We're going to wait until she's awake before we do more in-depth healing. I promise, she'll heal and be back to her old self soon enough." With that, she left, followed by two healers who rolled the cot out of the house into the front area. Taking a steadying breath, I followed, relief pouring through me at the news.

Thank the Goddess we found her in time.

Aris

Everything was a blur, mumbles and sounds mixing together as I tried to look around, my eyes refusing to focus on the flurry of activity around me. All I knew was I was half a numb blob and still felt like I was sitting directly in a fire. Weird sensations filled me, my body and mind slowly coming back to me as I realized there was a large group of people fluttering and shouting around me. I was laid on something soft, and someone was holding my hand.

"Sprinkles?" I whispered as well as I could, my mouth only partially working as I continued to wake up from whatever shit magic was pumping through my system. Caspian's ocean eyes widened, filling with tears as he looked down at me. He shouted over his shoulder before brushing a palm gently over my forehead.

"Cupcake, fucking hellsticks, you scared the shit out me," he exclaimed hysterically, his cheeks glimmering with tear tracks, but when I tried to lift my arm up to wipe them away, I felt like my wrist had been broken. Screaming, I stopped moving my arm. "Shh, Cupcake, try not to move, the healers are working through the damage as quickly as they can."

"What happened?" I questioned, my throat sore, though the burning had lessened the longer I laid on the cot. The rest of my guys' faces swarmed my vision, crowding around the bed with worried or angry expressions, but before any of them could talk, I heard Delilah's psychotic ranting screech over everything else.

"No! He's mine! You can't take my Torry away from me!" she screamed, her eyes bright red and her hair disheveled as she fought the witches who had secured her in power-dampening witch cuffs. When she saw me surrounded by my men, including Torryn, she seemed to completely lose herself, screaming incoherently as she thrashed around before being carted off.

"Did she... did she just call me Torry...?" Torryn asked in disbelief, his slack jaw and wide eyes making me laugh. His shocked expression turned to me as he watched me struggle to keep my giggles contained to settle the pain that flared. They finally subsided, my guys eyeing me like I had also gone insane.

"She wanted to be me, so she could have you, *Torry*," I teased. "Apparently, I'm not smart enough for you or some other crazy shit."

"Well, fuck everyone else. You are it for me, Aris," Torryn pledged, his seafoam-green eyes sharpening as he looked down at me, warm fingers brushing against my cheek. A round of enthusiastic agreement went up, making me a bundle of warm and fuzzy emotions. Another screech from Delilah had me looking over again, ruining our moment. Apparently, she'd heard what he said, and it didn't go over well. As she fully faced me, I noticed her face was disfigured, and part of her hair was pink. *No, she couldn't have meant that literally... right?*

"What happened to her face?" I whispered in a horrified tone, trying to peel my eyes away.

"She meant 'be you' literally. She was using dark magic and potions to become you. She only made it halfway there, though I have a feeling the potion was tied to your life force, meaning if she had succeeded, you would have been dead," Kye explained, his voice hollow, his words breaking with emotion.

"I'm okay," I promised, reaching up again and instantly regretting it. "Well... I will be."

"Miss Calisto?" A man I didn't know walked over from where he'd been standing near my cot. He had a healer sigil stitched on the breast of his shirt, so he must have come in with the others.

"Yes?" My voice cracked, the burn flaring just a bit but nowhere near as bad as before.

"I'm Healer Verisan, and I just wanted to ask you some questions before we continue our healing, is that alright?" I nodded, happy knowing they could help with the injury to my arm. "Do you remember what happened?" Once again, I nodded. "You were healed at the basic level, which should have alleviated any minor pain, but anything more extensive will require individualized attention. Can you tell me what hurts and if you know what caused it?"

I recapped what happened, the man scribbling down notes on a small witch's glass emblazoned with the capital crest. *Must be annotating it for the authorities or for records.* I purposely refused to look at my guys as their jaws clenched, and their eyes hardened, angry at what had happened but knowing there was nothing they could do about it now.

"So, the wrist is the worst, correct?" Healer Verisan

asked, tucking his notebook away in an inside pocket of his jacket.

"Yeah, I can't move my arm," I murmured. He nodded and got to work using his magic to slowly repair my body. Each injury felt like they started the healing process.

"Alright, Miss Calisto, that should be everything. We recommend getting some rest and taking it easy over the next few days. Your injuries are healed for the most part, but the more extensive ones like your wrist and the burns will require some time for the magic to fully heal. To help reduce any issues with your arm as the magic continues to heal you, I would wear it in a sling until early next week and the bandages on your wrists and ankles until Monday."

"Thank you," Torryn stated, his professor voice fully in effect as he shook the healer's hand. Leaving us be, he headed back toward the other officials who were going in and out of the building where I had been taken. We were on the outskirts of the city center in a home that was boarded up, no signs anyone even remembered its existence. It would have been weeks if not months before anyone found my body by pure chance.

"I have a question." I turned to look at them all staring down at me, fingers and hands resting on either my legs, arms, or hands. *They must be feeling the pull to keep contact. I'm glad the magic isn't pushing only me.* "I just remembered Delilah's eyes were red. At first, they were normal, then got redder the longer she talked. Was I hallucinating, or did it actually happen?"

"That's from her practicing blood magic; the stronger the spell or summoning, the redder the eyes," Drayce explained darkly before forcing a small smile and changing his demeanor. "Ready to head back to the inn, Angel?"

"Hellsticks, yes! I need soul cakes and Hex Mix as soon

as physically possible," I said emphatically, my guys laughing in response as I gingerly sat up and got off the cot. "Let's go," I smiled, my voice almost completely back to normal. I had no idea what she had given me to burn my throat, but right now, all I wanted was to chill and hang out with my guys.

Delilah might have kidnapped me, hurt me, and tried to steal my body with dark magic, but I was going to be okay. I had my familiar, my guys, and a chance to start fresh with no more threats looming in the distance. With them surrounding me as we walked, it turned out to be a pretty good Samhain after all.

It's the positive things in life that matter, right?

EPILOGUE

November 3rd
Sunday Afternoon
Aris

I made my way slowly to the headmaster's office, my arm cradled in the cloth sling to refrain from using it as the magic finalized its healing. The rest of me was sore, but the salves and other healing the witches had done during the Samhain festival seemed to have worked since my wrists and ankles were no longer burned. Mr. Stripes clutched tightly to my head, his fluffy tail swishing back-and-forth against my back and arm as we walked. He hadn't left my side after he was let out of that fucking cage, whether too scared about another incident or worried about me, I didn't know, but I couldn't complain. Honestly, I felt safer with him on my shoulder.

As I neared the headmaster's office, I found myself reflecting on the last couple of days. It had been rough as the healers had said it would be as my bone, wrist, throat, and burns healed, but my guys never left my side. Even Torryn had taken it upon himself to practically stand bodyguard outside my tower door. We had spent the day after everything had happened locked up in our rooms at the inn as I recovered before heading home yesterday. As soon as we were here, we resumed our relaxing, loungey behavior up in my tower, knowing it was now safe from Delilah and her crazy schemes.

I knocked against the wood, my tired body buzzing with nerves as I waited. Finally, after a few moments, I heard him give me the go-ahead to open the door. Taking one last steadying breath, I entered his office. Headmaster Tallis was seated in his office chair, a worn leather high back, as he eyed me with a glint in his eye I couldn't place. *He looks like a Summoner who had snared a Will of the Wisp, and that alone is enough to set me on edge.*

"Ah, Miss Calisto, please have a seat," he hummed boastfully, his hand gesturing toward the chair in front of his large, gaudy desk.

Giving him a small but polite smile, I did as he asked, Mr. Stripes climbing down from my shoulder to my lap before making himself comfortable in my arms.

"I would like to personally apologize for how we weren't able to stop the threat to you before it escalated. I want to assure you, we were working as hard as possible to catch the person responsible for these previous incidents," he cooed.

My smile widened until I felt like my plastic and fake grin would crack my face, but I didn't let my disbelief at his act slip through. *Yeah, buddy, that's exactly what my guys said.*

"I'm sure you did. Sometimes, things like that can't be predicted," I responded cheerfully, hoping this awkward meeting would be over soon. Something about him had me sitting straighter and more on edge than usual, although that could have been from the fact I had been strapped down and nearly sacrificed by a crazy witch only a few days earlier. He flashed me a smile before standing, making his way around the desk to sit against the edge of the ugly piece of furniture in front of me.

"Is, uh, that it, sir?" I questioned uncomfortably, his eyes sharpening as they looked down at me. His smile threw up a giant red flag, and Mr. Stripes shifted until he was back on my shoulder, in case I needed to leave abruptly.

"Miss Thana has been very talkative since she's been detained," he started, his lips quirking up in a friendly smile, but the vibe he was giving off was predatory. My adrenaline built in my body until I was buzzing with the urge to run.

"Well, I'm sure a witch as... unstable as her would probably have a lot to say," I attempted to be diplomatic, but it was a struggle. As he leaned forward, his fingers brushed the top of my shoulder briefly in a way that had me nearly shivering as my blood turned to ice.

"Aris, let's just cut the pretenses. I know about you and a certain member of my faculty," he murmured, his fingers brushing against my cheek. "And I called you here to see what exactly we can do to keep that little tidbit... secret."

Oh, shit.

RESTING WITCH FACE
BOOK 2 OF THE NOT YOUR BASIC WITCH SERIES

Coming December 2019

ACKNOWLEDGMENTS

Our husbands who supported us and cheered us on even when we were doubting our work!

Our PA Katie for keeping us sane when things got overwhelming!

Our alpha/beta readers—you guys are awesome!

Ash for dealing with our crazy and reading all of our stuff!

Finally, for all of our readers, this wouldn't be possible without you.

ALSO BY A.J. MACEY

Best Wishes Series:

Book 1: Smoke and Wishes

Supplemental Point-of-View Stories: Between the Wishes

Book 2: Smoke and Survival

High School Clowns & Coffee Grounds

Book 1: Lads & Lattes

The Aces Series:

Book 1: Rival

Book 2: Adversary

ALSO BY JARICA JAMES

Broken Silence (YA stand-alone RH)

Fae Knights Series

Book 1: Fae Bound
Book 2: Fae Sight
Book 3: Fae Strength
Book 4: Fae Eternal
Fae Knights Box Set

Master Reapers Series

Book 1: City of Souls
Book 2: Realm of Shadows

Obsidian Cove Supernatural Academy Series

Book 1: Call of the Siren

The Spirit Vlog Series

Book 1: Haunts and Hotels

Co-write with Chloe Gunter

A Pinch of Sass

Co-write with Rowan Thalia

Book 1: Into the Shadows

Book 2: Through the Woods

Coming soon: Monster (Academies of the Realms: 1)

STAY CONNECTED

For A.J. Macey:

Join the Reader's Group A.J. Macey's Minions for exclusive content, teasers and sneaks, giveaways, and more.

Newsletter sign-up at the bottom of the page at www.authorajmacey.com

For Jarica James:

Join the Reader's Group The Reaper Realm for exclusive content, teasers and sneaks, giveaways, and more.

Follow on Instagram @jaricajames for fun posts and behind the scenes looks.

Made in the USA
Middletown, DE
01 July 2020